MAKE ME *Yours*

Book one in The Stone Trilogy

RENEE HARLESS

RENEE HARLESS

Cover photo by pixabay
Cover design by Porcelain Paper Designs

RENEE HARLESS

More Books by Renee Harless

<u>The Stone Trilogy</u>

Make me yours

Make you mine

Make us more

<u>Welcome to Carson</u>

Coming Alive

Coming Together

Coming Consumed

Coming Altered

Coming Innocent

Coming Unraveled

Coming Unplugged

Coming Home

RENEE HARLESS

Make Me *Yours*

Book one in The Stone Trilogy

RENEE HARLESS

RENEE HARLESS

Prologue

THE SOUNDS OF CHAINS rattling against the concrete wake me from my drug-induced slumber. *Where am I? How did I get here?* Goosebumps spread across my paralyzed skin as I glance around the dark and barren warehouse.

Struggling against my restraints, I hear the faint voice whisper, "If you make any movements, they will only cut into your skin."

As the lone light bulb flickers off in the distance and as I glance around again in the light, I make eye contact with another victim.

Nodding my head towards the other person, I stop my wrestling and collapse fully onto the chair.

"Where are we?" I ask.

"I don't know. An abandoned warehouse along the harbor I think. I can hear some boats, every now and then."
Filling my lungs with the damp cold air, I feel my paralyzed muscles gain their strength.

"Why are we here?"

As a foghorn sounds in the distance, I can only hear the victim say, "... to kill us."

Chapter One

Five Months Earlier

"MALLORY? MALLORY, ARE YOU listening to me?"

As I sit and stare out into the emptiness of the park across the street, I barely take notice of the laughter coming from my kitchen as my friends play a drinking game. Deciding to ignore Madison's question, I sink farther into my couch cushion, hoping to become one with the piece of furniture. Typically, I am pretty outgoing and I enjoy spending time with my friends, but today I started feeling strangely melancholy about my life. Most days I find that I am happy and self-assured with what I bring into this world. I have a great job and a great set of friends. However, today my mother called and started asking when I planned to settle down. She was expecting grandchildren soon, after all. Only hindering my mood more, I found out today that my assistant is getting married to her prince charming at the age of twenty-two. Instantly, I felt jealous of her pending nuptials. I have had dates and one serious boyfriend, but none of those men were what I read about in my fantasy novels, even though I know they're completely unrealistic. I want a partner who makes my breath halt and pulse quicken, with just a glance. My only form of relationship is currently with my three best friends, who are happily intoxicating themselves, before we decide where to go for the evening.

"Never have I ever taken someone home with me from a bar," my roommate Mika yells before tossing back a shot of Goldschläger.

Mika and Madison seem to make it a point to go home with someone every weekend. Me? Not so much. I typically stay in my little bubble when we go out, but tonight I may find myself dancing along with the girls to knock myself out of this funk. I'm usually very shy when meeting new people, so used to caring for those around me, that I'm afraid of someone else taking advantage of my nurturing sense of personality.

Seth walks over to perch on the love seat, hands me a shot glass, and in a joking tone continues the game that is already in session.

"Never have I ever loved Seth," he says.

I toss back my shot glass. I do love Seth; he is one of my best friends. We met during orientation at the agency and hit it off as we were the only two in attendance around the same age. He works in the information technology department on a completely different floor than me, but we eat lunch together every day. I am acutely aware that Seth wants to date me, but I don't see him that way. I don't see anyone that way. I can feel my bubble of anxiety slowly forming as I consider that I will be alone forever. Right now, alone isn't half-bad. I don't have to inquire with anyone when I want to make plans or travel, but I miss connecting with someone. My one boyfriend, Derek, had been a nine-month relationship, my senior year of college. We were in the same media ethics course. Derek was my first for everything and once I gave in to his incessant pleading to have sex, he broke up with me. He said he had hoped I would have been more like Mika in bed. Yep, he had slept with Mika their sophomore year. I wasn't nearly as heartbroken as I should have been. That lack of emotion solidified the fact that he wasn't for me.

Seth is staring at me as I look at my empty shot glass and I know I must have been zoning out. I tend to do that sometimes when my inner monologues take over and it freaks him out. He asks if I am ok or if I need any water. I tell him I'm fine, and I was thinking about how my assistant is getting married. He smiles a large Cheshire cat grin.

"If that's what is upsetting you, you can always beat her to the punch and marry me," he says.

Rolling my eyes at his statement, he puts his arm around me and tries to kiss my neck, but I shrug him off. I force a polite small smile so my rejection doesn't seem as harsh. Seth seems to develop a need to touch me when he's drinking, and it makes me uncomfortable.

"When are you going to ask out that girl from reception? Her name is Stephanie, right?"

"Well, I've been thinking about what you said. Maybe I'll take her out this weekend," he replies.

Before I have a chance to consider Seth's statement, Madison, my other roommate, runs over to us and plops down on my lap. Yelling into my ear, she tells me that it is time to get ready and Mika wants to go to the new bar that opened down the street called Lucky 21. Lucky's is part dance club and part "extreme" bar. By extreme bar, I mean bartenders that put on a show, fire on the bar, and a hundred different types of liquor. It has been open for about two weeks, with lines that meet our row house three blocks away.

"Madison, how does Mika think we can get in? Is she going to find someone to hold spots for us in line? Like starting now?" I jokingly ask while glancing at my watch.

"Mika works with one of the bouncer's girlfriends. So tonight we got added to the VIP list," she says, between fits of giggles. "And...she wants to pick out our 'ensembles,'" she air quotes, "so that we coordinate."

Of course she does. Mika thinks of us as The Three Musketeers, or as she calls us, "M&Ms". I grumble at the thought of prancing around Baltimore in one of Mika's creations.

"Mallory, suck it up. You know you can't change her mind," Madison quickly adds in a tone telling me she does not want to argue about it.

With a strategy in place, the girls skip out the front door towards Mika's domain upstairs. A few seconds later, Seth tells me that he is going to head to his place and asks if I want to join him instead. I shake my head no, as he too heads out the front door.

Looking around my living room in the row house, I fixate on a picture of the three of us girls from college.

The night before graduation, we took the photograph when we decided to go to a fancy restaurant to celebrate.

I start looking at Madison standing on the end. She is a tiny little nymph in the photograph. Madison hails from Native American and Irish roots. With her jet-black hair, olive skin, and blue eyes she is absolutely breathtaking to look at.

Madison and I grew up together. Her family lived across the street from mine and we were always causing trouble. Her parents were like a second family to me; always taking me along on their vacations and mine did the same with her. We both went away to the University of Maryland together, where I studied journalism and media studies, while Madison studied business. Her goal in life was to own a chain of bakeries, which she has achieved. We shared a dorm room at UMD, which is where we met Mika. She lived across the hall from us and hated her roommate. One day, Madison and I walked back from class and entered our dorm room to find Mika had moved all her stuff into our two-person room. It was a tight fit for the rest of that semester, but the next year we got ourselves an apartment and began living together.

I glance next at Mika posing beside me in the photo wearing a tight green dress. She could be a daughter to Marilyn Monroe or a sister to Kate Upton and is just as tall. She towers over Madison and me. Mika has beautiful blonde curly hair, porcelain skin, and violet eyes. She has an endless amount of curves that perfectly shape her body into an hourglass. Oozing sex appeal, Mika knows how to get attention from men.

Her parents divorced when she was younger, and since neither wanted a small child after the separation, she went to live with her aunt and uncle. Mika loves her aunt and uncle more than her biological parents, though it isn't difficult to understand why. Both her mom and dad have remarried a few times and each has a handful of half siblings for Mika. She has only met a few of them because her parents try to pay her off to keep her from disrupting their lives. She spends the money on frivolous things that make her happy. Her upbringing caused her to have quite an attitude, which makes her perfect for her career as an attorney.

Despite her short temper, Mika will do anything for anyone. I know I should hate her for what Derek said, ages ago, or for the fact that she kept their relationship a secret from me, but I love her, and I try to practice the art of forgiveness. I feel bad for her sometimes. She will try to seduce and date anyone, and I think it boils down to abandonment issues stemming back to her parents. Once she sets her sights on someone, anyone around her better stay clear of her trajectory. She is terrified of being alone, and has a new date almost every night. If someone makes it past a first and second date, she will typically kick them out after the third. I have to give her credit though, because she is having more sex than Madison and I combined. I envy her as well sometimes; the way she carries herself with such confidence and won't take no for an answer. She always gets what she wants.

I think about Seth and how I would have pegged him to want to date both of my roommates instead of me. I know that they think he is gorgeous and I can't say that

I disagree with that observation. Seth is not what one would envision as an information technology person. He could be Chris Evans' identical twin. My preferences sway more towards the tall, dark, and handsome type; not the all-American pretty boys. Stephanie, the receptionist at my office, argues the case that I need to date him before he is snagged, specifically by her. Most of our agency already thinks we are together

Looking back at the original photo I'm holding, I scrutinize myself. I have unruly, waist length, mousy brown hair that I have to flat iron to keep from frizzing out of control. Occasionally, I can put some salt-water mouse in it and let it wave, but even that takes too much time. Typically, I tie my hair back into a ponytail or a French twist, but the night of the photo, Madison and Mika spent an hour curling it into beautiful tousled waves. The dress I'm wearing is a dark purple wrap dress that I received as a gift from my mother for job interviews. It was the nicest thing I had in my closet at the time and I'm lucky enough that I can still wear it to this day. Madison said the purple made my eyes pop against my pale white skin. My eyes are the only feature I like on myself. Though they are a little big for my face, they are this amazing color of emerald. I try to play them up with makeup, but I have no idea what I am doing most of the time.

Even with my medium height and slight frame, I blend into the background, next to the two beauties that are my best friends. It's no wonder they have men flanking them every time we go out. Not that I'm jealous; I would much rather sit at home, watching reality television and reading a trashy novel on my e-reader. The girls constantly remind me of my loner tendencies, which is how they trick me into joining them most evenings.

Placing the photo back on the mantle, I walk down the hall to my bedroom. Plopping back onto my bed, I sigh while passing glances around my bedroom. Noticing the click-clack of stilettos on the hardwood in the stairwell, I can hear the girls running down the steps outside my bedroom. I'm aware of the stiletto clap going in the opposite direction once they reach my living room and I realize they went straight for the kitchen before coming to find me in my room. They bring a shot of Goldschläger with them as they step into my bedroom and with a smile I throw my head back, letting the warming liquid slide down my throat.

"Mallory what's wrong?" Madison says.

With a dramatic sigh and whine I relent, "Do I have to go out?"

As Mika laughs, I turn my head in her direction and notice the bag placed behind her back.

"What do you have there?" I say with a tilt of my chin towards the hidden bag behind Mika's back.

"A surprise for you," Mika says as she hands me the bag.

Glancing inside, I pull out a beautiful bronze sequined dress.

It is a one shoulder, body hugging, design that will stop about mid thigh. It is very glamorous and very out of my comfort zone, but I am instantly in love with it.

Grabbing some sexy underwear from my bureau, I grab my new dress and move into the adjoining bathroom to put it on. Slipping the dress on, I am amazed at how well it forms to my body and how luxurious it feels against my skin. This must have cost Mika a fortune.

Treading back out into the bedroom, I see that the girls have moved into the living room and turn on some music to a dance beat I don't recognize. My feet slide into my favorite shoes and I turn to look into the full-length mirror resting on my wall.

With a strut towards the living room, the girls stop dancing and gasp.

"Mallory, wow!" Mika says.

Madison adds, "I have never, ever seen you look so sexy!"

"Thank you," I say, a little stunned and speechless at their reaction.

"Wait here, I need to get my camera!" Mika cries.

She is always taking pictures of us when we go out.

Propping ourselves onto my barstools, Madison and I lounge against the counter that separates the kitchen and living room while we wait.

When Mika returns, she sets the camera on the fireplace mantle and adjusts the timer, then rushes back over to us yelling, "Smile".

After losing vision temporarily from the flash, she bounds over to the camera to look at the photo. After analyzing the picture, she hands the camera to Madison, who smiles, and then hands the camera over to me. I look down and smirk at the three of us. Madison is wearing a gold skirt and Mika is a silver piece of scrap material draping across her chest.

"We look like the Olympic medals!" I exclaim causing us to fall into a fit of laughter.

Looking down at the photo again, my smile fades because I'm the one in bronze; the third-place trophy.

As we head out the door, I can't help but wonder where all this lack of self-confidence is coming from. Maybe I'm having an early mid-life crisis because I'm usually so self-assured. At this point in the trek, I have slowed my pace and I am at a significant distance behind the girls. Realizing my friends haven't even noticed, I decide to give it an hour or two at the bar, when they are too wrapped up in whomever they have met, and quietly slip out.

Chapter Two

AFTER PICKING UP MY pace, I quickly catch up to the girls as we stop at the entrance of Lucky 21. The other patrons are sending scathing looks in our direction, angry that we are skipping ahead of the line. Trotting up to the bouncer, Mika announces her name and gives an award-winning smile. With a wink and a grin, he asks for her number. I cringe and pray that this is not the co-worker's boyfriend; at least I hope it isn't or Mika will have some explaining to do at the office.

   Opening the door, he ushers us inside past the grumbles of those waiting in line. Glad I won't have to wait outside, I give a polite smile to the crowd to say that I am sorry and then I turn my smile to the bouncer and say thank you. He shoots a tight nod in my direction and then turns away quickly to address a few men in suits waiting at the door. I stopped for a moment to ponder his reaction and then realize Mika and Madison have again left me behind, again.

Walking farther into the club, I turn my head to the right, past a pillar, to find a beautiful room with a chandelier, pub tables, and a very regal bar. Narrowing my eyes, I decide this must not be the portion of the club the girls were mentioning to me. Moving forward, I head past that room a few yards and turn left. *Jackpot!* I can already see the girls on the dance floor with a drink in each of their hands. Boy, they sure do work fast. I meander farther into the room and take notice of my surroundings. Impressed, I find the bar towards the back and spot an empty stool. I also notice a few private booths that have been roped off, along with a stairwell that another bouncer is staffing. That area upstairs must be the VIP lounge.

The empty stool I was eyeing is still vacant when I finally make it over in that direction and I observe that the place isn't nearly as crowded as I would have imagined, considering the line outside. The bartender makes her way over to me and asks what I would like to drink, but before I order, I tell her of my observation. She laughs and says that in about thirty minutes, they will open the door to let in everyone. If the girls have already started drinking, on top of their pre-gaming, I know that I need to keep my head screwed on, so I order a kamikaze shot and a water. No indulging for me tonight.

After tossing back my shot, the stools beside me empty out, leaving me alone at the bar. Soon after, I become aware of some squeals gaining volume behind me and I know that my friends have found me. Turning around in my chair, the girls immediately start chatting to me about the group of guys they met on the dance floor. With a glance over her shoulder, Mika looks over to them, waves, and they smirk back. There are three of them and I know her dubious plan.

I smirk to myself as they each order a long island iced tea from the bartender. I'm going to have to get a cab for them because I can't carry both of them home. The bartender must notice my inner distress because I see that my kamikaze shot has been refilled. When I look up, she winks in my direction and I sag in relief. I'm glad someone is looking out for me.

After a few drinks, and with her skills in persuasion, Mika has convinced me to go out to the dance floor. For the next hour, the club quickly becomes crowded and I begin feeling slightly claustrophobic from all the bodies grinding against me. I attempt to tell the girls that I am going to get another drink, but I realize that they aren't paying any attention to me. They are each wrapped around one of the guys from earlier. How'd that happen? All three of us were dancing together just seconds ago. Frowning to myself, I head back towards the bar and find my stool still unoccupied.

As I sit down and order another shot and water, I see a group of beautiful women on both sides of me. Men trying to get a number, a dance, or even a glance in their direction, surround them. Typical, I think to myself as I take my shot and play with the straw in my drink. Two men that look barely of drinking age, ask to buy me another shot, but I decline them both. I try to be polite in my rejection, but each one call me a bitch when I tell them

I'm not interested. With a sigh, I look down at my drink and zone out, letting my thoughts drift to a tropical island where I meet a handsome man who sweeps me away.

As my brain comes back to reality, I notice that the stool beside me has been vacated and the woman on the other side is a beautiful red head in a skintight tan bandage dress. When she senses me staring at her she rolls her eyes and laughs and then says something to one of her male companions. They both turn in my direction and chuckle. With a roll of my eyes, I look back down at my drink and wonder if Madison and Mika are still entertaining their new friends on the dance floor.

Between my moments of imaginary fantasy, I hear someone talking over the music.   "Excuse me, miss. Is anyone sitting here?"
I keep to myself as I assume he is speaking to the beautiful red head or to the bartender. He has a strange accent. Not one I can place as English or Australian.

"Hello? Miss? May I sit here?" he says again and then touches my shoulder.
 I gasp from the contact as it feels like my shoulder has been set on fire from his tap. The startled motion causes me to knock over my drink onto the bar. The bartender rushes over to clean up the mess while I apologize profusely to her.

"I'm sorry, I didn't mean to frighten you," the man exclaims while masking a chuckle.

Looking up at him, I realize he is speaking to me and I immediately gasp. He is, without a doubt, the most gorgeous man I have ever seen. Hair that is thick, dark, and has a bit of wave to it, is styled in a tousled but sophisticated look. His jaw line is chiseled with a straight nose. Eyes of the lightest brown with a hint of gold that looks stunning against his olive skin. And lips that aren't too thin or full; they fit his face perfectly and are currently set in a sexy, but shy smirk. A bit of stubble graces his chin and that only enhances his godly appearance. The fitted three-piece-suit gives off the air of CEO or celebrity status. The snug tailoring allows me to see his strong, built, and defined body. His gaze upon me causes my body to warm and my nerves to shake. I recognize that he is smirking at me because he caught me checking him out and I haven't responded to him.

"You didn't, um, frighten me. I, uh, just wasn't paying attention," I say as turn and try to keep my face down, staring at the bar.

"Well, do you mind if I sit here, or are you holding it for someone else?"

"Holding it for someone?" I ask, peeking a glance in his direction.

"Someone like a boyfriend or a husband?"
I frown and turn back towards the bar.

"No husband or boyfriend. Please help yourself. I'm sure she would enjoy your company," I say with a hint of malice in my voice.

"Who would?"

Pointing to the seat beside where he stands I reply, "She would."

"Why is that?"

Like I really need to tell him that, he is beautiful and I know he is biding his time until the redhead is available for conversation. I know that she is more his caliber. With perfect timing, the redhead glances over to our new bar mate and unleashes her seduction skills.

"Hello, gorgeous. My name is Amber. You can buy me another drink," the redhead says as she holds out her hand.

He shakes it but only says hello in return.

Not completely worn off, she purrs, "Why are you wasting your time chatting with her? I am much more your league."

I scoff at her assertion, but also realize she is correct. Ignoring their conversation, I try to grab the bartender to settle my tab, but she tells me it has already been taken care of. Not questioning it and ready to leave, I turn in my stool to say good evening to the man seated next to me, but he seems to be preoccupied with Amber. He is standing inches from her face. Wow, she doesn't waste any time. Stepping away from the bar, I look around for my friends, but notice they aren't anywhere within this room. Concerned, I pull my phone out of my handbag and see that I have a text from Mika saying that they went with the boys to a local diner an hour ago. Is it already 1:30am? I must have been lost in my revelries longer than I thought. Goodness that makes me a horrible friend. To think that I was so absorbed in myself, that I didn't even notice them leave. This realization makes me feel terrible and as I stand pondering their retreat, I realize that I don't recall them coming to find me either. This understanding causes my fear for them to dissipate and allow anger to set in. They are the ones that asked me to come out tonight and then they left me here.

In anger, I turn to head towards to the exit of the room, but then the man from earlier jumps away from the bar and grabs my wrist.

"I'm sorry, that was rude of me," he says. "I wanted to let Amber know that she needs to learn polite manners. It is not kind to degrade someone to their face, let alone a stranger, especially when she herself is the one of the lower caliber."

Shocked at his outburst I ask, "You stood up for me?"

"Of course, it's not in my nature to bite my tongue."

My arm is starting to burn under his hand. Not from his grip, but from the sensation of his touch. This is such a bizarre reaction my skin is having, but maybe it is because I have been so out of sorts today.

"Thank you," I tell him, and as he removes his hand, it instantly feels like ice has been placed there instead.

Cocking his head to the side he asks, "Are you leaving?"

"Yes, I am. My friends left with some new male companions, so I'm calling it a night."

Once the words leave my mouth, I regret it. He could be a serial killer for all I know. I try to come up with a way to save myself, but I don't always think well on my feet.

He replies, "I can take you home later, if you'd like to join me for another drink."

"That is kind of you, but no. I need to get home. It has been a long week. It was nice to meet you…"

"Alex, Alex Stone."

"Well, it was a pleasure Alex. Enjoy your night."

As he stares at me, stunned to be discarded, I turn to leave. Running up ahead, he stops in front of me.

"Please? Please stay with me a while longer. I know you don't know me, but I am captivated by you. Just one more drink."

His words are a shock to my system and his sorrowful look melts my heart. I can't help but agree to his plea and I am in no rush, now that my friends have left me. With a nod of my head, I smile up at him and then he smirks at me and grabs my hand. I swear it is going to melt off from the heat of his touch.

We walk past the bar opening and head up the stairs to the VIP area. I'm not sure where we are going, because I stare at our fingers intertwined in each other. The butterflies in my stomach are one clue that I am highly attracted to this man. I've never felt anything like this.

During the staring match with my fingers, I don't notice that Alex has stopped in front of a pocket door and I run into the back of him, colliding into his entire frame. I instantly become entrenched with want as he wraps his arms around my waist to catch me and I can feel the heat pool in my lower belly. This reaction to a man is so completely unfamiliar to me, I worry that I won't ever feel this way again.

He looks into my eyes and just smiles, as if he can read my deepest secrets. I think he's going to kiss me so I lean in slightly, but instead he steps back and removes his hands from my waist. A shiver crosses my skin as his heat leaves my body.

Opening the door, Alex directs me to sit at a table nestled into the alcove before pressing a button on the wall and taking a seat across from me. Immediately, a server appears at our nook and stares at Alex. I understand her reaction, as he is a sight to be seen. Irritation envelops me as she only asks what he wants to drink and then steps away. The irrational part of me spurs forth and I make a move to leave. The second I go to stand, Alex slams the pocket door shut. Startled and bewildered by his reaction I find that he seems angry as well.

"I'm sorry she ignored you. That is not appropriate as a server and it will be dealt with," he speaks with such authority.

"Really, it isn't a big deal."

His tone softens dramatically when he speaks to me again. "Stay. I don't even know your name and I'd like to get to know you better."

"What difference would it make if you knew me better?"

"I'm not sure, but you seem to be worth knowing."

Hypnotized by his words, I move to sit back in my seat and stare at the table.

The server returns with Alex's drink and pretends to stumble while she places it on the table. At her obvious attempt at flirting, I roll my eyes and get up to leave. My small pride can't continue to take any more hits. While she is busy entertaining him, I hope to make a haste exit from the alcove. I walk as fast as I can through the hallway and down the steps that lead to the main entrance, stumbling out the door and into the same bouncer from earlier.

"You're Mallory right? Mika's friend?"

"Uh, yeah," I say as I look around quickly to make sure Alex hasn't follow me out, though I know he isn't far behind.
I don't want him to see which direction I go in or that I am walking home alone.

"I'm Brian, my girlfriend works with Mika; says she is a handful."

Laughing at his statement, "Yes, yes she is. I'm sorry Brian, but I need to leave. It was nice to meet you."

"Hey, do you think I can get your number before you head out?" Noticing a confused look on my face, Brian continues, "I'm sorry, it's so the club can let certain members know when we have VIP nights."

"But I'm not a member."

"Um. My list here indicates that you, Mika, and Madison are all VIP members for as long as the club is open."

"There must be a mistake; we didn't pay for a membership."

"Oh, well, the system says you have one, so I would use it. Can I put your number on record?"
Still confused, I repeat my number to him anyway.

"Thanks, Mallory, can I get you a cab?"

"No thanks, I don't live far. I'm just going to walk home."

"Are you sure?"

"Yep."

He hesitates and says, "Alright, it was nice to meet you, Mallory. Come back anytime. Have a good night."

"You too, Brian."

I start walking down the street heading back towards my home, feeling safe alone as there are a handful of people doing the same. When I reach my place, I stand at the top of the stairs leading to the main door of my house and peer down the street towards the bar. Suddenly, a commotion begins outside the front of the bar and I think I see Alex rushing out the door and pushing Brian. Goodness, what is that about? Abruptly, I see Alex jump into a waiting black SUV and veer off in the opposite direction. Confused at everything that has happened tonight, I turn the key to the main door and head inside my home.

I really wanted to get to know Alex better and I can't shake this feeling that he is important. In just a brief encounter, he brought about emotions in me that were completely new and foreign. I still feel the heat burning in my lower belly and I know tonight will be a long one.

As I open the door to my apartment, I begin to peel off my lovely dress. Turning to lock the door, I stand in my foyer donning my lavish lingerie. Leaning against the front door, I close my eyes and picture Alex's face while I bring my hands towards my chest. I imagine that his hands are massaging and kneading my breasts, while he whispers in my ear that he has never seen anyone as sexy and beautiful as me. My wonton thoughts continue as I let my hands trail down my stomach towards my pelvis.

The moment I begin to lead my fingers towards my mound, I hear the main door open followed by the laughter of Madison and Mika and two other men. With a grunt, I grab my dress off the floor, head towards the bathroom to wash my face, and get ready for bed.

Once settled in bed in my beautiful lingerie, I tentatively let my fingers pass across my shoulder and wrist, as the touches from Alex continue to linger on my skin. Lying in my chilled sheets, I close my eyes so that I can visualize Alex's face again. My vision is so vivid that I can I see his sexy smirk and golden eyes. I can feel this breath tickle my neck. My own hand reaches back to undo my bra and I let the straps slide down my shoulders as I envision his hands trailing along my collarbone, shoulders, and arms. I start to knead my breasts again and pinch my nipples, grasping them so hard that pain and pleasure become one. This form of ache is new to me, but it sets my core on fire.

I continue to tweak and massage my left breast, while I let my right hand trail down my belly towards my mound. My heart continues to pound in my ears as I think about Alex. The wax I recently received leaves my skin feeling smooth and slick. My panties are soaked through as my fingers glide along the pool of moisture. A man hasn't gotten me wet without his touch since I was nineteen and I am immediately thankful for my reckless decision to join him at the bar. My vision continues as I picture Alex's hand trailing fingers through my folds, while he begins to rub my already hardening nub. I am so turned on at this point that I know it won't take long for me to make myself come. As my breath accelerates, I spend A few more seconds of rubbing my breasts and clit before I explode on my bed. It has been such a long time since I have felt that type of eruption that I find myself smiling and drifting off to sleep.

RENEE HARLESS

Chapter Three

WAKING UP THE NEXT morning much later than I expected, I have the realization that my body is throbbing. Immediately escaping towards my claw foot tub, I try to erase any remnants of last night.

After an hour of soaking in my vanilla salt bath and catching up on my e-reader, I step out of my tub and decide to conquer the day. I put on my favorite weekend attire of jeans and a t-shirt and make myself some brunch. As I'm flipping some French toast, I hear a knock on the door and then a key turn in the knob. Madison and Mika come crawling through the door and drag themselves to the couch; both still wearing their clothes from last night.

I place a plate of French toast and bacon on the counter for both of them and send my evil glare in their direction. They both look up at me and frown.

Speaking first Madison says, "Mal, I'm sorry we left you last night. We got caught up in the moment."

"Yea, you didn't seem to be into our crowd last night," Mika chimes in.

"Well, thanks for asking how I felt about the crowd before you made that decision for me," I say. "Now eat some breakfast before I choose to go back to being mad at you."

"Mal, this is sooooo gooood," Mika says with a mouth full of food.

Smiling at her, I ask them how their night was.

"I don't even remember making it home. I think John and Ryan carried us most of the way," Madison states.

I look at them both and sigh. "Girls, you know better than that. I'm not your mom, but we aren't kids anymore. You can't get to the point where you don't remember getting home. That's what I was there for."

Disappointment etches across their faces so I try to lessen the blow by asking if they want to head towards the harbor with me this afternoon to watch the other patrons, but they both decline saying they want to rest.

After breakfast, Madison washes the dishes while Mika naps on my couch. I text Seth and ask if he wants to go to the harbor, but he is getting ready for a date with Stephanie. Apparently, he decided to take the plunge and she jumped at the chance to go out with him. Stephanie is a nice girl though and I think they would be good together.

Madison steps into my room as I grab my e-reader and she asks if she can nap on my bed. Giving her the go ahead, I head out the front door and walk towards the harbor. It is quite a few blocks away, but it is a glorious spring day so I don't mind. Stopping at a park, I decide this is a good resting spot. Locating an area shaded by a tree, I lean against it and begin to read. It's a story about some billionaire being a number of shades of fucked up. It's my first trashy novel delving into the realm of BDSM and I have to admit, it is pretty hot. I let myself get wrapped up in to the story and before long, I am feeling that ache again. I wish I had someone to help me release it, but I will have to rely on B.O.B. for that service later today.

When I finally pull my head away from my book, I notice that the sun is starting to set. Glancing at the clock on my e-reader, I see that it is 7:30 pm. Without moving from this spot, I have spent nine hours engrossed in the story. Who does that?

On the first of June, I see a group of black-suited men standing at the security desk of my office building causing quite a disturbance because they are blocking the path towards the elevators. Saying, "excuse me" to get by, they all look in my direction as I press the button for the elevator. A strange sense rushes over me and I feel that I have seen them before. Stepping inside the elevator and looking back towards the lobby at the security desk, I can see one of the men talking into his shirtsleeve. How strange. The doors to the elevator close and the car begins to ascend. A shiver crosses my body when I realize where I have seen them before; the night we went to Lucky 21. Maybe someone important was at the club that night. I imagine some governor's daughter lounging in the VIP area and giggle spurs from my lips, causing the other passengers to shoot dirty stares in my direction.

RENEE HARLESS

The car stops at every interval to let employees off on their level, so I have a few minutes before we reach my office on the 63rd floor. I move towards the right wall of the elevator and close my eyes, picturing the face that has haunted my every thought for the last three weeks. I don't know why I can't seem to get his image out of my head. Perhaps he drugged me or hypnotized my mind that night causing my subconscious to be completely focused on him. I snort as I consider those options knowing neither are the case. In reality, I can't get him out of my head because he is the only person to draw some sort of reaction from my body. My vibrator has been getting a work out these past few weeks because of him haunting my dreams. Suddenly, the jolt of the car from reaching the top floor wakes me from my inner thoughts. As I wait for the other passengers to exit, I swipe at my head noticing the faint glisten of sweat collecting along my hairline. All this anxiety from some dirty thoughts about a man I will never see again.

As I step out of the elevator, I offer a hello to my assistant Annie, who is in a heated conversation with Stephanie. Passing the front desk, I take notice that Stephanie isn't looking quite like herself. I hope her and Seth haven't called it quits already. Shooting a smile and wave in their direction, I continue toward my office.

Waiting for my computer to boot up I rummage through the files on my desk. I have a few creative designs for a clothing company that I need to go over with my Senior Account Director, but other than that, I don't have too busy a schedule today.

Annie walks in and hands me a sticky note about a missed call from earlier. I asked who the caller was and she replied that they didn't leave a name or a number, but said they would call back later. We gossip for a few minutes about the weekend and then I ask her about Stephanie. She glances around and then tells me that Stephanie won't say anything specifically, but hinted that she and Seth were having a fight. She prompts me to disclose if I know anything, but I am in the dark as well. Changing gears, we go over our daily calendar and I have Annie schedule a meeting with my Director this morning so we can go over a few creative pieces, then I begin to filter through my emails.

I stroll into my Director, Steven's, office at 11:00am. Steven is an older man with a very rotund waist and balding head. He has the jolliest personality and I can't help but think of him as Santa Claus. We have a great relationship and continuously joke throughout the workday. He starts our conversation by asking me if I'm tied down yet, like that will miraculously happen over a weekend, and then proceeds to try and set me up with his thirty-year-old son. I went on a date with his son once. It was the most boring date I have ever been on, but I try not to hold that against Steven. He just wants his children married and settled.

This morning we delve into the campaigns that I have designed for a clothing company and he selects one of the examples, which is my choice as well. We go over the rest of the presentation and he asks me if I want to be the one to present it to the company. This is completely unexpected and the opportunity catches me off guard.

"Steven, you have never asked me to present before."

"I know, but I think this will be a good opportunity for you. This piece, you designed it every step of the way. It is completely yours."

"Thank you, I would love to present this to them."

"That's great, Mallory. I also wanted to share a bit of undisclosed information with you. My wife and I discussed a few things this past weekend and it looks like I will be retiring from this agency in the next few days."

"What? You can't leave. I don't want to work for anyone else."

Steven laughs. "Mallory, I am years past retirement age with this agency and I have watched you blossom into a wonderful agent. I have enjoyed helping you succeed in your endeavors. I know we have been working together since you came on board seven years ago as first my assistant and then as a Junior Exec, but I think you will very easily fill my shoes." I must look stricken with emotion because he reaches out for my hand. "Mallory, what I am saying is in the next week they are going to hand my position over to you. It will not be posted to the public or internally for that matter. Annie will move into your current position and we will hire a new assistant for you both. I will stay on for a few months to help guide you through some of the agency's background pieces, but I think you will catch on quickly." He pauses and then continues, "So, Mallory, would you like to accept the position?"

I just stare at him, my boss, whom I have grown to love like a second father. "Are you serious? They are just going to give me your job?"

"You already do most of the creative work as it is. You don't ever need my opinion, though I do enjoy reviewing your presentations. It is a job you are already completing, Mallory. I've slowly passed down most of my projects to you so that it will be a seamless transition. So yes, we are just handing the job to you, if you want it."

"Oh my gosh, I want it, I do! I just don't want you to go."

With a boisterous laugh, he pats me on the back. "Great. I will get started on the paperwork from human resources and by the end of the week, you will be Senior Account Executive and Director Mallory Winston all before your thirtieth birthday. This will be your office so you can begin moving your things in as soon as you're ready."

"Wow, Steven...Thank you. This means so much to me."

"I know it does, you will do a fantastic job. Now let's go tell Annie and maybe you two can go over your current projects."

"What about your current projects?"

"Mallory, you already have them."

That thought makes me smile. He is such a wonderful boss. I hope Annie loves working for me as much as I enjoy working for Steven.

"Oh, Steven, before I forget, did you see the group of men at the security desk this morning?"

"I did, I believe they are upgrading the building's security features. Maybe some of the big wigs were harassed outside of the office, I'm not sure. But extra security can never hurt."

"Well, that makes sense. All right, let's go spread around the joy. And, Steven, thank you again, for everything."

With a wide smile, he ushers me out the door towards Annie's cubicle. We ask her to join us in my office and she enters hesitantly as if she is about to have a heart attack. I laugh to myself at the grief stricken look on her face. Once we sit down at my desk, we tell her the good news. She bounces out of her chair and hugs me. She has had a spectacular year, first with her engagement and now with a new position. As she thanks us an infinite amount of times I remember how exhilarating it felt to be in her exact position six years ago. I teasingly ask her to calm down and to go call her fiancé to inform him of the great news. Steven leaves the office, following behind Annie, and reminds me again to start moving my things into his old and my new office.

Staring at the wall in my soon-to-be old office, I can't help but be overjoyed with the incredible year I'm having.

Chapter Four

THE ELEVATOR DEPOSITS ME on one of the lower floors as I plan to meet Seth for lunch and tell him my good news. After excitedly telling him about my morning, he gives me a hug as he steps away from the table. I trim my lunch hour short so that I can run to the florist shop across the street. I want to place some flowers on the coffee table in my new office.

As I browse the flower shop, I spot my favorite calla lilies in an exquisite shade of purple placed in one of the window settings and I immediately ask the employee to ring them up. As I cross the street, I notice a dark head of hair and broad shoulders a few yards ahead of me and I instantly think of Alex. This stranger looks remarkably like him. I slow my pace on the sidewalk as to not frighten any of the passersby. My pulse starts to quicken and my heart beats faster as if I am running a marathon. I am saved from embarrassment when he continues to walk past my building so that I may duck inside the door quickly and make my way to the elevators, collapsing against the wall.

Once the car stops on my floor, I begin collecting my emotions. Glancing in her direction, I head towards Stephanie, but she grunts at me when I ask how she spent her weekend. Confused at her dismissal, I continue to walk towards my new office adding more pep in my step.

Stopping at the doorway, I push on the handle and the door opens to a beautiful corner office overlooking the street. Straight ahead of me is a deep mahogany desk that could easily fit four people. To the right are a love seat, coffee table, and two wingback chairs. They are perpendicular to the window and overlook the ground below. To the left of my desk is a small conference table that will sit eight people. Placing my flowers onto the coffee table, I glance out the window and I see a few black town cars pull up towards the entrance of the building. Steven mentioned the new security and I consider the possibility that the people in the cars are the reason for the upgrades. With a shrug of my shoulders, I walk over to my desk and begin to unload the files Annie brought in while I was at lunch.

About an hour into placing my files inside the filing cabinet, I receive a buzz from Stephanie.

"Ms. Winston, you have a visitor."

"I don't have anyone scheduled. Did they give a name?"

"No, Ms. Winston, security called up. However, this guest seems like he is urgent to see you. Maybe it is important. It could be about your new job."

"Oh, you are probably right. Please send them my way. I'm in Steven's old office. Thanks, Stephanie."
"You're welcome. Oh, and congratulations, Mallory," she says, her voice holding a hint of resentment.

Shuffling through my files again, I completely lose myself into the sorting project.

"Good afternoon, Mallory."
Startled by the voice, I look up towards the door to see the man that has been frequenting my thoughts. Alex stands in the doorway greeting me with a dazzling smile and I am taken aback by how striking he truly is. My dreams haven't been doing him justice.

"Ms. Mallory Winston. You have been a very difficult person to track down since you ran from me at the club and left me no name. I was able to bribe the owner of Lucky 21 to give me your information." He pauses and glares at me, not offering an opportunity to interrupt. "You see, Mallory, I have found myself in a dilemma. My problem being that I can't seem to get you out of my head. I envision your face everywhere I turn. So I have something I need to discuss with you, but first, I have a very pressing matter that you need to address." As I catch my breath and cock my head to the side slightly, he continues, "Why did you leave me that night?"

Minutes pass as he stares into my eyes waiting for my response, anger and desire crossing through them. Realizing that I haven't answered his question, I respond with traces of vulnerability lacing through my tone.

"You, um, seemed more interested in the waitress than me, so I left," I whisper while looking down at my desk.

"Interesting," he says while tapping the tip of his long finer on the stubble of his chin. "I apologize for her behavior. I was not interested in what she was offering. And she didn't seem to take the hint either." Allowing his words to seep into my head Alex takes a dramatic pause. Continuing to speak, he lets his voice purr like velvet across my skin. "I am sorry that we have lost all of this time due to a small misunderstanding."

With a deep sigh, I look up at him and gaze at his masterpiece of a face. His eyes show profound sincerity and he truly appears remorseful for the server's actions. Sensing my forgiveness, Alex promptly shuts the door behind him and walks forward.

"Your receptionist mentioned that you received a promotion today. I want to take you out to celebrate." His accent makes my stomach flutter while the demand in his voice causes goose bumps to grace my skin.

"You would?" I stammer out.

"Yes, I would," he says as he gently rubs his thumb across his lower lip, hints of desire in his eyes. "I will have my driver Gregory pick you up at 7:00 pm this evening. I have your address."

Continuing to walk around my desk, he stops and stands in front of my chair. Using the armrest, he turns the chair so that I am facing in his direction. The passing of electricity between our bodies causes the air to crackle around us. The long fingers I previously admired now stroke down my forearms until his hands meet mine. He tugs at them so that I stand directly in front of where he is positioned. Too stunned to react, I stare into his magnificently golden eyes as his finger reaches up to trace along my collarbone.

"Ms. Winston, I feel that since meeting you, I have not properly existed these past three weeks. I don't enjoy feeling this out of control within my world."

Trying to steady my voice, I lick my lips and weakly speak. "I have a confession to make, Alex."

"Oh yes? And what would that be?" he says as he continues to trace my collarbone.

"I haven't been able to stop thinking about you either. You haunt my dreams."

Alex begins to lean in closer to my body. "That is good news, Mallory, as I have dreamt about you as well. But we will have to delve into my dreams later as those will require little to no clothing," he whispers into my ear.

As his words tickle across my ear and neck, my breath becomes shallow and my heartbeat accelerates. I hope he can't tell how he affects me. Slowly, as if asking me to deny him, Alex reaches his hand behind my head and grips my hair, while his other hand winds around my waist. His nose traces along my jaw line and I am frozen in this spot.

"Mallory," he whispers.

Tilting my head in his direction, he seals his lips over mine and I can feel the craving in his kiss spread throughout my entire body. He places small pecks on the corners of my mouth and lips and then he tilts my head back using his grasp on my hair and brushes his tongue against mine. What starts as a slow, sweet kiss turns heated very rapidly. With my body taking over, I reach my arms around Alex's neck and pull him closer so that I can feel him pressed against my frame. Resuming his control over the kiss, Alex grabs my left leg and hitches it around his hip. The same hand sweeps over towards my behind and tightens its hold. A gasp escapes from my throat and I move my mouth away from his. He begins to place kisses along my neck and jaw line. Tilting my head back as I slowly rock my hips back and forth, I can't help but think that this is the most amazing kiss I have ever experienced.

Some echoing shrill bounces along my office walls and I know our moment is broken. I jump away from Alex's arms and answer the page from Stephanie.

"Ms. Winston, Seth wants to know if you want to go out to celebrate tonight."

With a glance back at Alex, I see he has a grimace placed over his perfect mouth.

Smiling as I respond to Stephanie, I speak sweetly into the intercom, "No, thank you, Stephanie. Please tell him I have plans."

Alex speaks up, "So you will come with me tonight?" sounding like a child filled with excitement.

"Yes, I would love to join you."

The childlike smile turns into a very sexy smirk as he says, "I will see you at 7:00pm. We have much to confer. And Mallory..."

"Yes?"

"You should wear this dress tonight. I am intrigued by the opportunities it may offer me," he whispers into my ear as he reaches for me again.

My body shivers at his seductive words as he turns to leave. When the door opens, he turns his head in my directions and winks.

Immediately following Alex's exit, Annie comes barreling into my office.

"O. M. G., Mallory! Who was that? Is he a model or something? He was the most beautiful man I have ever seen," she inquires as she continues to stare at his retreating behind moving down the hall towards the elevators.

I smile at her description because I feel that same way. "His name is Alex; I met him a few weeks ago. He asked me to dinner tonight."

"Get out of here, Mallory! Run to Vegas and marry that good-looking piece of meat tonight!" Annie exclaims as she rapidly fans her face with a file folder taken from my desk.

As we both burst into laughter, I ask her to help me file my stack of designs. Before we realize it is 5:30 pm and time to head home.

Entering the main room of our house, I glance up the staircase. Madison left yesterday for a business conference in Texas so she won't be home for a couple weeks. Mika, I am sure, is working late again. So I feel a bit disappointed that I have no one to share my good news. Grabbing my phone from my bag, I decide to call my parents to share my promotion with them.

"Hi sweetheart, how was your day?"

"Mom, I had a fantastic day. I got a promotion at work."

"That's splendid news honey. What will you be doing?"

"Well, Steven is retiring so they are giving me his position. No interview or anything. I will be Senior Account Executive and Director Mallory Winston."

"Baby, I am so happy for you. How are you celebrating with the girls this evening?"

I decide not to mention my date with Alex. My mom is itching for grandkids and since I am the oldest, she has been hounding me to get married.

"I will probably wait to celebrate when Madison gets back from her round of conventions in two weeks. So tonight, it will just be me, a glass of wine, and some trashy TV."

"Well, there is nothing wrong with a night like that," she says through her laughter. "Mallory, I need to go check on dinner. I will pass along your good news to the rest of the family. Congratulations. We love you."

"Thanks, Mom. I love you all too."

As I hang-up and release a sigh. I miss them. Richmond isn't too far away; I need to plan a visit soon.

After ending my call, I glance down at my watch and notice that it is already 6:15pm. Realizing that there isn't a lot of time to get ready I stumble into the bathroom and take a shower making sure to buff and shave every inch of my body. As I let my curling iron heat up, I blow dry my hair and then walk into my bedroom to decide what to wear. Alex seems like the domineering type and he told me to wear my wrap dress this evening, but I want to wear something that I haven't sat in all day. There was no mention of where we were going so I'm not sure what to choose. Sifting through my closet, I pull out one of my special event dresses. The dark purple strapless dress glides over my body with the hem landing just above my knees. Forging through the bottom of my closet, I find some cute black heeled sandals to finish off my outfit. Back in the bathroom, I attempt to curl my hair into waves and apply some makeup. My smoky eye attempt is a disaster so I clean my face and apply some mascara to give myself a more natural look. At 7:00pm on the dot, the main entrance doorbell rings, starting my heart in a gallop. Taking deep breaths, I grab a black quarter length sweater and head out the door to meet Alex's driver, Gregory.

Waiting at my door is a very tall and large man, in his late thirties, with very kind blue eyes. As he introduces himself as Alex's driver and head of security, I ask him why Alex needs a head of security. With a boisterous chuckle, he ignores my questions and escorts me to the back of a waiting town car and he steps into the driver's seat. The trip is taken in silence, as I don't trust my nerves enough to ask hundreds of questions regarding my date. In an attempt to relax, I glare out the window and notice we are on Light Street, which is only a couple blocks from the inner harbor area. Abruptly, the car turns onto an adjacent street and stops in front of an expensive steakhouse.

As Gregory assists me in exiting the car, the valet ushers me to the door of the restaurant and the host immediately guides me to a private room off the main dining area. She moves aside to let me enter the room and I see Alex standing beside an empty chair beckoning me forward. A dark gray suit with a dark purple silk tie and pocket square adorns his frame. The suit and accessories must have been chosen to match my dress from earlier. I'm secretly glad that I chose the same color palate when I changed. With a released breath, I take a tentative step towards the chair and attempt to sit down.

Pushing my chair towards the table Alex whispers in my ear, "You look delectable this evening, though I am a tad disappointed you aren't wearing your wrap dress. I had visions of untying it later."

Reaching around to take off my sweater with shaking hands, I gasp as Alex's hand brushes across my bare skin. Our touch has not only affected me, but I can hear Alex's breath hitch when his fingertips trace along my shoulder.

He leans down to speak again, his warm breath whispering across my ear, "I cannot say I am saddened by your alternative choice of attire for the evening. This dress has wonderful possibilities as well."

The waiter steps forward to pour our water as Alex moves around the table to sit in his chair.

"Mallory, I took the liberty of ordering for us this evening."

"Thank you. I've never eaten here before, it seems quite extravagant."

"You will enjoy it," Alex says and then continues, "I want to apologize for my actions at your office earlier today. I do not normally lose control in that manner, but I was drawn to you in that instant."

A deep shade of blush dances across my cheeks in remembrance of earlier.

"That's ok, Alex. I enjoyed it," I whisper as he nods in understanding and shifts in his chair, obviously adjusting himself.

Our wine and meal arrive and we begin to exchange your typical first date banter. Alex has an older brother and a younger sister, Nicholas and Abigail. He studied medicine at Oxford University and he is here volunteering his time at a local institute. I asked him where his accent came from and he said he was born and bred in the English countryside. It was a bit strange that he wouldn't divulge what his parents or siblings do for a living, but I wasn't disheartened.

With a sexy smirk gliding along Alex's lips, he inquires about my family with great interest. I explain to him that my parents gave birth to me at the age of twenty after being married only a year and that we have a very close relationship. At age nineteen, my twin brothers are ten years younger than I am and they are both currently enrolled at Virginia Polytechnic Institute to study architecture. The discussion of families makes me miss my own and the saddened look on my face pulls the attention of Alex.

"Mallory, is something wrong? Is the food not to your liking?"

"Oh no, Alex, the food is wonderful. I have never had a meal this mouth watering," I say shaking my head quickly. "Just all this talk about family is making me miss my own."

"I understand. I have been here for only a month and I miss my family as well. It was different when I was at University. Now that I choose to be on my own, I miss them more."

As we finish dinner, he grabs the waiter's attention and orders us dessert. Chocolate cake for him and crème brulé for me.

"You don't look like someone that indulges in chocolate cake often," I say to Alex, skimming my eyes across his muscular chest.

"I have quite the sweet tooth and we are celebrating. Of course, I will have to devote extra time at the gym for this luxury."

At my answering giggle, a huge grin spreads across his face and I could stare at his perfect smile for days.

"Was there something else you wanted to discuss this evening? I remember you mentioning something in my office."

"Yes, I did and I still do, but we have barely started our night. We will discuss more later."

"Later?"

"Patience, Ms. Winston."

We exit the restaurant and I slide into the town car as Gregory holds the door for both Alex and me. As the car begins to move, Alex trails his fingers up and down my elbow to my wrist so softly it feels like a feather. I wonder if he can hear my heartbeat speeding up. The car stops suddenly and I glance outside to see we are stopped in front of the science museum. One of my brows arch as I look toward Alex in a confused manner and he shakes his head. As he helps me to exit the car, our fingers intertwine around clasped hands and he pulls me toward the planetarium. Walking though the entrance, I observe that there aren't any other patrons. A guide shows us to our seats toward the back of the stadium and then the show promptly begins. As a narrator points out the constellations in the night sky, I sit mesmerized by the vision before me.

"This is breathtaking," I whisper to Alex.

"Yes, it is," his voice slightly deeper than earlier.

Sensing his gaze on me, I turn my face in his direction. With the heated blush creeping across my cheeks again, I am thankful for the darkness of the room. Grabbing my hand, Alex rubs small circles onto my wrist in a seemingly nervous gesture.

"Mallory, I want to discuss something with you."

"Uh, Ok?"

"I will only be here until the end of July and then I must head back to England for some business regarding my family."

"Oh," I respond letting the disappointment seep into my voice.

"Do not be upset my lovely; I want to spend every remaining second I have here, in your company."

"Oh," I say trying to sound more excited but instead it comes out sounding a bit husky.
The circle he is rubbing onto my wrist is sending sparks in a straight line towards my pelvis.

"I want you, Mallory, all of you, for the next sixty days. I want you to be at my disposal. I want you to give yourself over to me, body and mind, so that I have complete control over you. I can guarantee that you will never have experienced such pleasure. We have an overwhelming connection. I know you can feel it, Mallory. What I'd like more than anything, is for you to give me a chance to explore it."

His words cause me to think back to the BDSM novel I have been reading.

"How? Will I have to sign a contract with limits and safe words? Will you hurt me?"

"No, of course not, Mallory. I would never hurt you," he rushes and rubs his hand across the back of his neck before taking a deep breath continuing, "I have never done this formally so forgive me for not explaining this properly. We will only need a contract if you feel you need one, but I'm here for only a short time. I will gladly have my lawyer draw one up if you find it is necessary. We don't need to focus on explaining our limits now; we can discuss them during certain scenes. I can tell you are inexperienced by the way you react to my touch, so please trust me enough to know that I won't cross any lines. I will push your limits, but I will never step beyond what I believe you can handle. We can have a safe word of your choosing; though I hope we would not ever need to use one. Mallory, I have never wanted to explore this world with anyone beyond those that have already been enlightened."

"So, you want me to submit to you? Call you sir or master? Wear a collar? Do everything you say? I'm not sure I can do that. I mean, I'm used to doing what is expected of me, but I don't think this is the same thing."

"You can call it what you want, Mallory, whether it be a relationship or domination/submission. I would prefer you call me sir, not master, as that is what I am accustomed to in my life. As far as a collar, you will need to wear something that shows that you belong to me," he says as he strokes his knuckles softly across my cheek."I have something in mind that I think you will be pleased with if you accept my terms. Also, you will only need to follow my commands when we are together. At your work place and alone with your friends you are free to act how you desire. And remember, Mallory, I can only do what you allow. You will always have power over me, my dear," Alex concludes with a gentle smile across his mouth and eyes.   Without hesitation, I take a deep breath and make a request. "I would like some time to think about it. May I ask a question or two?"

"Of course."

"How many others have you had this lifestyle with?"

"Not as many as you would think. I would only consider two an actual relationship. One when I first began and realized I thrived on control. That relationship lasted through my undergraduate term. And then there was a second affair that lasted while I went through Medical School."

"Why did they end?"

"They both met someone that fulfilled them more than I could. They are both happily married and one is expecting their second child. I am very pleased for them both."

As a sigh of relief escapes from my lips I purge forth, "What made you seek control like this?"

Visibly clenching his jaw to hold back his anger, Alex says, "I have already answered your two questions,

Ms. Winston, and normally I would seek some form of retribution in regards to questioning me more. But considering your curiosity of our proposed relationship I suppose I can give you another answer."

"I'm sorry, I didn't realize —"

Cutting off my words he exclaims, "To answer your question, no particular person, situation, or upbringing brought me into this lifestyle. When I began having sex, I noticed I liked to dominate my partners. I looked up others that practiced the same manners as myself and learned some of the basics in establishing these forms of relationships. I tend to favor the consensual but informal side of the affairs. It's not nearly as sad a story as those books, I am sure you have read, describe," he says sending a sexy smirk my way causing me to blush again. "Mallory, please consider what I'm asking of you. If you need a day to consider, please take it. I want this to work and I want as much time with you as I can, but this is all I can offer."

He kisses the back of my hand as the show in the planetarium comes to a close. When the house lights come on, I look around at the empty stadium.

"Alex, where is everyone else?"

"I booked this showing for us."

"You did? Why did you do that?"

"I have my ways, Ms. Winston, and I don't like my intentions questioned. I wanted some time alone with you so I ensured that it would happen. Of course, it is a shame you didn't wear your wrap dress, we could have created a better show than those of the constellations." The meaning laced within his words shoot electricity to my core, triggering me to bite my lip. "You look even more beautiful when your cheeks turn that shade of pink."

As the guide escorts us out of the planetarium, we head towards the waiting car with Gregory standing by the open door.

"Does he always sit and wait for you?"

"Not always, but I requested his services for tonight since I knew we were going to have wine with dinner."

"Oh."

Sliding into the car, Alex reaches across the back of the cushion and pulls me toward his side so that I am situated snuggly beside him in the center of the seat. He seems content with this arrangement so I rest my head on his shoulder as he begins to stroke up and down my arm. We don't have a far trip before reaching my home so I fight my eyelids against sleep.

After everything Alex revealed, I have a lot to consider if I want to spend more time with him. It pains me to think that this may be the last time that we see each other. At that realization, a sigh escapes my lips. With a glance down at me, he kisses the top of my head making me feel special, treasured. Falling in love with him would be far too easy. This notion is what has me the most scared about our potential affair.

The car stops in front of my home breaking this content bubble I have encased around myself. Ever the gentleman, Alex ushers me out the car and moves to walk me inside. I open the main door and we stop in front of the entrance to my apartment, each unwilling to let the other go.

"Would you like to come in, Alex?"

"Thank you, but no. I have a few things I need to take care of back at my place," he replies as he rakes his fingers through his thick mane of hair in a seemingly nervous gesture.

"Oh, okay. Well, thank you for a lovely evening; I had a wonderful time."

"You are most certainly welcome, Ms. Winston," he says as he hands me a business card. "Please contact Gregory no later than 4:00pm tomorrow if you decide that you would like to pursue this with me."

"I will let you know either way, Mr. Stone," I resolve as I stare up into his golden eyes and find myself getting lost in their pools of color.

Leaning forward, Alex rests his forehead against my own.

"Please say yes, Mallory," he whispers.

I reply in the same hushed tone, "I just need time."

"I understand. I am trying to be a patient man, which is not something I am familiar with," he says as he takes a deep breath. "This may be the last time we will see each other and I really want to kiss you."

My gaze flickers down to his lips and my tongue darts out to wet my pout.

"Ok," I reply.

Swooping in before I even finish the word, his mouth is so urgent and passionate against my own. It's as if he needs to capture my soul through this kiss and change my heartbeat match his own. My body is pinned against the front door by his weight and the ardor in this kiss seizes the air in my lungs. Nothing I have ever experienced can come close to how I feel in this moment. Roaming along my body, one of Alex's hands finds itself massaging my right breast, while his left hand starts to hike up the skirt of my dress. That same hand meanders over to the front of my panties and pushes aside the lace, trailing his fingers through my slick folds.

"Ms. Winston," he groans. "You are so wet for me. Your body already knows what it wants," Alex whispers along my mouth.

His right hand tugs down the top of my strapless dress and the cups of my bra and at the upward thrust of my breasts Alex leans down and promptly licks around my nipples, spending a minute on one and then switching to the other. I hear him groan as he sucks a nipple into his mouth, sounding more insatiable every second. His finger starts to circle around my clitoris, burning a fire in my womb. Knowing I won't last much longer, whispers of his name escape my throat and I gasp as the sensation takes over me.

As reality slowly drifts back into my senses, Alex adjusts my dress and trails kisses up my neck to my ear.

"That was the most beautiful thing I have ever seen. I look forward to hearing from you tomorrow, Ms. Winston. Have a pleasurable night," he says as he places each long finger in his mouth, licking at my essence. When he steps out of our embrace, I see he needs to adjust himself and it builds my confidence to know that I affect him as much as he affects me.

"Good night, Mr. Stone."

RENEE HARLESS

Placing a quick peck on my lips, he steps out the main door towards the awaiting car.

Treading into my home, I grab a bottle of water from the kitchen and drink from it quickly, hoping to cool off my heated skin. It is only then that I realize the significance of what he is asking of me, to give myself over to him completely. To lose all sense of who I am when in his presence. Can I do that? I like to believe I have a more domineering personality. An Executive Director would need to have the capability to dictate those around her. On the other hand, I am always making sure everyone around me is taken care of before I do anything for myself and my confidence has plummeted recently. Maybe this relationship is what I need, to have someone take care of me, not to have to look out for anyone else, to have someone else appreciate what my body has to offer. I sigh aloud as I weigh the pros and cons of this potential relationship. I could really use a glass, no, make that a bottle of wine to think this over, but it is too late at night for that.

Standing in my bathroom, I shrug out of the dress and lingerie. In the mirror, I stare at myself and ponder what Alex sees in me. What makes him think that I am different from any other woman he has met? I cock my head to the side and squint my eyes in the mirror looking for something, anything, to help me make this decision.

That night I find myself again staring back at golden eyes that carry the spirit of my soul with them.

Chapter Five

THE NEXT MORNING, I have more energy than normal; certain that with my tossing and turning I would be exhausted today. After throwing on some black fitted pants, a pink silk button down blouse, and nude sandals I grab my bag and head out the door. Left with enough time to stop by the coffee shop across the street from my office, and since I normally don't make this stop, I decide to pick up three more coffees for Steven, Annie, and Stephanie.

Stepping into the lobby holding the drinks, I notice that there are at least four more security guards added to the staff. As I continue onto the open elevator, their heads all pop up as I pass and one of them speaks into his shirtsleeve. Strange, I think to myself. Making my way to my office, I see that Stephanie is on the phone at her reception desk so I place the drink onto her counter. Rewarded with a huge grin I continue on, glad that she seems to be having a better day than yesterday. Outside of another director's office I find Steven and I pass off his drink into his waiting hands. Annie steps into my office a few minutes later saying that she was up all night finalizing the guest list and has already had three cups this morning, but is in dire need of another. Filling me in on her evening, she discloses that her and her fiancé decided to get married August 1, two months away. Maybe Alex will still be here and we can go together, even as friends.

"Hey, Annie. Can I bring a date to the wedding?"

"Definitely, I had you down for a plus one. Who are you going to bring? Please say that hunk of man who was here yesterday."

"Maybe. We went out last night and had a great time, but he is pretty busy, so we will see how it goes."

"OOOHH, you will have to fill me in later. Steven needs me to go make some copies real quick. I know he wants to go over the HR forms with you as well."

"Ok, thanks."

Once Annie leaves my office, I shoot a text to Madison. She is the only person I know that you can ask any question and she won't fish for details. She won't sugar coat her response either.

> **Mallory: If you were given 2 months to do something crazy and exciting, but may lose yourself in the experience, would you?**
> **Madison: How would I lose myself?**

Mallory: You would look at aspects of your life
differently. Things that made you happy
before, may not again. But you would
have this moment in your memory
forever and that moment made you
happy.

Madison: Hm…. I'd go for it. Everyone should
want me to be happy anyway.

Mallory: Thank you.

Madison: Something I should know about?

Mallory: Nope

Madison: All right. I miss you girl. We need to
go out when I get back.

Mallory: Yes, we do. We need to celebrate, I'll
tell you about it when you get home.
Love you Madi.

Madison: Love you 2 Mal.

A knock on my office door breaks me of my inner
turmoil.

"Steven, you don't need to knock, this is still your
office. Your name is on the door."

"Not for long, they are changing it out on
Friday."

"Wow, so soon?"

"It's not soon, I wanted it done yesterday," he
chuckles. "Now about these HR forms. We just need to go
over your change in benefits, pay grade, and security
access."

"I didn't think about any of that yesterday."

"I didn't want to overwhelm you. Anyway, let's get started."

We read through, fill out the new benefits form, and sign for my new security access card. Steven shows me how to log into payroll for Annie and the new assistant when he starts tomorrow. Apparently, one of the other executive's son will be my assistant.

"Thank you, Steven, for everything."

"No need to thank me, but you are certainly welcome. I have a few meetings this afternoon and I would like for you to join me so we can do some formal introductions."

"Sure, just grab me when you're ready."

The morning passes as I complete my task of sorting old design files. With a few free minutes, I reach into my purse and fiddle with the business card Alex handed me yesterday evening. I know what I *want* to do, but I am not sure if that is what I *should* do. Fear inhabits my heart as I am afraid to lose myself in Alex's possession, but I don't want to regret my decision to tell him no. Instantly I listen to my heart, make my final decision, and dial the number on the card. There is no answer and the call goes straight to voicemail. With a deep breath and shaky voice, I leave a message for Gregory to share with Alex.

For the first time in seven years, I eat lunch alone. I'm sure that Seth went to lunch earlier with Stephanie. After finishing my sandwich, I head back upstairs to my office where Steven finds me minutes later and ushers us into a large conference room for my introduction to the rest of the senior staff. Most of the Directors and Vice

Presidents I have met throughout the years and send me a welcome smile. The CEO asks for an update on my current campaigns and I explain my designs and current clients, seeming to impress everyone with my workload. Steven assures them that I know these projects better than anyone else does and that I would present the clothing campaign to the client tomorrow.

As I head back to my office to prepare some documents for the other directors, I find that it is already 5:00pm and I haven't received any messages. With a reluctant grab of my purse, I stroll towards the elevators where Steven joins me and we ride down to the lobby discussing what he is going to do during his retirement.

Saying goodbye to Steven, I head towards my car and notice a bright red convertible double-parked in front of my Mini Cooper. As I try to figure out whose car this is, I don't notice the man standing on the other side of my Mini Cooper holding deep purple calla lilies.

"Good evening, Ms. Winston."
At the sound of a stranger's voice, I scream placing my hand over my heart.

"Geez, Alex, you scared the crap out of me," I say while catching my breath. "Are those flowers for me?"

"Yes, they are," he says with a small smirk as he lets his gaze travel up and down my body.

"They're beautiful."

"Not nearly as beautiful as you," he says as he moves around the car to stand in front of me.

"How did you know that they were my favorite flower?"

"I didn't. I took a guess since they were on your office coffee table yesterday. I am glad I assumed correctly."

"Did Gregory give you my message?"
Leaning down he places a sweet kiss on my lips.

"Yes, yes he did. Are you ready to go? We can take my car and Gregory can drive yours."

"Gregory is here?" I say while glancing around. "Why can't I follow you?"

"Yes, he is. He stepped into the lobby momentarily, but should be out shortly. And I want you in the car with me, Mallory."

I smirk and reply, "And so it begins."

He guides his hand across my cheek, lingering on my jaw line, and then leans down and says, "Sweetheart, you have no idea," he breathes out.

Gracing me with a heart-stopping kiss, coughing in the background startles us both from our moment. Turning, we find Gregory standing a few feet from where we are and heat rushes across my cheeks in embarrassment. With a quick hello and wave, I hand him the keys to my vehicle and I walk over the sports car. I hope he's able to fit in my pint-sized vehicle. Alex ushers me into the car and then moves to his side, gliding elegantly into the driver's seat.

"What kind of car is this?" I ask.

"This, sweet girl, is a Jaguar F-type. She was a thirtieth birthday present from my parents."

"When was your birthday?"

"Three weeks ago. The night we met."

"Oh, I had no idea!"

With a small shrug of his shoulders and toss of his hand Alex replies, "It is not a problem, meeting you was the best present I could have asked for."
Reaching over to grab my hand, he places a gentle kiss on my knuckles.

Answering my unspoken thought, Alex says, "We are going someplace special so that we can answer one of your questions."

"Which question?"

"You will be pleased with the answer, Mallory. Believe that."

"Yes, sir."

Alex turns his head quickly in my direction and inhales rapidly.

"Oh baby, you don't know what you do to me when you say that," he responds with a sexy grin.
I answer his smile with a smirk of my own.

We glide onto the highway and hum of the car puts me at ease. Whipping in and out of traffic gracefully, he pulls off the highway and enters an area I have never ventured to before. Parking the car, he leads me towards a store across the street.

"A jewelry store?" I question.

"I have ordered our item prior to today, but we can still browse. You look most beautiful when you are excited." Turning in his direction with a large grin on my face, I grasp him in a giant hug.

"Thank you," I whisper into his chest, holding back the unannounced tears that threaten to fall at my joy.

The welcoming staff greets us as we walk into the store. One employee acknowledges Alex directly and then they step away to the back of the store to retrieve the item. Strolling along the lit-up glass containers, I am mesmerized by all of the diamond engagement rings. A two and a half carat, round, brilliant stone with a white gold band has caught my attention and I am halted in place. It is simple and classic and by far the most exquisite ring I have ever seen.

"Find anything you like?" Alex says in a humorous tone.

When I glance up, I am met with a smirk and a wink.

Pointing to the ring I was admiring I say, "I may buy that for myself one day, just to look at on my hand."

"You are a funny girl, Ms. Winston. Let's go home."

Thanking the staff, we head back towards the car.

"Were you able to get what you came for, Alex?"

"I believe so," he states with a secretive smile on his lips.

As we head out on the highway, Alex glances at me.

"Mallory, I hope I am not being presumptuous, but I would like you to stay with me this evening and every other evening until I leave."

Shaking my head slightly, I can't help but wipe my now clammy hands on my legs. Taking a deep breath to calm my nerves I turn in Alex's direction and lick my lips before saying, "I'd like to stay tonight. Other than celebrating with the girls next weekend and picking a time to visit my family, I can stay every night."

"That pleases me, Ms. Winston. Perhaps if things are going well I can join you when you visit your family," Alex responds with a quick glance in my direction and a coolness in his voice that does little to calm my nerves causing me to focus on a small piece of his statement.

I begin to hyperventilate at that notion. "Why would things not go well?"

"Calm down, Mallory. We don't have a signed contract with terms and a stated timeframe. If you are unhappy or want out of our arrangement, I will let you go. That's all."

My attachment to Alex is already reaching an alarming state and I can't imagine being without him, yet I know next to nothing about him. We are only having a short-term affair so I shouldn't be surprised that Alex would have no difficulty letting me go. Sensing my unease, Alex grabs my hand and squeezes before letting go to down shift the car.

Turning off the interstate, we stop at a few lights before coming to a halt. I tentatively glance out the window to see we are in front of The Braxton building. *Holy shit*, I think to myself. A valet comes around to guide me out of the vehicle, while a second valet retrieves the keys from Alex.

Taking my hand in his own and clasping the jewelry bag in the other, Alex guides me towards the wall of elevators inside the lobby. Releasing my hold temporarily, he takes out a key and selects an elevator that, he says, will lead to his penthouse. The elevator pings to his floor and we step out into a small vestibule to face two double doors on the right.

RENEE HARLESS

Opening the door, Alex guides me inside and on a tour of his home. He says he shares it with his family when they visit, but that he owns the property. To the left of the foyer is a guest room decorated in an array of blues. Heading to the main living room and dining room, I admire the color of the walls, which are a soft brown, similar to the color of his eyes. The wood trim around the room has been painted white, while all of the furniture is a dark, rich hue with accents of green and blue placed throughout. We walk through the dining room into to the family room, which has a large gray sectional facing an enormous television, light gray walls, and artwork with pops of bright colors. Across the family room stands the kitchen with dark wood, light gray countertops, and stainless-steel appliances. I find that Alex's style is very masculine but clean and modern. Stepping through another door off the kitchen, we walk back through the foyer. Alex points down the hall, says there is a butler's pantry at the end, and then points to my left showing a guest bedroom of yellows and whites. To the right there is a powder room and a media room. Stopping at a set of double doors Alex leads me inside and I am in shock at the size of this bedroom. Walking to the left down a small hall, I find an oversized bed in silver tones against walls of dark purple. Off the bedroom is a sitting area with a small library and a bathroom that is much larger than my bedroom. There is a gigantic built-in tub as well as a large walk-in shower. Continuing my hunt, I ignore a locked door in the hallway and head towards the balcony off the master suite.

The sun is beginning to turn the heavens into a mirage of brilliant pinks and purples across the night sky. I find Alex perched against the railing, waiting for me with open arms. Rushing into his hold, I rest my cheek against his chest as he softly strokes my back.

"I ordered dinner from the concierge when we arrived. It should be here shortly. I hope salmon will suffice for the evening."

"It will thank you. I would love to cook for you one evening. I enjoy cooking, but it is hard when it's only for one person."

Smiling at my offer Alex says, "I would like that. I have something for you."

Holding a blue box out for me, I step back from his grasp and open the package. Inside is a classic heart tag necklace. Gazing at the simplistic beauty of the necklace, I am in shock to receive such a remarkable gift. Looking closer I notice next to the traditional heart charm is another heart. This one is open and made of diamonds. As my fingers glide across the stones, Alex acknowledges my fascination.

"I am assured by the jeweler that this open-heart charm can withstand a weight of 100lbs, as can the chain." A horrified expression must cross my face because he quickly clears up his statement. "Not that it would be necessary, but you may enjoy a little leash play. We can discuss that when the time comes."

Nodding my head, I reply, "Thank you, Alex. It is beautiful."

"A beautiful necklace for a beautiful woman. This will be your collar, Mallory. It will be inconspicuous and no one will know what it stands for, but every time you glance at it you will think of me and what I can do to you and you to me." He takes the necklace out of the box and clasps it around my neck, letting his fingers linger along my neckline for a few extra seconds. "Come, dinner should be here," he says.

Stepping back into the house we move to the dining room. Placed on the table are two trays of food and a chilled bottle of champagne. Pulling out a chair for me, Alex busies himself pouring each of us a glass of wine and arranging our dinner plates, before sitting down himself. Raising his glass Alex makes a toast.

"To new beginnings and arrangements."
Joining into his toast, I raise my glass and try to stifle any looks of apprehension. Not quite sure what I am expected to do, I wait for Alex to begin eating, and then I dive in. The salmon has a cinnamon glaze on it, as do the carrots, and they are both mouth watering.

"Ms. Winston, you seem out of sorts," Alex says taking note of my quietness.

Wanting to aim for honesty I twirl my wine glass stem between my fingers as I tell Alex, "I'm sorry sir; I am just a bit nervous."

Setting down his utensils Alex looks into my eyes. "You are doing a splendid job already in regard to waiting for me to prompt you to your actions."

"That's not why I'm apprehensive. I'm, uh, nervous about the sexual side of our relationship. I mean, I'm not naive; I know what this relationship entails. It's just that I have only had sex with one person and that was only a couple of times. He was disappointed in me and dumped me because of it."

"I see," pausing, and then continuing, "Ms. Winston, you and I both know that a well orchestrated performance relies on players from all sides. If he believed your performance was lacking then he is just as much, if not more, to blame than you are. If he knew you were inexperienced, he should have guided you like a conductor. I believe that we will make beautiful music together. We have a very heated connection to the point where I find it difficult to keep my hands off you. Wouldn't you agree, Ms. Winston?"

"Yes, sir," I reply, trying to control the blush that I feel creeping up my face.

"I'm glad we have the same opinion. Now I will ease you into all of our sexual endeavors. We will not begin at a starting point beyond your current boundaries. With that being said, all this talk about performance has me itching to taste you," he says as his tongue peeks outside his mouth and he licks his lips causing a burst of desire to pool in my belly. "I would like you to go into the master bedroom, take off all of your clothes only leaving your undergarments, and stand beside the foot of the bed."

Without hesitation, I move quickly to the bedroom and follow his command.

RENEE HARLESS

Chapter Six

ENTERING THE BEDROOM, I begin removing my clothes, folding them, and placing them on the floor in front of the bed. Not wanting to disappoint Alex, I stand on the right, beside the end of the sleigh bed with my hands clasped in front of me, waiting. I remember all of my books saying that girls knelt and were positioned a certain way. Alex hasn't instructed me on anything particular so I continue to stand and keep my head down. In this position, I stare down at my feet and realize that I need a pedicure. The thought makes me giggle and as the noise escapes my lips Alex chooses that moment to walk into the room.

"Are you giggling, Ms. Winston?" Unsure if I am allowed to speak, I look up into Alex's eyes in horror. "You may speak."

"Yes, I'm sorry, sir."

"What, pray tell, have you found so amusing?"

"I hadn't noticed that I needed a pedicure, sir. My polish is chipped."

"Well I can't say that I understand your humor, but as I am not a female I will not seek punishment for your break of silence." Continuing into the room Alex comes to stand in front of me tilting my chin up with his finger. "You are quite lovely to admire, Mallory. I hope to meet your expectations."

My expectations? I thought I was here to please him.

"Ms. Winston, you have done a magnificent job thus far. From this time forth, whenever I ask you to prepare yourself, I would like you to come directly to this room and strip down as you have and then put this on." He shows me a soft, silk, black nightie. It is nicer than anything I have ever slept in. "Once you have put on the garment, I would like you to continue to place your folded clothing on the floor and stand where you are with your head down. Do you have any questions?"

"Yes, sir. What do I do the remainder of the time I am with you?"

"You can continue to act as you normally do. I will instruct you if you displease me. Understand?"

"Yes, sir."

"Good. Now a few details, Ms. Winston. Are you on birth control?"

"Yes sir. I received my shot two weeks ago. And I received a clean bill of health from my doctor at that time too."

"Very good. I am clean as well and I can show you the documentation if you wish. Next, I am under the assumption that you will not breathe a word of our actions outside of this apartment. It would hurt your blossoming reputation as well as my own and I would hate to come after you for slander or defamation."

"Oh, goodness no! I would never say anything," I rush out, feeling slight trembles rack my body. My need for him in this moment completely tops my apprehension about our arrangement.

"I know, darling. Calm down. I just needed to verify. Finally, I do not typically have females stay the night with me. I either have Gregory take them home or send them to the guest room across the apartment. But since our time is short, I would enjoy having you in my bed the remainder of my stay."

"Yes, sir," I whisper with a bowed head, trying my best to hide my smile at the thought of sharing Alex's bed.

His stare lingers on me for a moment before he speaks again, "You are much better at this than you believe, Ms. Winston. You have been very willing to give up your control. I am finding this quality in you extremely sexy." Alex takes the black nightie away from me and tosses it on top of my clothes. "We won't need that tonight. You look divine in this set of pink lingerie, Mallory. I may have to buy you more of these."

With his few sexual words, I am already dripping with desire for him. The pink panties I am wearing are soaked and my nipples are poking through my lace bra, aching to be touched. Reaching forward Alex pulls me up against him, rubbing my erect nipples against his chest. With a delicate touch, he traces my jaw line with his nose and nips at my ear.

"You smell so good, Mallory. I can't wait to taste you," he says as his gravelly voice glides across my face.

A moan escapes my mouth at his spoken words. All of my hesitation about our situation dissipates as his mouth reaches my own. All of our desires are portrayed in this kiss. Strolling down my back, his hand reaches my behind as my hands drape around his neck and I lift my legs to wrap around his waist. I can feel his erection through his pants and I find myself growing even more in wetness. One of his hands grips the hair close to my head and my nipples begin to ache from rubbing against his chest.

Suddenly, I feel myself placed on his bed with my legs hanging off the edge. Alex bends down and glances up at me past his dark thick lashes. The smoldering stare stays on me as he reaches up to hook his fingers around my panties. As he tugs them down my legs, I can hear my breath quicken.

"Unhook your bra and take it off," he orders. Following his command, I toss my bra towards the floor at the end of the bed, hoping it lands with my pile of clothes. Gazing at my bare body, heat and want pass across Alex's eyes.

"My god, Mallory. You are the most breath-taking woman I have ever seen."

Reaching towards my knees, he spreads my legs farther apart. Closing my eyes, I can feel kisses trail from my heel, up my calve, and stop at my upper thigh. Switching to the other leg, Alex performs the same routine. The fire in my lower belly ignites and I swear that one touch to my center and I will explode. I'm amazed at this man's talent as just his lips on my legs are bringing me to the brink. My breath starts to speed up as he kisses closer to my core and then I gasp as he licks my folds. Sliding his tongue a few times, he then reaches up to part the sensitive skin, causing me to release a moan. As his tongue enters my center, my hips begin to move on their own accord. Stretching my center with his fingers, he begins to circle his tongue around my throbbing nub of nerves. As the nibbling on my clit continues, I realize I won't be able to hold back much longer, letting out a startled moan as I explode. The orgasm is so strong that I see stars. Alex continues to pump his fingers in and out of me, waiting for my orgasm to subside.

Standing quickly, Alex begins to remove his clothes and in a blur, all of his clothing lands on the floor. Slack-jawed at his beauty I take a moment out of my lustful haze to appreciate his body. My gaze travels across the broad and muscular shoulders, down to the taught muscles across his abdomen, downward to the athletic build of his thighs. Even his naked feet are gorgeous. Alex is a work of perfection. Growing wetter by the second, I'm knocked out of my fog when he begins to move closer.

Moving me farther onto the bed, Alex whispers, "I'm sorry, sweetheart. I wanted this to be slow and sensual, but I can't control myself. I need you now."

"Yes," I let out as a moan.

His mouth meets my own and Alex plunges into me a second later. He thrusts inside me twice, but abruptly stops. With his erection still inside me, I can feel his heavy breathing against my neck.

"You feel so good. I don't want to hurt you, but you're so tight."

He begins kissing me again, but I pull away and rock my hips, urging him to continue.

"Please, don't stop, Alex. It feels too good."

Placing more kisses on my neck, he reaches around and hikes one of my legs around his arm. Starting slowly, Alex rocks back and forth, but soon the thrusts come harder and faster. Nothing has ever felt this good. Wanting him deep, I dig my heel into Alex's back and after figuring out my intention; he turns me over on the bed. Lifting me by my waist, he pulls my body up so that I am up on my hands and knees and he enters me from behind. This is the deepest penetration I have ever had and it is a bit painful at first, but that feeling is quickly overshadowed by pleasure. Alex pulls me back using my hips at the same time he thrusts forward. I can feel his sweat dripping off his chest and onto my back. As the pleasure continues to grow, I can feel my body begin to shake at the intensity.

"Not yet," Alex says behind gritted teeth.
I try to hold back my climax, but the feelings of pleasure are hard to withstand. Reaching his pinnacle, Alex spanks me hard and I let go at the same time his hand makes contact with my skin. Falling into a heap on the bed, we both try to steady our breathing.

Lifting me into his arms, Alex moves off the bed and carries me into the bathroom, sitting me on the edge of the tub. While he starts the water, and adds some bath salts, he lifts me again and we settle into the bath. As Alex positions me across his lap, I tuck my head into his neck. Scooping up water in his hands, he pours it over my shoulders.

"Do you want me to wash you?" he says.

"Can I just sit here with you instead?"

"Sure, sweetheart. I enjoy having you in my arms."

Relaxing into the warm water, wrapped in the arms of the man of my dreams, I fall into a peaceful sleep. Moments later, I wake up to find myself being carried to Alex's bed.

"Sleep well, darling," Alex declares.

I reply behind a sleep-filled voice, "Alex, can you set an alarm for me? I need to be up for work at 6:30am."

"Anything for you, beautiful. Get some rest." Folding me into his arms, we drift off to sleep.

*   *   *

The buzz of the alarm echoes across the room at 6:30am and I look across the bed into Alex's sleeping face. He is a stunning man and I can't believe that he is mine for the next two months. Rolling onto my back, I stretch and then get out of bed heading towards the shower. Joining me a minute later, Alex pins me against the tile wall, pulling my legs up to wrap around his waist as he kisses me fervently. My core was dripping the minute I saw his face this morning so he glides into me easily. One of his hands pins both my wrists above my head and he moves his mouth from mine to start nibbling at my neck as he continues to pound into me.

"Oh, baby, I am so close. You're so hot and wet. I won't hold out much longer," he pronounces.

"Yes, Alex, yes," I moan.

His erection thickens inside me and soon he spurts out his seed. With one more thrust, I let go of my climax. Resting our heads against the tile, he breathes heavily into my neck.

Minutes later Alex utters, "I'm sorry I interrupted your shower. When I saw you get out of bed naked this morning I couldn't help myself."

I smile an innocent smile at him and answer, "Alex, you can interrupt me anytime."

His answering smirk causes my heart to speed up, but he quickly realizes my thoughts and shakes his head. Instead of another round, he grabs a loofa. From my head to my toes, he cleans me, paying special attention to the area between my legs. Pouring his shampoo in my hands, I wash my hair and then offer to wash his back. Once we finish removing the scent of sex from our bodies, we step out of the shower. Grabbing heated towels from the rack Alex wraps the material around my body. Time has escaped both of us and knowing that I need to leave soon, I decide to throw my hair into a French twist. Only then do I realize that I don't have anything to wear for work. I huff and stare at my clothes on the floor from last night.

"Mallory, what's wrong?" Alex asks, concern laced in his voice.

"I don't have anything to wear to work today and I have a major presentation to give to some clients."

Grabbing my hand, Alex walks me towards the locked office, where a walk-in closet stands across. He directs me towards the back of the closet where I find a slew of clothing all in my size.

Speaking to me with downcast eyes, seemingly embarrassed, Alex says, "I wanted you to have everything you need here so that you feel more inclined to stay with me. In the dresser in the center you will find an array of lingerie in your size."

"How do you know my size?"

With his hands now firmly placed on his sexy hips Alex replies, "Mallory, I know everything I need to."

"Thank you, sir. These will be lovely," I say turning quickly from Alex to hide my blush.

I open the dresser drawers and find a number of lace bras with front clasps and matching panties. Naturally drawn to the purple pair I snatch up the lace attire and put them on. These are much sexier than my normal undergarments. Turning towards the racks with clothing, I decide on a gray pencil skirt and bright green silk top. Feeling my skin ignite in a scorching heat, I glance into the full-length mirror to find Alex's stare burning into me from behind as I pull the clothing off their hangers.

"You are quite the site, Ms. Winston. I could watch you for eons of time."

I blush and stutter, "Thank you, sir. I'm running a bit behind so I need to get dressed."

"As you wish."

"Oh and Alex, have you seen my necklace? I had it on last night, but I can't find it now," I say as my hand strokes across my naked neck.

"I took it off of you when you fell asleep in the bath. It is resting on the counter in the bathroom," Alex assures me.

"Thank you," I say as I rub my hands over my crossed arms. "For everything. For letting me have this time with you."

"You are most certainly welcome and believe me, I should be thanking you. Breakfast is waiting for you in the kitchen when you are ready. I have left another item for you on the kitchen counter as well. It is to only be used for me as it has been pre-programmed." Coming closer to where I stand he gives me a sweet kiss on my lips. "I have to head to the Institute, so Gregory will help you receive your car from the valet. I will be there late this evening, so I will collect you around 8:00pm at your home."

"Yes, sir," I pause and gaze into his eyes. "I hope that you have a good day, Alex. I will see you tonight." I stand on my toes and give him a kiss on his lips.

Before stepping out of the closet, he kisses my forehead and trails his hand down my arm to my hand. After Alex steps away, I finish getting ready, grab my necklace from the bathroom, and head towards the kitchen. I have about fifteen minutes before I need to leave so I take my time to enjoy the omelet that is waiting for me.

Gregory introduces me to the concierge and advises him that I will be staying with Mr. Stone for the remainder of his time here this summer. My Mini Cooper pulls up to the entrance and I say goodbye to Gregory before heading towards my office building. Alex lives a bit closer than I do so I am here earlier than normal. With the extra time, I decide to tackle the last-minute pieces on the storyboard for my presentation at 9:00am.

Time slips by and before long, it is time to meet with the client. Grabbing my file and storyboard, I head towards the conference room. Along the way, I stop at Stephanie's desk and ask her to send the clients back when they arrive. I position my items in the room and wait. My clients are a brother and sister team, Kyle and Lily Johnson, that began designing clothing as a hobby, but have had much success designing clothing for celebrities. Their goal is to open a few retail stores so they can sell to the average consumer. They aren't much younger than I am and I am astonished at all they have achieved at such an age.

Arriving on time, we delve into the campaign pieces I have fabricated for them. Seemingly happy with our progress, I wrap up our meeting with the hopes that the campaign will be finished soon. Scheduling our follow up, I walk Lily and Kyle to the door, but on the way-out Kyle lags behind so that we are alone.

"Ms. Winston, I see that it's around lunch time. I would love if you would join me."

"Mr. Johnson, is this invitation business or personal?"

"Well, I'd like it to be personal, but it can be business if that makes you feel better," he chuckles.

Nervously I giggle and answer, "I appreciate your honesty, Mr. Johnson, but unfortunately, I don't believe in seeing clients outside of the office, whether it is personal or business related."

"Ah, I take it you have a boyfriend then."

Smiling as I think of Alex I reply, "Yes, I do."

"He is one lucky man, Ms. Winston. I hope to see you soon," Kyle states as he moves towards the door.

As he steps out, I wonder to myself what just happened. I am not accustomed to men asking me out. Now I find myself with a gorgeous man as my lover and another attractive man interested in a date with me. If this doesn't give my self-confidence a kick in the butt, I don't know what will.

Leaving the conference room, I stop by Annie's desk to give her a few projects to add to the campaign. She will learn the ropes by working on these small changes and I am happy to pass them off to her. Dropping my things off in the office, I glance into my purse for a piece of gum, but the unopened package from Alex grabs my attention. Lifting it from my bag, I untie the box and see a brand-new phone charged and ready to go. Unlocking the screen, I see that there is a waiting message prompting me to open the messaging app.

> **Alex: Good morning beautiful girl. I hope that
> you impress your client as much as
> You impress me.**

I feel a smile adorn my face as I read his message and I quickly fire back a reply.

Mallory: Hi Alex. The clients loved my campaign. All is well, but busy. I am looking forward to tonight. Thank you for the phone.

Waiting for a few moments, I set the phone down when I don't receive a response. It was nice of him to get me a new phone. My current one is on its last leg. Then I remember he said I could only use it for him. Perhaps we can negotiate and I can pay him a monthly fee to use it as my primary phone. I doubt he would want me to go without a usable device.

The calendar on my computer flashes that it is noon so I decide to head down to the cafeteria for lunch. There is a baked potato bar today so I indulge in a few extra calories after the sexual workout from last night and this morning. Seth only joins me at my table for a few minutes before huffing out of the room after receiving a message on his phone.

The new assistant started today, but I haven't gotten to speak to him much. He's been working closely with Annie, learning all her past duties. Something about him seems a tad off, but I can't put my finger on it.

Back at my office it is a busy afternoon with conference calls the remainder of the day. Steven wants me to introduce myself to all of the clients so that they become more familiar with me taking over their projects.

Before I know it the day is ending, but I stay a bit later than normal and reach my home around 6:30pm.

RENEE HARLESS

After eating a quick dinner, I turn on some music and lie on the couch hoping to catch a nap while waiting for Alex. My body and mind are exhausted from the past two days. Startling me from my deep sleep, I can feel myself being lifted from the couch and my skin burns where Alex's hand touches me.

"Sleep, beautiful girl," he whispers into my ear.

Placing me on my bed Alex slowly peels off my clothing. The bed dips slightly and I turn my body in that direction to find Alex resting on his side facing me. I want so badly to memorize the shape of his body with my fingertips, but I am too exhausted to move.

"Thank you," I whisper as he pulls me closer. With my head resting along his shoulder and our legs intertwined we drift to sleep.

Chapter Seven

THE NEXT MORNING, I wake up in a set of cold sheets. Listening for Alex in the house and hearing nothing, I realize that I am alone. Not completely sure if I dreamt that Alex was here, I stretch and get ready for work. While grabbing a granola bar from my kitchen, I see my necklace sitting on the kitchen counter. Anger surges through my veins. Furious that Alex hasn't left me a note to excuse his quick exit; I toss the necklace in my bag and head out the door. During my car ride, I replay the previous night in my head causing my emotions to change from angry, to hurt, then to a combination of the two. I know he is busy and may have only left early this morning, but my feelings are hurt that he didn't say goodbye.

Entering my office, I steer clear of Stephanie and Annie. Once they see the anger written across my face, I know that they will pry me for details. At my desk, I stare at my email program and then pull out my phone. No missed calls, no voicemail, and no messages. What the hell? Did I say something in my sleep to make him upset with me? With utter confusion added into my heady state, I try to focus on my projects.

My day passes in a haze and I haven't been even remotely productive. Everyone can tell that I am upset so they seem to avoid me at all costs. As I step into the elevator I glance at my phone again, still no messages. Not sure if I am supposed to go to his place tonight, I head towards my own.

Once I walk into the main entrance, I notice Mika is upstairs. Normally I would go up to her place and catch up, but I am not in the mood tonight. Instead, I let myself into my apartment and head toward my bedroom. After throwing on a pair of short gym shorts and comfortable a long sleeve t-shirt, I pop a bag of popcorn in the microwave and grab a glass of red wine.

"Popcorn and wine; the dinner of champions," I say out loud to myself causing me to release a chuckle.

Turning on the television, I see that *The Notebook* is playing. My emotions couldn't bear to watch that film tonight, so I turn the channel to The Food Network and settle in for a marathon of *Diners, Drive-ins, and Dives*.

After finishing off a bottle of wine I am about to start another when I hear a knock at the door. Heading towards the noise, I trip over the leg of a barstool, twisting my ankle.

"Fuck," I shout as a twinge of pain spirals up my leg.

Hopping over to the foyer, I am holding my leg up as I open the door. Expecting to find Mika on the other side, I am taken aback to find the Adonis I have been angry at all day.

Noticing the pain in my face and my leg in my hand Alex rushes forward asking, "Mallory, are you ok? Did you hurt yourself?"

Staring up at his beautiful face, I notice that his eyes look tired and he has a bit more stubble than usual.

Through gritted teeth I declare, "I'm fine I just tripped over the barstool, that's all. Why are you here?"

"Because I want you in my bed."

"Why?"

"Why what, Ms. Winston?" Alex asks impatiently, sighing as he says my name.

"Why did you leave and not say anything? I thought…I thought you didn't want me anymore. That I did something to disappoint you," I say as a tear escapes from my eye, surely from my alcohol-induced state.

Taking note of my distress, he grips me in his arms.

"Oh baby, no. I have never wanted someone as much as I want you. I just didn't want to wake you up. You look so peaceful when you sleep. I had an important call to make back home and it was early due to the time difference."

"Oh," I say in embarrassment. Leaning into him, I nuzzle his chest and continue, "but you didn't message me at all today. I wasn't sure where to go when I was done with work."

He tilts my face up with his hands and says, "Ms. Winston, I apologize for my mistake. It will not happen again... I have missed you today, Mallory. Let's go home."

Gazing into my eyes, asking for permission, he beckons me with a kiss so soft and sweet I can feel my heart melt. He moves around my home turning off the television and lights. After grabbing something from my room, he lifts me into his arms and carries me out the door. After double-checking that the lock is secure, we continue towards the town car where Gregory waits.

The ride to Alex's home is unbearably silent, the only noise coming from the radio. A phone rings startling us and Alex reaches into his suit pocket, answering it quickly. It is then that I remember I need to ask him about the new phone.

"Stone," he answers abruptly. "Yes, I will return the end of July. Yes, please have it ready. Thank you," he says into his phone's receiver before shoving the phone back into his suit pocket.

"Alex, may I ask you a question? It's about the phone?"

"Sure, darling."

"Well, my current phone is on its last leg and I was wondering if I could use the phone you gave me as my primary phone."

He pauses to consider my request, rubbing his finger back and forth across his lower lip, which I now realize is a contemplative gesture, he answers, "I definitely wouldn't want you to go without a way to contact your family. So yes, you may transfer your contacts to that phone. Is that all?"

"Yes, well, I have one more thing, but it isn't very important."

With a huff in his voice at a lack of patience, Alex says, "Out with it, Mallory."

"Ok, um, Annie my Junior Exec is getting married August 1. Will you still be here?"

Shaking his head in disappointment Alex takes my hand and presses a soft kiss across my knuckles before saying, "No, darling. My last day in the states will be July 29. I have a prior engagement for my family that Saturday, as well. I'm sorry; I would have loved to accompany you."

"Oh, that's okay," I reply, trying to keep the disappointment out of my tone. "I just thought I would ask so I didn't wonder if you could have stayed. I will see if Seth can join me."

"Who is Seth?" Alex says as anger flashes in his eyes.
"He's a friend from work, we eat lunch together most days, and he hangs out with me and the girls on occasion."

The car stops and Alex rushes out abruptly, but doesn't wait for me. Rising to my feet quickly I rush towards the elevators to catch up with him. Pulling me in behind him, he turns me against the wall of the car.

"Do not flaunt your men in front of me, Mallory. I am a possessive man and I do not share," Alex articulates.

Stunned into silence by the tone of his voice, I can't even begin to tell him that I do not see Seth as anything more than a friend.

When the car stops, we stroll quickly through his home with his hand gripping my wrist. Stopping in front of the media room, I have yet to see, he opens the door. The walls in this room are a dark gray, like charcoal, with a long, taught, black leather ottoman assembled in the center. Along the wall there is an intricate art piece with different sized, non-connecting squares, that are in an overall shape of a circle. Placed along another wall is a piece of furniture that resembles a dresser. On top of the dresser is a series of colored candles and a few decanters filled with liquid. Along the other side of the wall, there is an armoire to match the dark wood of the other furniture. The pieces make the room very dark but warm.

"Mallory, you have disappointed me and in doing so, you deserve to be punished. I had hoped that we would have a nice reconciliation this evening, but this will be equally as enjoyable for me. Ms. Winston, do you know why I have been disappointed?"

I stare at him bewildered at his change in personality. Punished? I had only been spanked as a child a few times, though I did enjoy his spanking the other night.

"Mallory?" he says angered.

"Uh, yes, sir," I answer swiftly knowing that mentioning Seth is what spurred this. And I can't really blame him, because I know I'd throw a fit of jealousy if the roles were reversed.

"Good. Now go stand in front of the medallion on the wall. Take off all of your clothes, fold them, and place them on the floor beside you. Then stand with your legs apart, facing the room."

Once I am standing in front of the medallion, I see that the piece is a bit more sinister than I originally thought. It has a few restraints attached to it in varying locations. This epiphany jolts my emotions with nervousness. I take off my clothes and fold them in a hurry, not wanting to displease Alex further. Turning to face the room, I spread my legs wide and as I do, I find Alex standing in front of the open armoire. One of his hands holds a plastic paddle with holes placed throughout and in the other hand he holds what looks like a whip with a number of strips at the end. From this distance, the end of the whip also resembles a dildo. My apprehension grows as I become unsure of his intentions. Alex grabs one more thing from a drawer within the armoire and then stalks over to where I stand.

"Normally, I would enjoy seeing you walk around with a dual cock gag in your mouth as a punishment, but neither of can afford the humiliation, so I will use pain instead," he begins.

"Can you tell me what you have and plan to do, sir?"

"As you are new to this lifestyle I will describe the toys only. I typically like to perform scenes with the element of surprise. This one," he says and holds out his hands, "is a paddle that will whistle when being used." Holding out his other hand he continues, "This one is a flogger with an attached dildo. This flogger can be used for pleasure or pain. And these are nipple clamps that attach to your collar." He pauses and then hisses at me in anger, "Mallory, where is your collar?"

"I'm sorry, sir. It is in my bag, sir." I rush out and keep my head down.

I can hear the disappointment as Alex releases a deep breath and I can feel the desire in the room change as he leaves. Moments later, he stalks back into the room with my necklace in his hand and he fastens it quickly around my neck. He strokes bits of cold metal across my chest then attaches the biting nipple clamps to my breasts; overly tightening them causing me to gasp in pain.

"Turn around and raise your arms. Keep your legs spread," he demands. Following his command, he straps me onto the medallion. Hissing into my ear Alex exclaims, "For every hit you receive you will count out loud. I will begin with twenty lashings from the paddle. Your safe word will be purple."

With my nod in agreement the hits begin softly at first, starting at my calves, then moving to my thighs and behind. As the sixth hit is announced, the pounding starts and I find myself beginning to cry from pain. He pauses momentarily as I can barely gasp out the number ten.

"You are a lovely shade of pink. Don't forget about the safe word if it becomes too much," he says as he dips his hand between my legs. "You're dripping with honey, sweet girl. Your body enjoys this."

I can hear him taste his fingers and groan. The lashings continue until I can barely speak or stand up from the pain. Needing to endure this, for him, and for myself, I swallow my pride and refuse to use the safe word.

The paddle drops to the floor as Alex halts his movements. Turning my head to the side, I see him move toward the dresser and drink something from one of the decanters. Pacing back to me, he starts to remove his clothing. As I watch him, he stares into tear stained my eyes.

"I would have preferred you to undress me this evening, Ms. Winston. Maybe another time," he says as his collared shirt joins his jacket on the floor.

Next, he removes his belt and pants and is left standing in a v-neck undershirt and boxer briefs. Reaching behind his head, he lifts and removes his shirt. Pulling down his boxer briefs, I continue to stare and notice my mouth going dry. Alex's body is all tight chest with six-pack abs and the v-cut that girls dream about. Obviously, he spends a lot of time at the gym. Looking down at his erection, I shouldn't be surprised since I have enjoyed it already, but I am shocked at its length and thickness.

"Taking in your fill, miss?" he asks.

"I'm sorry, sir," I reply nervously, tucking my chin to my chest.

"I don't mind, your body is equally as enchanting," he says as his fingers scroll down the chain draping my chest and tug on the nipple clamps.

"Ah," I shout as pain and pleasure ripple through my breasts.

Skimming down my body his hand glides across my mound toward my folds. Strong fingers slide back and forth along my center.

"Oh god," I say through a moan.

"Do not force me gag you, Ms. Winston," Alex exclaims with force. "Be quiet. This is for me not you. You are not allowed to come," he continues.

I shout in my head a slew of profanities, as he steps away and grabs the flogger. My upper back and arms are met with soft light strokes.

"This won't do," Alex seems to say to himself. The flogger drops to the floor with a whoosh. Soon, he removes my restraints so that I can be turned around and then they are placed back.

"Much better, more skin to liven up," Alex says as he walks away.

Grabbing the pants lying on the floor, he reaches into his pocket and pulls out the dark purple belt that goes with my wrap dress. That must be why he went into my bedroom.

He comes back to where I am restrained and wraps the belt across my eyes tying it in the back.

"This will heighten your senses, Mallory," he says as the flogger brushes lightly across the front of my body.

All too soon, he begins to lash me. Sharp strips of pain shoot across my legs, arms, and stomach. He strikes my breasts numerous times causing a current to lace through them. Moisture drips down my inner thigh as my body craves a form of release. Minutes, or hours, pass and I am numb to the pain, only feeling the burning desire.

Ending his torment, he unhooks the restraints on the medallion. With so little strength, I practically topple over myself as Alex guides me to the ottoman in the middle of the room. Leaning me across the furniture, I note that it is a bit higher than I expected. Pulling restraints from under the ottoman, he attaches them to my wrists. I feel Alex stroke his hand softly down my back and across my behind. Ending at my pool of heat, he inserts two fingers into my core.

A husky tone vibrates from Alex's mouth as he says, "Mallory, your body is so turned on right now. It likes to be punished." He continues to stroke his fingers in my core hastily bringing me closer to the edge. All too soon, he removes his fingers. "This will be quick Mallory; and remember, my pleasure not yours. You may not come."

Thrusting his erection into my body, I focus on his movements. As his erection grows, he continues to pump harder and faster and I can feel him close to his release. As to not disappoint him again, I scatter my brain full of thoughts related to work and family to keep my release at bay. Miraculously, I am able to hold off my climax as he spills his seed in me and then leans on my back; both of our breathing heavy from the exertion. Alex sits up quickly and removes my restraints and blindfold. Stroking my hair, he lifts me into his arms. As my eyes adjust to the dimmed light as he carries me into his bedroom and gently lays me on his bed.

Stepping out of his bathroom, his hands carry a bottle of lotion.

"This will help with the pain and keep you from bruising. May I rub it on you?" he soothingly asks.

I nod my head yes, as I continue to lay there as tears of pain well up in my eyes when he rubs the lotion over my body.

"Please sweetheart, don't cry here," he says in a shaken voice.

In reply, I whisper, "The lotion burns."

"I know. I am sorry. You did a wonderful job." Tenderly turning me onto my back, his thumb traces under my eyes, wiping the tears that have fallen. Leaning in, Alex gives me a soft kiss.

"I don't want you to do that again," I tell him.

Concerned, Alex asks, "Is this too much for you, Mallory? We can stop this if you need to. I understand that it isn't for everyone."

"No, please," I say, pleading though in pain. I'm not ready to lose him yet. "It just wasn't what I had expected. I'll do better, I promise."

"You are a wonderful submissive, Ms. Winston. Always eager to please me. Now lay back and rest. I will get you some aspirin and water and then we will go to bed."

"Yes, sir."

When he steps out of the room, I think how this one act of punishment caused him to release all of his anger and disappointment from my actions. Once he was finished he was incredibly sweet. Maybe I need to find a better form of release instead of bottling my emotions inside.

Alex walks back in with a glass of water and a bottle of aspirin and then hands me both. I sit up to take the medication and then unclasp my necklace and rest it on the nightstand along with the glass of water. Lying back in the bed I turn onto my side to face the alarm clock and make sure it is set for the morning. Being the gentleman he is, Alex waits for me to get comfortable and then he kisses my forehead before stepping out of the room. It is only 10:30 pm, but I am exhausted. Closing my lids, I fall asleep quickly and for the first time since meeting Alex, I don't dream of golden eyes.

Waking with a heavy arm wrapped around me and a warm chest pressed against my back I am utterly content. Alex must be able to sense that I am awake because he starts to press kisses to my shoulder blade.

"How do you feel?" he asks.

"Not nearly as sore as I expected."

"Good, that lotion is great. I buy it overseas."

Quickly the room spins as Alex flips me onto my back, resting on his elbows above me. He plants sweet kisses along my face, eyelids, and nose. Once he reaches my mouth, he starts kissing me with a fervent passion. He massages my tongue with his own and starts to rock back on forth against me, pressing his growing erection against my thigh. With a few stokes, he teases me by inserting the head of his penis into my core and then pulling back out to rub along my nub again. Moisture is dripping from my opening as he ignites heat over my entire body. I've never wanted to feel someone become a part of me as I do with Alex. Slowing his movements, Alex gazes down at me and bites his lip. *Wow,* I think to myself. That is the sexiest thing I have ever seen. Hesitating for only a second, he pushes forward and I can feel the tip of his penis rubbing against my g-spot. While kissing and nibbling on my neck, he thrusts slowly in and out of me. My hands reach around to his shoulder blades and I grip the tight, flexing muscles. My vision starts to blur as I inch closer to my climax, only a few more thrusts and I will go over the edge.

He whispers in my ear, "Don't leave me, Mallory," as we come together.

This was the first time we had regular, missionary, vanilla type sex and I thought it was the best thing I had ever had, not that I had much to compare it with. Against my chest, Alex rests his head, the breath from his nose tickling my neck. Moments like these are why I could easily find myself falling in love with Alex Stone. I will need to harden my heart for the next two months because it would be a big mistake to lose myself to him.

My fingers stroke through Alex's soft and thick hair for a few minutes.

Breaking the silence, I murmur, "Alex, I need to get ready for work."

"Stay with me today."

Softly I look at him and grasp my bottom lip between my teeth. "I can't. I have to finalize my new position today and tomorrow."

"Alright," he replies, his mask sliding into place, and moves off of me.

Working my way off the bed, I notice most of my muscles are sore, but I don't see any bruising. Quickly, I take a quick shower and braid my hair in a fishtail design. In the closet, I pull on a pair of pants, a silk shirt and cardigan, and black flats. Satisfied with how I look, I make my way back to the bedroom and clasp the choker around my neck. Alex is snoring softly and I lean over to press a kiss to his forehead. I close my eyes and inhale a hint of his scent, memorizing every flavor in the fragrance, then make my way out of his place.

RENEE HARLESS

Chapter Eight

THE MORNING SEEMS TO drag on as I anticipate seeing Alex this evening. My mind is off picturing different scenes involving the two of us, causing Seth to leave at one point during lunch at my lack of companionship. In the afternoon, Annie comes into my office and plops down onto my couch, startling me from my midday trance.

"Annie, what can I do for you?"

"Oh nothing, I just wanted to admire your view."

"How is the wedding planning going?"

"Great, we have everything ready. I am going dress shopping this weekend."

"Oohh that is exciting!"

She studies my excited expression looking for any hint of sarcasm and then her gaze lands on my choker.

"Hey Mal, when did you get that necklace?" she says through a pout.

"No, silly, I, um, well—" I begin to stutter out before she interrupts.

"Did that hunk of a man buy that for you?"

I have to chuckle and agree with Annie's recollection of Alex. "That hunk of a man's name is Alex. And yes he did."

Annie steps closer to admire the jewelry. "I haven't seen one with that other heart charm on it. Did he have it customized for you?"

"Yea, I guess so."

"Isn't that sweet? Well, I'm sure you're busy, holler if you need me."

"Will do," I reply.

Without any new campaigns to work on or calls to make I head over to the seat Annie just vacated. I find myself staring out the window daydreaming about Alex. Visions of his hands on me, my fingers running through his hair, and his mouth pressed against my own.

My office phone begins to ring, knocking me from my illusions and I find myself in a heated conversation with a past client. By the time 5:30pm rolls around, my mind is exhausted and my emotions are on thin ice.

In my car I turn on the radio and listen to Mumford and Son's "I Will Wait For You." Smiling to myself as I sing along, I remember Madison returns from her conference tomorrow. I wonder if Alex wants to join us in our celebration dinner for my promotion. I maneuver my Mini Cooper up to the entrance at The Braxton and I toss my keys to the valet. Stepping towards the elevators, I realize that I don't have a key for the penthouse. Noticing a man in a shirt that says SECURITY, I walk over to his desk.

"I'm sorry, sir, but I am staying with Mr. Stone and I don't have a key for the elevator," I say politely.

"Do you have your visitor security tag?"

"My what? I'm sorry I don't have one of those. His head of security, Gregory, introduced me to the concierge and a few staff members, but I don't see them here. If you could just let me up —"

Interrupting my statement, the security guard says, "I'm sorry miss I cannot do that. Mr. Stone is an important resident and I am under strict orders to not breach the security of any of our residents."

The look he sends me is one of disgust and he speaks in such a condescending tone that tears begin to well in my eyes. Turning away from the desk, I head towards the exit. Taking a moment to compose myself, I reach into my purse and dial Alex's number.

"Please pick up, please pick up," I mumble to myself.

"You're late, Ms. Winston," Alex scoffs.

At my fear of being punished I let a few stray tears escape from my eyes. "The security guard …won' let me up… And I don't have a key … or a card," I say taking deep breaths to calm down.

"Mallory," Alex begins in a completely different tone than the one I heard a moment earlier comes through the line. "Sweetheart, calm down. I will get this sorted out. Please stay where you are."

An older woman overhearing my end of the conversation hands me a small packet of tissues.

"Thank you," I say to her as we exchange small smile.

Moments later, I hear an elevator ping and an exasperated Alex rushes over to me.

"Darling, are you okay?"

Nodding my head, I twist my hands within each other waiting for Alex's mood to change.

He continues, "I'm sorry for the misunderstanding with security, I am going to take care of it. Wait here, okay?"

Placing a gentle kiss on my forehead, Alex stalks towards the security desk. I cannot hear much of what is said, but I can see Alex practically shaking in fury.

"I'm sorry, Mr. Stone, but it is our policy to only grant access to those given security tags," the guard attempts to explain.

Alex begins to shout, visibly frustrated with the situation, "She has them! I picked them up this morning so that I could give them to her when she arrived here. All you had to do was match your database with her driver's license."

The security guard looks embarrassed and apologizes, "I'm sorry sir, you are right. My apologies for causing you to come down to sort this matter."

Ignoring the guard, Alex heads back in my direction. Like the flip of switch, Alex's once angry demeanor is now full of sweetness and sincerity as he wraps an arm around my shoulders and leans down to press a soft kiss on the top of my head.

"Come, love, let's head upstairs," he says pleasantly and I follow him to the elevator.

That evening we spend our time watching the television and eating crab cake sandwiches on the couch.

"Alex, Madison comes home tomorrow," I begin, "and I think she plans on at least going to dinner. Would you like to join us?"

"Thank you for thinking of me, but no. I want you to enjoy your time with your friend."

"Are you sure? I would prefer your company."

Chuckling he adds, "Yes, darling, I am sure. I have plans tomorrow evening so this works out well."

"Ok, well if you change your mind the invitation stands."

Taking my plate, Alex moves it to the coffee table. He swiftly grabs my hand, tugging me up, and we begin walking towards his bathroom. As Alex fills the tub with water, he pours some lavender oil.

"How is your skin?" he questions.

"It doesn't hurt anymore."

After removing the cardigan I'm wearing, Alex unbuttons the camisole, tossing them into a pile on the floor. He trails his hands down my arms and back up, across my collarbone. His hands slide effortlessly down my breasts and circle the skin exposed above the bra, hardening my nipples instantly. Continuing their downward path, his hands hook into the waistband of my trousers. Catching his fingers around the belt loops, he yanks, causing me to step forward. Kissing me hard, he begins to undo my pants as my desire blossoms. Alex slides the trousers down my legs, bending in the same motion so that he rests before me on his knees. I kick off each of my shoes and he helps me to step out of the pant legs. Kneeling before me, Alex trails his nose along my panty line inhaling my scent.

"You smell divine."

His words, mixed with the timber of his voice, causes me to instantly pool into my panties. It is astonishing that my body is so wet and he has barely touched me. Seconds later, he hooks his fingers into my underwear and rips them to shreds allowing his tongue to sweep forward and lick against my folds. Continuing to explore my center with his tongue, he stretches my legs farther apart with his arms. Nimble fingers spread my folds apart as he focuses on pleasuring my clit with his tongue. Joining in, I begin to knead my breasts through my bra. He must be able to sense my closeness to the brink because Alex suddenly inserts two fingers into my core and starts to pump. Shouting Alex's name, I explode seconds later.

Trailing kisses up my belly and between my breasts, Alex finally lands on my mouth. The taste of my essence on his lips and tongue cause my body to begin heating up all over again. Unclasping my bra, I let it fall to the floor, then reach up, and twist my fingers into Alex's hair. With heavy lids, Alex steps back and cuts off the water.

"Undress me, Mallory."

I comply, working quickly to unbutton his collared shirt, throwing it into the pile with my clothes. Tugging his v-neck shirt up, he helps to pull it off his chiseled body. My hands trail across his muscles as I lean forward to plant small kisses along his chest. The heartbeat coming from his chest starts to pound faster as I

kneel before him and undo his trousers. Hooking my
fingers into the band of his pants, I pull them and the
boxer briefs towards the floor. His beautiful member
springs forth and I have the sudden desire to take him
into my mouth. I help Alex step out of his pants and then
I lean forward, letting my tongue trail a path along his
penis, circling the head.

"Oh god," Alex hisses between his tightly
clenched teeth.

Shooting a glance in his direction, I find his head
is resting back and the muscles in his arms taught. Taking
him fully into my mouth, I push him as far back as I can,
feeling the head of his cock brush against the back of my
throat. Using one hand to stroke the base of his shaft and
the other to massage his balls, I start to slide him back
and forth in my mouth switching between sucking and
licking. Relaxing my jaw, I suck his balls into my mouth
and massage those with my tongue, hoping he is getting
the same pleasure from this as I am. When I begin
sucking him again, I can feel his penis begin to grow in
size.

"Baby, I'm going to come. Swallow it for me," he
demands.
Soon I feel liquid pulse down the back of my throat and I
continue to suck to get every drop. His heavenly taste
brings forth a moan from deep in my throat.

With his head titled back, Alex takes a moment to
catch his breath before pinning me with his steady gaze.
One cocked eyebrow in place, he says, "Ms. Winston, that
was…unexpected."

Stepping into the tub, Alex beckons me to follow him. The bath is very large, like the size of a small pool. Situated against one of the tub's sides, he pulls me to sit in front of him with my back to his chest.

"The lavender will help your wounds," he states.

"Oh," I say intrigued by his statement. Then I continue, "Well, it smells lovely."

"You smell lovely," he responds as he relaxes into the water, wrapping his arms around my waist and resting my head on his shoulder.

One of his hands travel upward and he begins to knead my breast. Soon I feel his growing erection start to press into my back. His other hand travels lower to tease my center while his expert mouth places soft kisses along my neck and ear. Reaching behind me, I wrap my fingers in his hair and close my eyes to revel in the moment. I love his hands on me, touching me, caressing me. He makes me feel cherished in these moments.

Suddenly stopping, Alex removes my hands from his hair and then turns me around. A hand wraps around my braided hair and pulls me in for a frenzied kiss. Pushing off the wall of the tub, Alex comes to sit in the center. He positions me so that my legs are straddling him and then impales me onto his cock as I whimper into his mouth from the sensation. I am burning with want for him and I can't seem to ride his cock fast enough. One of his arms snakes around my waist and he begins to thrust up as I bear down. We break away from the kiss and lean our heads back as we continue to pound into each other. Brilliant colors flash behind my eyes as we come simultaneously.

When we begin to calm down Alex growls into my ear, "I am nowhere near done with you yet."

He stands quickly, causing more water to slosh over the sides of the tub and then reaches out for me. Standing, I grasp his hand and then follow him out of the bathroom. We stop in front of the bed and Alex leans down to kiss me. Our heated kiss continues where we left off in the tub and our hands start roaming over the other's body. In mid kiss, Alex moves on the bed and I follow.

"Mmm, I haven't gotten my fill of you yet. I'm addicted to your taste," he says as he flips me around so that I am straddling his face. Alex immediately inserts his tongue into my core and I moan at the sensation. Leaning my head down, I take his erection into my mouth. As he sucks on my clit and pulses his fingers in and out of me I lick and suck his cock between my lips while stroking his base. I feel Alex insert his thumb into my tight rosette and then replaces his thumb with two fingers. I gasp, never having anyone touch that spot before, although I am amazed how incredible it feels. Not wanting him to stop, I groan as I feel myself start to reach that point. The sucking action Alex has unleashed onto my clit becomes stronger and he pumps his fingers faster. As I edge towards my climax, Alex moves me around on his body. He quickly thrusts the head of his massive penis into my core and another earth-shattering climax quickly ensues. A pause in his movements allows me time to come down from my hedonic state. Still pumping his fingers in and out of my rosette, my breath turns heavy as Alex starts to move inside my center.

"Oh, darling girl, you feel amazing," he claims, as he pounds harder causing another climax to build in my belly.

As Alex reaches his point, a low pained moan of pleasure falling from his mouth. I reach mine. Falling back onto the bed, Alex pulls me against him.

Both taking a moment to catch our breath I glance around Alex's bedroom and notice the lack of pictures, of anything personal. Turning back to gaze at him, I get lost in his eyes as the setting sun sends a warm glow across the room. Taking in our euphoric state, I press a gentle kiss onto his chest before using this opportunity to question my lover.

"Alex, I want to know more about you. I want to know about your life; the things you like and dislike."

As a deep sigh rumbles through his chest, he replies hesitantly, as if expecting this question, "I know, beautiful. I wish I could tell you more about myself, but I am already growing more attached to you than I should. There are things I cannot tell you and it is for the better. I swear that to you, love."

Exhausted from everything we have just experienced and the change in our conversation, I close my eyes and drift off to sleep.

I wake the next morning to find Alex stroking my hair and whispering into my ear, "You are so serene when you sleep. Did you enjoy yourself last night?" Opening my eyes, I unleash a glorious smile in his direction.

"I'm just a bit sore for obvious reasons, but last night was amazing," I reveal as I sit up in bed I wrap the sheet around my chest, "May I ask how last night was for you?"

Blush donning my cheeks, I stare down at my hands as Alex reaches across and threads his fingers in my hair tilting my face up towards him.

"Mallory, last night exceeded any expectations that I may have had about our relationship. I will take us any way I can. And yesterday was brilliant." My grin widens at his statement. "Ms. Winston, you have a beautiful smile," he expresses as he presses a gentle kiss on my forehead.

"Thank you."

Tossing a glance at the alarm clock I jump up; I have fifteen minutes to get to work.

"Shit," I say to no one in particular.

Scrambling off the bed, I jump into the shower and finish quickly. My hair is still in the braid from yesterday so I take it down and let it wave down my back. Chuckling behind me, Alex laughs as I run like a maniac into the closet. I decide on a black and white sheath dress and throw on some hot pink Prada shoes. This is a record for me as I still have five minutes before I need to leave. Walking back into the bedroom I leave Alex with a heated kiss.

Calling out to me Alex says, "I will call you this weekend, Mallory. I hope that you enjoy your night."

"I look forward to hearing from you, Mr. Stone. I'll see you later."

Recalling our brief words before falling into slumber, my drive to work is laced with visions of Alex's secret life.

RENEE HARLESS

Chapter Nine

MY DAY PASSES QUICKLY as I spend most of it in the human resources office filling out paperwork and setting up the payroll system. Madison calls me in the afternoon to let me know she is home and buried under a pile of laundry. I excitedly tell her that I will be home around 5:30pm and that we need to go out to celebrate tonight, though I don't mention what we are celebrating.

Entering my home at the end of the day, I can hear noises upstairs so I drop off my bag in my living room and then head upstairs to join Madison.

As I engulf her in a welcoming hug she asks, "Hey Mal, what are celebrating?"

"Well, it turns out that Steven decided to retire. So, I am now Senior Account Executive and Director Mallory Winston."

"Oh my gosh! That is fantastic news," she shouts enthusiastically. "I am so happy for you!"

"Thanks. How was your conference?" I inquire.

"Eh, it was as expected. I met a few good-looking guys, but overall pretty uneventful." She pauses, cocks her head at me, and grins. "You look different, Mal. Something happen while I was gone?"

"No, nothing happened," I rush out.

With no intention to disclose my new relationship to her, I decide to stay silent. Madison wouldn't approve of my decision knowing my heart will be broken by the end of summer, though she unknowingly helped me make my choice.

"Hm…" she begins and asks, "Since it is your night where do you want to go to dinner?"

"I was thinking The Cheesecake Factory. Does that sound good?"

"It sounds fantastic. Is Mika coming?"

"I don't know; I haven't seen her in a while. I'm going to head downstairs to change."

"I'll call her. Did you go shopping without me? I want to borrow those shoes."

Glancing down, I see the pink Prada's I slid onto my feet this morning. Thinking of Alex I realize how much I miss him already.

Pushing aside the hangers of clothes in my closet, I pull out a cream-colored shift dress. My lingerie is switched out for a nude colored lace bra and panty set before I slide the linen dress over my body. While I stroke mascara through my eyelashes, I hear my phone buzz. Glancing at the screen, I see that I received a message from Alex.

Alex: I will miss you tonight darling.
Mallory: I will miss you too. Are you sure you
**   can't join us?**
Alex: No I can't. My guest will be here shortly.
Mallory: Ok see you later.

I close out the app and slip my feet into the pink Prada's just as Madison comes barreling through my door. She is adorned in a gray satin mini dress.

"You look cute, Mal. Mika wants to meet us at a bar later. She says she has had a rough week."

"Ok, that sounds good."

"Hey, what's that? When did you get a new phone?"

"Oh, um, it's a perk of the new job," I exclaim too quickly.

Eyeing me speculatively with a slant in her eyes and a cock of her head she says, "Alright."

As we finish our meal at The Cheesecake Factory, Madison and I catch up on the past two weeks.

"So who is he, Mal?"

"Who?"

"The guy that has you glowing. You're in love."

"No, I am not."

"Yes, you are. What's his name?"

I stare at my glass and spin the stem between my fingers.

I whisper, "His name is Alex…I met him a few weeks ago when we went to Lucky 21."

"Was he the one in the sexy suit? He had been eyeing you all night."

"He was?"

"Yep. Nicely done, he is a fine specimen."

"I was so embarrassed. I didn't realize he was trying to talk to me."

"Why wouldn't he want to talk to you?"

"Men never talk to me."

She unleashes a loving smile in my direction, pats my hand in a motherly gesture and says, "That's because you're beautiful and they are intimidated by you. No one wants to be rejected by the most stunning woman in the room."

"Madison, are you crazy?"

"No, I'm just telling you what the guys say when they talk to Mika and me. We try to tell them that you are sweet and kind, but we can't seem to convince them. You're a great wingman for us without even trying," she says through laughter.

I toss my napkin at her and reply, "I didn't realize I was intimidating."

"Well none of that matters because you found someone that had the balls to talk to you any way."

Releasing a heavy breath, I utter, "We've only been dating since Monday and I think I've already fallen for him."

"I'm not surprised. Your mom always used to say that once you fell, you would fall hard and fast."

"I was trying so hard not to. It isn't going to end well for me."

"Why?"

Through a sigh, I wrap my arms around myself and I pronounce, "He leaves for England at the end of July. Our affair is only temporary. He says he wants to spend all of his spare time with me up until that point, but when he leaves we will be over." As a shiver passes over my skin, I can feel a lone tear trail down my face.

"Oh, Mal. I don't think he will find it as easy to leave as you'd like to believe he would. But either way, you should enjoy the time you have with him while he is here. I like seeing your eyes alive and happy"

"Thanks, Madi; you're right. I'll just take it one day at a time."

Raising the last of her wine to make a toast, I raise mine in unison.

Madison declares, "To your new job, new love, and new beginning."

"Cheers."

Making our way down the street to a new bar and grill called Shotti's Point, Madison unleashes her inquiry.

"Now that we got that out of the way, how is the sex?"

"Geez Madi, maybe I don't want to talk about that," I exclaim in an embarrassed tone, blush creeping along my chest, neck, and cheeks.

She stops and stares at me tapping her foot.

Placating her I say, "Okay Okay. The sex is absolutely amazing. Better than anything anyone has ever described to me."

Knowing about my relationship with Derek, Madison asks, "Is he taking care of you, Mal?"

"Yes, he is. I'm his top priority."

"Nice," she shouts between giggles. "Next time you guys go at it can you record it so I can get off to his voice? I have a thing for accents."

My body bursts with laughter and I stumble through the door.

"Madi, you are too much. I am not recording us having sex so you can listen. That is beyond weird."

"Well, just ask. I'd pay him."

"Ha, not going to happen."

Searching for Mika, we find her surrounded by men at the bar, and settled on top of a barstool. Madison runs up and gives her a giant hug and I follow. We saddle up to the stools on both sides of her and order our drinks. The bar is hosting karaoke tonight and we sing along to most of the tunes.

Mika leans over towards me asking, "So you're seeing someone?"

"How did you know?"

"Madison mentioned it a few minutes ago. She says he was the one in the suit at Lucky's."

I notice a hint of anger in her voice at the mention of me having a boyfriend. Mika was always much closer to Madison, but we have always gotten along.

Confused by her interrogation I reply, "Yea, that was him. His name is Alex."

"Well I'm glad he found someone once I turned him down," she says with a saucy grin on her face.

"What?" I ask taken aback by her words.

Mika explains, "Yea, when I went to the bathroom he asked if I wanted to come home with him."

Internally questioning the truth to her statement, I ask, "Why would you tell me this?"

"I just thought you should know. I don't want you getting too far ahead of yourself. Men like him are all the same. They say one thing and do another."

Knowing Alex has always been honest with me, I try to keep myself from believing her. Taking note of the despair arriving on my face, Mika turns away and heads towards a table of guys to flirt. Mission accomplished, I'm sure.

Madison moves to the stool Mika vacated and says, "Don't listen to her, Mallory. She is being a total bitch. I don't think that really happened with Alex."

"What if she is right, Madi? I barely know anything about him. He could be exactly as Mika described."

"Mal, you're a smart woman. You wouldn't be with him if you thought he would even remotely resemble what she described."

"You're right," I say grabbing her in a small hug.

"Hey, I'm going to head over to that table of guys and hopefully get a date...or some free booze, come with me."

As I shake my head in response she moves along to her conquests.

The next few hours I watch the karaoke tournament going on and join in a few of the songs. I don't drink often, so the alcohol passes through me quickly and I can feel myself starting to catch a buzz. Swiveling on my stool, I attempt to catch Madison's attention, but I don't see her anywhere. Waiting a few minutes, I ask the bartender if he has seen Madison or Mika, but he says they left about half an hour ago. What

RENEE HARLESS

the hell? Madison and I walked here, not that I could drive home. Slamming my drink onto the bar I steeple my arms on the bar and rest my head in my heads, taking a few calming breaths.

Pulling my phone from my purse, I start to browse my list of cab companies when I stop on Gregory's number. I really want to see Alex and he told me to use his driver if I needed to. Looking down at my watch, I see that it is only 11:30pm. It isn't too late to call. Hesitating, I press the button to call Gregory and he answers after two rings.

"Ms. Winston."

"I'm sorry, Gregory, I know it is late, but my friends left me at a bar and I don't have a ride home."

"I would be glad to pick you up, Ms. Winston. Where are you located?"

"I'm at Shotti's Point."

"I will be there in ten minutes, Ms. Winston. Please be waiting for me by the door."

Waiting outside as instructed, I see Gregory pull up to the bar ten minutes after ending our call. Right on time.

"Good evening, Ms. Winston," he articulates.

"Gregory, I am sorry to call you so late, I'm sure you were relaxing with your family."

"My family is in England for the time I am here, Ms. Winston," he says as he guides me into the car. "Where am I taking you this evening?"

"I'd like to go to Mr. Stone's place, please."

"I do not think he is expecting you tonight. I have been informed that he has company."

In my rush to find a ride, I hadn't thought to call
Alex. Wouldn't he want to see me? Unless what Mika
said is true and he has a different kind of company he is
entertaining.

Shaking my head from my inner monologue, I say
to Gregory, "I cannot go back to my place because I
would run into my two best friends whom have so
courteously ditched me, again. I don't have anywhere
else to go."

Gregory shoots me a sympathetic look in his rear-view
mirror and drives away from the bar.

The car pulls up in front of The Braxton and the
valet helps me exit. Gregory follows me into the elevator
leading to Alex's penthouse and we ride the car in eerie
silence. As the doors to the elevator open, we are greeted
with boisterous laughter. Laughter that I determine is
Alex's and another that is female.

Glancing over to Gregory I ask, "Who is she?"

"I'm not sure, miss. Mr. Stone does not discuss his
guests with me. Besides you, miss."

Anger flashes across my face. This emotion mixed with
alcohol is not a good combination.

As I step forward, Gregory grabs my arm and
asks, "Are you sure you want to go in there, Ms.
Winston? We can go downstairs to my home and you can
sleep there. When you have cooled off in the morning
you can come back and speak with Mr. Stone."

In the background, we hear a female say, "Alex
we can't do that, she'll know."

Pulling my arm from Gregory's grasp, I stomp
towards the family room and kitchen. Shock rocks my

system as I turn to see Alex and a beautiful blonde sitting on his couch, leaning into each other. Neither of them notices me as their backs are turned in my direction. I feel very alone at that moment, not just because Gregory hasn't followed me, but because Alex is seeing someone else. As I am about to step forward to confront the two lovers, a small, bubbly brunette bounces up beside me. I look at her as she says, "Hi!" and then she continues into the room in a whirlwind. Turning my gaze back to the lovers, Alex twists and notices me standing there.

Startled Alex inquires, "Mallory, what are you doing here? Is everything ok?"

Glancing from him, to the blonde, and back again, I can vaguely hear him say, "Oh bugger."

The brunette that was beside me looks confused and stares at Alex. At his mortified expression, I begin walking briskly towards the elevator holding back tears. Mika was right and I'm an idiot.

Hoping to make the elevator move faster, I press the down button numerous times. Gregory smartly escaped the madness. Just as the elevator doors open, Alex pulls me back by my arm, but I can't look at him. I try to pull away, but he cages me against the wall to keep from escaping.

"Mallory, why are you here? Is everything ok?" he asks as he begins to wipe the tears from my face.
I shake my head no, as I cannot from a coherent sentence.

"Sweetheart, I will explain everything to you in a moment. It most certainly isn't what you think. Now, why are you here?" he asks concerned.

Gazing into his eyes, I see truth, sincerity, and vulnerability in them. He looks devastated that I am about to leave him. His expression assures me that I have made the wrong assumption. Alex doesn't share and he wouldn't expect me to share either. He told me that himself.

I catch my breath and explain, "They ditched me, again."

"Oh, darling. I'm sorry."
Warm arms pull me into a tight hug and I let the tears fall feeling safe wrapped in his arms. The electricity is passing back and forth between us and I can hear my heartbeat rise from the contact.

He pulls back from our embrace and places a sweet kiss on my lips before saying, "Come, I will introduce you."

Taking my hand and reassuring me along the way, we walk back into the family room. The brunette has moved into the kitchen while the blonde remains on the couch. Looking down I see that the blonde is very pregnant. Vomit rises in my throat as I start to consider that it is Alex's baby.

"Mallory," Alex says pulling me from my inner torment, "I would like to introduce you to Vanessa. Vanessa is the woman from medical school I mentioned to you. She is here for a conference about genetic testing. Vanessa was unable to bring her husband and son with her this time so I offered to let her stay with me for the evening."

Cocking my eyebrow towards Alex, I find it strange that she would be staying with her ex lover and that her husband is okay with this arrangement. Especially when Alex punished me for mentioning a male friend. Assessing the situation, I visibly relax after mentally deciding to trust Alex. At my resolution, I can see Alex unclench his fists and the lines relax on his face. He seems to have been preparing for a fight, maybe to fight for me.

"Vanessa, Alex has mentioned you. It is a pleasure to meet you," I say politely.

"Mallory, I have heard so much about you this evening, I feel as if I know you already. It is a pleasure to meet you as well. I apologize that Alex hadn't mentioned I was staying with him. He can have such bad manners and I most certainly can see why you would be upset. I apologize on behalf of him and myself," she replies sweetly as she shakes my extended hand. Her kind smile eliciting one of my own.

"Thank you, I am sorry to interrupt your evening."

"Don't be silly, please join us. I'd love to get to know you better."

Just as sweet as Alex had described, I am finding it hard to picture her partaking in a BDSM scene. Moments later, the bubbly brunette walks in and sits a drink in front of me and then smacks Alex on the head. He winces at her contact.

Holding out her hand she says, "Hi, I'm Abigail or Abi for short. I am this bonehead's wonderful sister."

Through a giggle, I shake her hand and reply, "It is nice to meet you, Abi."

Alex speaks up, "I didn't know Abi was coming, she showed up right after you left this morning." He then shuts his mouth quickly as if he hadn't intended to mention that I have been staying the night.

"Alex, you're 30. I know you're having sleepovers. What I want to know is if you plan on giving me a niece or nephew soon?" she asks without faltering as she cocks and eyebrow in question to her brother.

Chiming in Alex asks, "Abi, can't you bother Nicholas about kids? He is already married you know."

"Psh, his wife is a snooty bitch and won't have kids because being pregnant will make her look fat. You're my only hope."

Downing the drink, she sat in front of me, I laugh to myself at her statement.

Sitting on the couch, Abi and Vanessa gossip with each other as Alex drapes an arm around my shoulder pulling me close. We talk about my dinner with Madison and our drinks at Shotti's Point. He seems very angry at the decisions my friends made this evening, telling me he would be crushed if something happened to me.

After a few minutes, I peek up at Alex and say, "Alex, if you don't mind, I am beat and would like to head to bed."

"Sure, I'll walk with you," he says. Turning towards the girls on the couch he adds, "Ladies, I will be right back."

"Goodnight, Abi and Vanessa. It was great to meet you both."

We walk back to the bedroom; Alex holding my hand and I say, "Alex, I'm sorry about barging in this evening. I was upset and wanted to see you. Gregory had said you weren't expecting me, but I came anyways." Stopping to shut the door, he turns to face me and threads his fingers in my hair.

"Baby, I am not upset you are here. I am actually thrilled that when you were upset you came straight to me. That is what I want; I want you to need me," he says sincerely.

"I do need you," I respond eyeing him up and down in his casual attire of denim and cotton.

Leaning down he seals our lips in a passionate kiss and walks forward to press me against the closed bedroom door. As he pulls my hands above my head, gripping both wrists in one of his hands, he moans into my mouth while grazing his hips against my own. We continue to kiss as his other hand grabs the hem of my dress and pulls it up to my waist. My panties disappear as he tears them apart with his nibble fingers. He inserts two fingers to massage my center and crooks them to rub the spot that will send me over the edge. Gasping into his mouth, I break the kiss and rest my head against the door as my breath begins to speed up. Alex leans down farther, biting and sucking along my collarbone, causing the embers in my belly to ignite. As I find myself reaching the pinnacle, Alex's thumb rubs my clit and I sky rocket towards pleasure. Kissing me softly, he pulls his hands away and helps me undress completely before guiding me to the bed.

"Goodnight, Mallory," he says prior to kissing me again and heading back out to his guests.

Chapter Ten

MY BODY CAN FEEL the weight of Alex's arm draped over me and I turn over to face him in the morning sun, smiling to myself. With his dark lashes fanning across his cheeks, lips slightly parted, and one arm resting under the pillow he is picturesque in bed. My eyes memorize his defined muscles and the way his body looks with the silver bed sheet draped over his pelvis.

Sighing to myself I ask, "How did I get this charming man?"

The bed jostles as I exit and Alex repositions himself onto his back, moving the arm from under the pillow to rest above his head, his other arm resting across his stomach. I grab my phone from my bag on the floor and turn on the camera setting. I take a picture so I can always remember that I spent two months with this perfect man.

To make myself look somewhat presentable for Alex's guests, I grab a pair of gym shorts and a long sleeve shirt from the closet after a quick shower. During my journey to the kitchen, I notice no one else is awake, so I decide to make everyone French toast and coffee. I veer towards the pantry to grab all of the ingredients and get started making breakfast. As I flip the first piece of toast, I feel large hands glide around my hips and rest on my waist underneath my shirt.

Alex nibbles my neck and I moan in a husky voice, "If you keep doing that I am going to burn breakfast."

"I can't help it. You look delectable this morning," he says as he rubs his growing erection across my backside.

Tilting my head towards his face, I am rewarded with kiss. As I continue making breakfast, I find that Alex still looks amazing wearing black cotton lounge pants and a loose t-shirt. Watching me work, he sits at a bar stool with a cup of coffee and gentle smirk presiding on his face.

"Ms. Winston, you have gorgeous legs, I may require you to show them off more," he says between sips of coffee.

"Are you crazy? My legs are beyond pale," I reply with a chuckle." But maybe we can compromise and I can wear stockings."

With a tap of his finger on his chin Alex contemplates and replies, "I don't know."

"I can get thigh highs and wear a garter belt. I have a feeling you would enjoy seeing those."

"Oh, I would. We may need to go to a shop and pick a few things out."

Placing his plate in front of him, I lean across the counter and kiss his lips. "I would only ever do that for you, Alex." I explain.

"Damn right," he says as he smacks my ass when I turn back towards the stove.

Vanessa and Abigail come out to join us thirty minutes later and thank me for breakfast. We make easy conversation and I laugh at the banter between Abi and Alex. I can tell they are very close.

Vanessa stands to leave the table saying, "I have to head out to catch my flight. Alex, thanks for letting me stay and, Abi, it was great to see you again. Please let me know when you're in Wales next." She walks over to me and leans in, grabbing me in a hug. "Mallory, it was wonderful to meet you," she whispers to me. "You're perfect for him. He will screw up, but please give him a chance to make it right."

Her words leave me stunned as she stands and moves to hug Alex and Abigail. As she grabs her bags out of the family room, she winks at me. How can she tell I am perfect for him? My gaze lands on Alex and he smiles at me, melting my heart yet at the same time causing my core to clench. Abi subtly coughs breaking the moment between Alex and me.

"So, what plans do you two have today?" she asks Alex.

"I don't believe we have anything planned. However, it is still early. Mallory, would you like to go to Cross St. Market?"

"Sure, I love to walk through the market. The florist there is wonderful. Maybe I can pick up some flowers to liven up your place," I say.

"Can I tag along with you guys?" Abi inquires.

"Sure, Abi. I'd love for you to join us," Alex says. "Mallory, why don't you take get ready. I want to talk to Abi for a bit."

"Yes, sir," I answer with a wink.

Wearing a light blue sundress, I make my way back into the family room and I overhear part of Abi and Alex's conversation.

"So, you haven't told her?" Abi asks.

"No, Abi. And I have no intentions to do so."

"Why not?"

I step into the room and interrupt their discussion by asking, "Tell who, what?"
I have a sneaking suspicion the "who" is me. Alex glares at Abi who is giving him quite an evil look.

"Abi and I were discussing if my mother was aware of my return home the end of summer," Alex replies, but the way he doesn't look directly at me lets me know he doesn't plan on telling me what they were discussing.

I squint at Abi who then looks away so I turn towards Alex and question, "Why wouldn't you tell her when you are coming home?"

"Well, my mother wants to see me married off. If she knows when I am coming home, she will surely have women lined up for me to date. I haven't prepared myself for that."

Hoping to learn more about Alex I say, "That sounds horrible. Is your mother that bad?"

"No, she is actually quite wonderful, but her need to marry off her children is a flaw to her character. If things were different I would love for her to meet you." A hint of a smile adorns my face, but I am torn at his words. Mulling over his comment I wonder what he means by different.

Abi speaks up trying to clear the tension in the room, "Mom would love you, Mal. She doesn't travel to the states often, but if you ever visit England, you should look her up. She would love to take you to her garden. Those flowers are her other babies. I am a bit jealous of them."

Laughter erupts from her like a volcano as she finishes her sentence and heads towards her room.

Finding a few moments alone, Alex and I move towards each other in the family room.

"Everything ok, Ms. Winston?" Alex solicits.

"Yes, sir. I am sorry again for interrupting your evening."

"I was happy to see you, Mallory. I missed you last night. I enjoy your company."

"I like Abigail and Vanessa, they seem lovely. My friends on the other hand, are on my shit list."

"I can't believe they left you there. That isn't safe for any of you. If something happened to you because of them, they would be on my shit list as well."

Placing light strokes along my face with the back of his hand, he leans forward, kisses my forehead, and then steps toward his bedroom.

RENEE HARLESS

Resting on the balcony located off the living room, I lounge on one of the Adirondack chairs overlooking the harbor. The morning is extraordinary today and I unwind in the breeze off the bay. Abi joins me minutes later and sits in the chair beside me staring at the water.

"You're changing him, Mallory," she states nonchalantly as she tugs at the edge of her shirt.

"Excuse me?" I say offended, crossing my arms defensively.

"Oh, sorry, I don't mean in a bad way; it's definitely good. You're changing him for the better. He is less closed off, he seems happy."

"I don't think that it's from me. We've only been dating for a week."

"I know it's from you. He mentioned meeting dark haired beauty a month ago and it turned out to be you. He called me that next day and said he had met someone important and was frantic he couldn't find you. He hasn't been the same since. Normally, he would have chewed my head off for showing up unannounced. Instead he seemed quite excited to see me." She pauses and turns towards me then adds, "You are perfect for him and I know you are different from the others, Mallory. I hope he realizes that before it is too late and he messes up."

I consider her words and notice the sheer sincerity in her eyes.

"Thank you for saying that, Abi. I adore your brother, but we agreed that this relationship was only temporary. I know he is willing to let me go at the end of July and I am preparing my heart for that day."

Abi stares at me and as she is about to speak again Alex walks out. I am stunned into silence at his beauty. His wet hair glistens in the sun. He has on a pair of low-slung jeans that fit close to his legs, black converse shoes, and a tight, fit, gray t-shirt that shows off every ripple of his chest and abdominal muscles.

"My two favorite ladies lounging on my balcony; what more could I ask for?" he declares.

I begin blushing at his statement and Abi laughs at my reaction saying to him, "Charmer."

Heading out of Alex's building, we wait as Gregory pulls up in a large SUV. Alex ushers me into the back seat and Abi sits in the front. When we arrive at a crowded Cross St. Market Alex and I hold hands as we walk behind Abi. She wants to see, smell, and taste everything and I can't help but laugh at her enthusiasm.

Explaining her reaction Alex says, "Everything in England is completely different. You'll see one day." Then he places a gentle kiss on the palm of my hand, but my heart has clearly zoned in on the last words of his sentence. One day?

During our leisurely walk, I ask Alex if I should call him Dr. Stone.

"You could, but it's not necessary."

"What do you do at the institute?"

"I help the research teams. They'd like to hire me as a full-time employee, and I have considered it, but the timing isn't good right now."

Trying to keep the conversation light, I stop in front of the florist area and point out a handful of tulips, peonies, and hydrangeas that I think would look well in

Alex's apartment. The sales person wraps them up and we continue towards a seafood joint for lunch.

While eating my meal, I instinctively feel eyes boring into me. I turn to see Stephanie glaring at me from a table across the restaurant and Seth looking in the other direction. Uncomfortable with the situation, I turn back to the group at my table.

Reaching out to grab my hand, stroking his gently, Alex asks, "You ok?"

"Yea, I'm fine. I just had a moment."
Pressing his lips in a slight frown, he looks at me as if he doesn't believe me, then squeezes my hand and continues his conversation with Abi.

As we return to Alex's home, Abi and I head out onto the balcony we vacated earlier. Joining us a few minutes later, Alex brings with him a bottle of wine and glasses.

"So, Abi, when do you head back?" I ask.

"I'm not sure. I have a few friends across the country I plan to visit, so I may stay around here for another couple days, but I have no timeline."

"Wow that must be exciting. I've only ever seen Maryland, Virginia, and North Carolina. My family didn't really have the luxury to travel, but we vacationed close by. I don't even think I have any friends outside of Maryland."

Changing subjects quickly and dismissing my comments, Abi shouts, "Hey big bro, can we eat at that seafood place on the harbor? I could go for some shrimp!"

"Abi, we just ate!" Alex exclaims. But the way the love for his sister shines through his eyes, he gives himself away with his mock anger.

"I know, but it's not too early to decide on dinner."

"Whatever you say, sis. But sure, we can go down to the harbor for dinner."

"Great, I'm beat from that entire sensory overload this morning. I'm going to head inside and take a siesta." Finishing off her glass of wine, Abi heads inside leaving Alex and me alone on the balcony.

The moment Abi shuts the door, Alex walks over to where I am sitting, lifts me up, situates himself on the chair, and then proceeds to place me on his lap.

"You look beautiful today, Mallory," he whispers as he strokes my neck with his nose.
At the slightest touch from his hand, the burning sensation activates over my skin and I close my eyes.

"Th-thank you. You look sexy, as always," I stutter as I shift slightly, trying to get some relief from my tightening core

"Sexy, eh?"

"Yes, don't pretend you don't realize the effect you have on the female population. I enjoyed watching all of the women gaping at you today while we strolled along the market."

"I believe you are delusional, Ms. Winston."

"On the contrary, Mr. Stone. It is you who are delusional."
Leaning in, I place a soft kiss on his lips and then he rests his forehead against my own.

"What you do to me, Ms. Winston," he seems to say to himself.

Smiling up at him I ask, "Do you mind if I join you and Abi this evening? I am still upset with Madison and Mika, so I don't really think I should go home."

"Certainly. I thought it was implied that you would be joining us. I told you I want you near me as much as possible before I leave."

"I'm sorry. I didn't want to disappoint you by assuming I was to tag along."

"You are perfect, Ms. Winston. Have I told you that recently?" Alex says as he trails a finger up and down my neck and collarbone.

"Not today, sir," I respond with a smile.

Turning me on the chair so that my back is against his chest Alex begins to massage my breasts through my dress and suckle the skin along my shoulders and neck.

"Mmm. Ms. Winston, I want you now. Stand, take off your panties and hand them to me, then sit back down on my legs facing towards the railing," Alex commands.

Following his instructions, I can hear the soft hum of a zipper pulling down as I finish his demands and stand facing away from him. With an unfamiliar boldness, I hold out my hand with my panties dangling from my fingers. My breath and heartbeat have accelerated to a wicked pace and I can feel my fingers trembling as I anticipate Alex's next move. He snatches the panties from my hands and I proceed to sit on his lap. My hips are lifted suddenly, so that he can slide his lower body forward and pull me back against him. Placing my legs on the outside of his, I can feel his erection slide along my folds. My desire for him in this instant causes a moan to release from my lips. Hoping to hit my throbbing spot, I rock my body back and forth. Alex tilts me forward and then he lifts his hips up. Without time to react, he enters me swiftly and we gasp simultaneously. He starts to pump me up and down holding onto my waist and he does the same with his hips. The feeling is incredible as he fills my core to the brink. My body wants him to stop because he is hitting me so deep, but he is creating such intense pleasure that I can't imagine him ceasing. As he continues to drive us both forward, I can feel myself pushing closer to the edge. I try to hold back my explosion, but I sense he is getting near to his peak as well. After reaching forward to rub my clit with his hand, we reach our conclusion together and both lean back, Alex onto the chair and me onto him.

Wrapped up in bliss, I hear Alex announce, "That was spectacular, Ms. Winston."

"Yes sir, it was."

We tread into the house and head towards the bedroom. Lying down on the bed, I watch Alex as he unfastens his wristwatch.

"You are quite a sight to behold, Ms. Winston," Alex says as he stands there in all of his sumptuousness. Crossing his arms across his tight chest, he says authoritatively, "Touch yourself, Ms. Winston. Begin with your breasts and move your left hand to your already slick folds, and then fuck yourself with your fingers."

Nervousness surges through me and bow my head momentarily. But as desire courses through me remembering how passionate I feel when Alex is turned on I do as he says letting my right hand massage my breast and pinch my nipples, while my left hand travels down to my wet sheath. My hand slides back and forth saturating my palm and fingers. As I insert two fingers into my core, I close my eyes to pretend that it is Alex. I envision his naked body and I can feel his hands instead of my own. My body is still reeling from our earlier exertion.

"Oh, I am so close, Alex. May I come sir?"

"Fuck, baby. I can smell your sweetness from here," he says with a husky voice.

Opening my eyes, I see him leaning against the wall separating the bedroom and sitting area. One of his hands is stroking his pulsating cock through his unzipped jeans, while he watches me pleasure myself behind his heavy eyelids.

"No, Ms. Winston. You may not come yet," Alex demands.

Moaning at his rejection of my request, I try to slow the force of my fingers, but my impending upsurge continues to grow. Closing my eyes again, I focus on trying to hold back all of my pleasure.
As I open my eyes again, I find Alex standing in front of me.

"Stop," he utters.

I pull my fingers from my core and I place both hands on the bed. Sweat beads grace along my hairline and my breathing is heavy.

Demanding me, my Adonis says, "Flip onto all fours, Ms. Winston."

Abiding by his command, I position myself on the bed as he has asked and he moves onto the bed to kneel behind me. As soon as I find my place in the correct position, Alex swats his hand across my behind.

"Ow!" I shout out in a startled gasp. I scream from the shock, not the pain.

He slaps in a circle, moving from right cheek to left cheek then to my center. As hard as he is hitting, I feel no pain. I welcome each hit. After five rounds, he moves his hand across my core.

"Darling you are dripping. You enjoy this pain, don't you?"

"Yes, yes sir. I will take anything you give me." Two more slaps follow and then he inserts his index finger into my core and his thumb into my rosette. He pulses them in and out slowly and leans his body slightly forward, tugging on my hair with his other hand.

"You may come now," he whispers into my ear.

At his words, my body bursts into an eruption. He crooks his finger, continuing to rub my center and drains the rest of the orgasm from my body.

As I come back to my senses, Alex twists me so that I am up on my knees facing him and he slams mouth against mine in a brutal kiss. I would give anything to have someone want me for the rest of my life, the way Alex wants me in this moment.

"Wrap your legs around me," he whispers between heated kisses.

As I squeeze my legs around him, he falls forward onto the bed catching himself with his arms. Pinned beneath him, I start to rub my folds against his erection.

Continuing to kiss me feverishly, my body begins craving him again.

"Do not release your legs unless I move them. Understand?"

"Yes, sir."

Moving back to a kneeling position, Alex swiftly enters my body. There will be no sweet love making with him right now. The pounding of his body into mine causes me to slide against his silk duvet. Adjusting our position, Alex reaches down and tilts my hips upward allowing him to rub against my inner spot. When he maneuvers himself again, he moves his hands beneath my back to grip my shoulders. He is pounding into me so hard, I am afraid I will black out. Sensing my discomfort, he bends down to kiss me and then tugs my bottom lip. This bit of pain causes my resurgence of a climax to push forward. Through my peak, I can sense Alex letting go along with me.

As we both come back from our climaxes, Alex moves to lie beside me. Wrapping his arms around my waist, he places a gentle kiss on my lips and I think to myself that I have never felt as treasured as in this very moment.

Chapter Eleven

WRAPPED IN OUR PERSONAL cocoon, Alex and I lose ourselves in each other for an untold amount of time since. Banging on the bedroom door snaps us out of our fantasy.

Abi shouts, "Guys, come on. I'm hungry."
I reply to myself with a "humph" and snuggle my face into Alex's sweaty chest.

"She will continue to bang the door until we respond," Alex says to me then yells out, "Give us a few minutes, Abigail."

As I smile into his chest, Alex whispers into my ear, "As lovely as it would be to lie in this bed with you all day, I believe we need to reenergize with some food." Looking up at him with a pout on my lips, he bends and kisses my mouth. Reaching up, I tangle my fingers in his hair bringing him closer to me.

"Come, darling; let's not keep the child waiting. There is lotion in the bathroom for your bum," he states.

"Fine. Would you mind rubbing it on me?" I ask as I walk into the bathroom to grab the bottle and then stand innocently in the entryway.

Walking to me, Alex gently takes the bottle from my hands and motions for me to turn around. He tenderly rubs the lotion onto my raw behind and as he rubs in small circles, his fingers begin to brush against my center. A gasp escapes my mouth every time he softly touches a fold or skin of my inner thigh, causing my lower belly to inflame again. My body can't seem to get enough of him.

"It seems you have awakened something in me, Ms. Winston. I appear to be insatiable in my cravings for you," Alex proclaims as he continues to rub circles around my body intimately.

"I'm yours, sir. Take me. Please."
Continuing to shift his hand back and forth, my hips rub against his hand, looking for more friction.

"Bend forward slightly, Mallory, and hold onto the door jamb," he says before he enters me slowly, as if he is afraid to hurt me.

His thrusts are unhurried and steady and through unstable breaths Alex says, "I won't last long. Seeing your pink behind had me burning at every rub."

"I'm so close, sir," I respond as my grip on the doorjamb tightens, whitening my knuckles, when his speed begins to pick up.

Soon we are rocking at a fiery speed and I let out a scream as I feel both of our bodies come apart. We both gently move to the floor and rest against the wall.

My limbs have gone limp since experiencing the handful of orgasms in such a short time frame, and luckily I have stayed conscious as the banging on the bedroom door resumes.

"Alex," Abi cries, "are you even out of bed? I am hungry."

"Alex, I promise that was not my intention when I asked you to rub lotion on my ass."

He chuckles as he gracefully moves us off the floor, "Sure it wasn't, Ms. Winston. I still enjoyed myself all the same." Smiling up at him, I kiss his cheek and then clean myself up.

This evening I decide to wear a short, a-line, coral colored skirt with a loose-fitted, off-white tank top. Some cute rhinestone sandals join the ensemble and I add a chunky necklace I found in the dresser. After a few minutes of dressing, I make my way out into the living room where Alex and Abi are waiting for me.

As I am pulling my mess of hair into a ponytail I say, "Sorry to keep you guys waiting."

Wearing his same attire from earlier Alex answers, "We weren't waiting long."

"Oh Mal, you look adorable," Abi says before turning to look at her brother and inquiring, "Can we go now?"

"Yes, Abi; we may leave now," he replies with a secret grin gracing his lips.

Running back into the bedroom and calling from over my shoulder, I announce, "Alex I need to grab my phone so I can text Madison and Mika," while they head towards the elevator.

As Abi leads us out of the car to the lobby, Alex wraps my hair around his wrist and pulls my head back. He leans down, plants a heated kiss onto my lips, and then continues out of the elevator shaft. His sudden burst of passion halts me to my spot. When I recognize the elevator doors beginning to close, I catch myself and begin to move again. After catching up to Abi and Alex, Alex reaches out and wraps an arm over my shoulder as Abi places her hand on the crook of his elbow of his other arm. Intertwining my hand into his, I rest my head onto him.

We only have to walk a short while until we reach the restaurant. Since we didn't call ahead, Abi gives them her cell number to call us when our table is ready and we head out onto one of the harbor docks to enjoy the setting sun on the water.

As I lean against the railing of the dock, Alex wraps himself around me and rests his chin on my shoulder. We stay like this for a few peaceful moments taking in our surroundings, seemingly one person, as my heart beating in time with Alex's.

Lost in separate thoughts we are startled when Abi bounds over to us. "Hey guys. They had a cancellation. Our table is ready," she announces.

After following Abi back to the restaurant, the host seats us at our table.

Once we are settled I ask, "So, Alex and Abi, what do you all do back home in England?"

Abi replies, "Well, I just graduated with a degree in marketing, focusing on branding, and Alex, as you know, is a doctor. But he isn't a practicing physician. He concentrates on research; specifically, genetic research. He wants to find better detection and treatment for Prader Willi syndrome."

Listening to Abi describe their studies, I stare at Alex and pronounce, "Alex, I had no idea."
Not flattered by his sister's listing of his achievements, he shrugs at my response.

Ignoring Alex, Abi continues, "Alex has a wild side though and that is what earns him all of his money. Well, the money that doesn't come from our family. He owns a formula one racing team that I don't know much about it, but his driver wins all the time."

"Holy shit, really? What an adrenaline rush," I exclaim, astonished.

Alex nods his head and looks down at the table, as if he is embarrassed of his second occupation. Reaching under the table, I capture Alex's hand that is resting along his thigh, and link our fingers. Sending in my direction a heartbreakingly beautiful smile, I return it with one of my own. We continue to beam at each other while Abi places a dinner sampler order that we all plan on sharing.

A light voice startles my and Alex's moment by shouting, "Can you two please stop eye fucking each other?"

We both turn our heads quickly towards Abi with horrified looks upon our faces.

She persists, "Seriously, we are out in public. I was getting all worked up and hot just sitting here. Alex, I don't know how you plan to leave here in a month with the way your two were just mentally screwing each other."

"Yes, well, work and mum aren't going to leave me much of a choice," Alex retorts as the waiter arrives with our meal and places the heaping plate of seafood onto the table.

From under the table, Alex squeezes my hand and then releases me. As we dig into to the shrimp, oysters, mussels, and crab legs, I look up momentarily from the mass of food on my plate to find Madison and Mika seated at the table across the restaurant. Wiping off my hands, I check the phone in my purse but find no missed calls, no texts, and no voicemails. Realizing they actually left me out of their dinner plans, I try to finish my meal, but I no longer taste any of the succulent flavors of the seafood. I absentmindedly move portions of my food around while I sit sullenly at the table.

As Abi heads towards the rest room, Alex leans into me and whispers, "I'm here to take care of you. What's wrong?"

I look up into his eyes and pause before revealing, "They're here."

"Who?"

"Madison and Mika. They're eating dinner on the other side of the restaurant. They didn't even invite me."

Seeming to contemplate my words Alex responds, "Well, perhaps there is a misunderstanding."

"We have a house rule; if anyone goes out to eat, we always invite the others. It has been like that since college. Even if one of us went away for the weekend, we always invited the other to dinner. It was sort of an inside joke. They have never, not invited me."

Just as I finished my explanation, Abi walks back to the table and we halt any further discussion.

After settling the bill, Alex pulls my hand towards his mouth, places a kiss along my knuckles, and sends me a wink.

Turning in Abi's direction Alex declares, "Abigail, please wait outside for a moment. Mallory and I saw some friends we want to say hello to quickly."

"Sure," she answers.

Once Abi moves from the table, I ask Alex in my distress, "Alex, what are you doing? I still have to live there. I don't want to make it worse if they are upset with me."

Alex stands from the table and grabs my hand while speaking, "Trust me, Ms. Winston. If there were any hope of continuing your friendships with these women, they have diminished it this evening. If I recall one of them is Mika correct? And she lied to you about meeting me. That is no way to treat any friend. So in reality, they will now only become your house mates once I leave."

The tone he uses while speaking to me compels me to realize he is right. Somehow, along the way these girls are no longer the friends I once knew. Mentally I ask myself how long I let them walk all over me. With my new resolve, we stride over to the table occupied by Madison and Mika.

Siding up to their table I announce, "Hi girls! I want to introduce you to my boyfriend, Alex Stone." Both staring at me, mouths agape, as they make quick glances to Alex. I can see jealousy burning in both of their eyes; green does not look good on them. I continue on, "Alex, this is Mika and Madison. I grew up with Madison and I met Mika in college."

In his perfect speech Alex says condescendingly without them even noticing, "Evening ladies, it is a pleasure to finally meet you. Mallory constantly talks about her friends. I apologize for snagging her away for dinner plans so quickly this evening that she didn't have a chance to see you, though she did send you a message inviting you along." Mika and Madison are speechless as he continues, changing his voice from playful to angry very quickly. "On a side note, I have a few choice words for you ladies," Alex whispers harshly while leaning into their table, his grip on my hand ever increasing. "It is not wise to leave a bar or club with strangers and leaving your friend unaware of your plans. One, something could happen to you and she would be none-the-wiser. And two, something could happen to her and you would be just as much at fault as the criminal. And let me be clear that if anything ever happens to her, because her two friends left her somewhere alone, I will personally see that you two are held as accomplices to the crime." With terrified looks spread across their faces, we start to walk away and then in the blink of an eye, Alex turns back towards the table. "Oh, and one more thing," he says angrily as he faces Mika, "I do remember you. You are the tramp that threw herself at me and then when I turned you down, you proceeded to sit on my lap and grind against me. I do not tolerate liars especially those that lie to my girlfriend. It would be wise of you to stay away from me and from Mallory or I will quickly have you disbarred."

Sauntering away, Alex exits the restaurant with me trailing behind him.

"Mallory, did you get to say hi to your friends?" Abi asks curiously, noticing the back-away stance of Alex.

"I did."

The anger continues to roll off Alex in waves as we walk back to The Braxton.

Leaning into the ear of my powerful man, I whisper, "Thank you for saying everything I wish I was strong enough to say."

As we stop at a cross walk with a crowd of people he turns towards me and says, "Mallory, I promised you I would do anything in my power to protect and care for you. Unlike your friends, I will always keep my promise."

Peeking up at him, I wrap my arms around his waist pulling him into a hug. He proceeds to wrap his arms around me and kiss the top of my forehead. We stay like this until the crosswalk light changes.

Entering the apartment Abi hollers in question, "Hey guys it's still early, do you want to watch a movie?"

"Sure," we reply in unison.

Grabbing the remote, Abi places herself on one end of the sofa while Alex sits on the other end with me resting up against him.

"Can we watch 'Paranormal Activity?" Abi solicits.

We both nod our head as an answer.

"You can cuddle up against me if you get scared." Alex utters in a joking manner.

In between laughs I say, "I will keep that in mind, but unfortunately I love horror flicks and I have seen this movie a lot."

An hour later I am jostled awake as Alex lifts me into his arms and I see that Abi has already moved from the couch.

Alex whispers into my ear, "Sleep, love."

Waking sometime during the night, I feel fingers kissing my skin, trailing back and forth along my side.

"I know you're awake, Mallory. I can hear your breath hitch at my touch."

He reaches his hand up to my face and I turn onto my back. Stroking his thumb along my cheek, he slants forward to kiss me on both corners of my mouth and then his tongue strokes my upper lip begging for entrance. Opening my lips, his tongue probes the inside of my mouth as his fingertips trace a path of fire down my skin. With no direction in mind, his fingers outline my collarbone, breasts, nipples, ribs, navel, and thighs in sensual and measured strokes.

"Alex, may I touch you?" I ask and without hesitation he places my hand directly over his heart and gazes devotedly into my eyes.

Tracing his chest and taught stomach, my hand draws light circles across his body. Light kisses are placed along my collarbone causing me to falter my perusing of his body. Quickly, he grabs my hand and places it with the other, both alongside my head on the bed sheets, interlacing our fingers together. Resting above me he places a kiss on my lips filled with so much emotion, I am taken aback by its sincerity. I attempt to portray all of my feelings for Alex in my returning kiss; I want him to know that I love him. The words can't ever be said between us, but I hope to convey my love for him whenever we are together in moments like this.

Between kisses Alex discloses, "You. Are. So. Sweet. I. Need. You. Now."

I want him to make love to me as he slowly enters me inch by tantalizing inch. As he pushes forward, I whimper from the light soreness I feel from our escapades earlier in the day.

"I'm sorry, darling. Am I hurting you? I can stop. I know I was rough earlier."

"Please, Alex. Don't stop. You feel too good," I say as I lift my hips slightly, meeting his thrust.

"Your body feels amazing. I could stay inside you forever. Your tight, wet, cunt welcomes me every time. I can't get enough."

"Please, Alex."

"Please what, Ms. Winston?"

"More. Please. Please, make love to me."

He quickens his pace only slightly and leans down to kiss my neck.

"I love seeing you wear my collar all day, but seeing you naked with my collar on is an aphrodisiac in itself," he says eliciting a moan from me at his words.

Untangling one of his hands from my own, he moves it to my backside. His thumb enters my tight rosette, giving me even more pleasure and bringing my proximity to the brink closer with each thrust. Adjusting my hips slightly so that his body rubs my clit as well, the triple surge of pleasure becomes too much and I let go in his arms.

Easing back into a slumber, I can sense Alex quietly cleaning me up before he slips back into bed, wrapping his arms around me.

Through my veil of unconsciousness, I can hear him murmur, "This has been the best week of my life. I am sorry that it can't last any longer than the two months I am here. I wish we had met sooner, my love." Pausing he continues, "You will make someone very happy one day and I will be jealous of that man for all eternity." Brushing a strand of hair from my face, he kisses my forehead and finishes, "Sleep well, darling."

Waking in the morning light, I find an empty bed and hear laughter out in the living room. I don't remember much from last night, but I am very sore, everywhere. Glancing over to the side of the bed Alex usually lays, I find a single purple rose on the pillow. I don't know what different colored roses mean, other than red means love, but perhaps Alex chose this rose because purple is my favorite color. Taking the delicate flower in my hand, I move to the bathroom placing the rose on the counter and stepping into the hot shower.

"Good morning, beautiful. Can I get you anything for breakfast? Abi has made some pancakes," Alex announces.

"Abi cooks?" I ask.

"Only breakfast food, like her brother," he chuckles.

"Well, I would love some pancakes. Thank you." As I bend down to kiss him, he affectionately pulls me onto his lap.

"You looked so serene this morning, I couldn't bear to wake you," he says as he loosens the sash on the robe and slides his hands inside to rub my back.

"Alex, Abi may see," I exclaim.

"No, she just went to her room for a shower so we have a few minutes. I told you I don't share," he says as he nips at my neck

"I'm sorry, sir."

"No harm. How do you feel this morning?"

"I am pleasantly sore, sir. I think you wore me out yesterday."

"I suppose that I can let you rest today."

"That is kind of you, Mr. Stone. Maybe I will feel better this evening."
Wrapping my arms around him, I rest against his sitting frame as he continues to stroke my back beneath my robe.

Minutes pass and Alex breaks our silence by asking, "Mallory, how do you feel about baseball?"

"I love baseball. The Orioles are my favorite. I've never been to a game though."

As he ties the sash back onto my robe he continues, "Well, how would you like to go today? There is an afternoon game at Camden Yards and I have tickets."

"Oh, my gosh, seriously?" I exclaim as I jump off Alex's lap and hop up and down in excitement.

He snickers "I will take that as a yes."

As I continue to dance in my exhilaration, Abi comes back into the room and inquires, "Mal, you ok? My pancakes are not that great."

I stop dead in my tracks realizing that she has witnessed my ridiculous dancing.

With bright red cheeks, I turn to her and say, "Damn Abi you sure are a buzz kill. Alex is taking us to the Orioles game today. I love the Orioles and I have never been to a game."

"Oh, we go every time we're in town."
Walking back over towards Alex I plant a very loud and very wet kiss on his lips.

"I am so excited! What time is the game?" I call out.

"It begins at two so we have plenty of time. Help yourself to some breakfast."

Chapter Twelve

CAMDEN YARDS IS PACKED and as we are directed to
our seats, I can't help but wonder how Alex got a hold of
these. They are three rows back from home plate and
usually reserved for season ticket holders. My two
companions are amused by my excitement; I must look
like a little kid at an amusement park. Blushing in
embarrassment, I continue to gaze at the baseball
stadium.

"I'm sorry, Mallory. I forget what it is like to be
some place you dream about. Please take it all in. You
look quite adorable when you're in awe," Alex says as he
leans over to me and kisses my forehead.
On a mission, Abi scampers off to go get us some lunch
and beer.

Enjoying our few moments alone together, I wrap
my hand in Alex's and I lean into him whispering,

"Thank you so much for this, Alex. You have no idea what this means to me."

"You're most welcome, Mallory. It is a pleasure."

"Oh, and thank you for the rose this morning; purple is my favorite color."

He hesitates momentarily, as if wanting to say something more, but decides against it.

Instead, he replies, "I know, darling. Though, it isn't nearly as striking as the woman I left it for."

"Are you sure you have only had two girlfriends? You're quite a romantic you know."

"Only for you, sweetheart. I told you I'd do anything to keep you near me for the next two months."

Abi comes bounding up the stairs moments later, trailed by two young stadium ushers carrying all of her purchased food and beer.

"This wonderful country has men always wanting to help out a lady," she says as she turns to face the boys carrying her goods. "Thank you, gentlemen. I can take it from here."

They both blush and scamper off.

"You are horrible, Abi," I say with a chuckle.

Watching the game, I am riveted to my seat. Alex and Abi keep talking about cricket or some English game that I don't understand, but they don't distract me from my love of the Orioles. During the seventh inning stretch, we all stand with the rest of the stadium and move into stretching positions. Abi even tries to complete yoga poses where she stands, causing her neighbors to laugh. The Orioles are ahead by three runs so I am relaxing into my seat when I notice the camera for the large screen making its way over to our section. I see the couple four rows behind us show up on the screen and kiss. The cameraman must have noticed Alex's and my hand tangled together because he quickly closes in on us. At first Alex doesn't notice, so I pretend I don't either, though I know my cheeks speak differently. Abi points out the screen to Alex and he grins widely, leans towards me, and pulls my face into a very heated, barely PG-13 kiss. I am so lost in the sensation of Alex's lips gliding across my own that I barely register the crowd hollering beside us. When he finally lets me up, we grin at each other for a small moment. He kisses my forehead and after placing his arm over my shoulder, we finish watching the game. Most of the crowd is still in awe from our throws of passion that they are more content watching us than the game.

The Orioles win the game and before leaving Alex even manages to get me a signed baseball from the pitcher. Of course, while I receive the baseball from the pitcher, Abi collects his phone number.

We walk back to Alex's home and decide that we would stay in for dinner. Since neither Alex nor Abi cook, I will be the one grilling steaks and steaming vegetables. Thirty minutes later, we sit down in companionable silence to enjoy our meals.

"Well, I'm beat, that sun wore me out and my flight leaves early in the morning," Abi says as she tosses her long hair behind her back nonchalantly.

"Thanks for stopping in, Abi. It was great to see you. Let me know when you return to England," he announces as he stands to give her a hug.

Walking over to me, she pulls me into a tight hug.

She squeezes all of the air from my lungs and whispers, "Mal, I want us to keep in touch. I programmed my number into your phone, so you call me anytime. Perhaps when I travel back this way we can meet up."

"Sure Abi, I would like that. Are you sure you need to leave so soon? I am glad that we had the chance to meet."

She hugs me again and moves towards her room. Alex's phone rings moments later and he hesitates to pick it up after glancing at the screen.

"I need to take this, Mallory. Please go prepare yourself in the bedroom," he declares before moving towards his office.

I move quickly to the bedroom and disrobe from my clothes, folding them onto the floor beside my designated spot. The black nightie is folded in my nightstand and I remove it. Sliding it on, it glides over my skin.

Making my way back to my designated spot, I stand in position and I can vaguely hear some shouting coming from Alex's office. Twenty minutes have passed and my legs are beginning to stiffen from being locked in the same position for this amount of time. After an additional twenty minutes, Alex strolls back to the bedroom.

"Lovely. You may look up, Ms. Winston. Follow me."

He has changed into a pair of gray gym shorts with no shirt. I have to refrain myself from wiping my mouth to catch any drool that may have slipped out from staring at him, as he is quite a sight to behold.

Following him into the media room Alex commands, "Please stand beside the medallion, facing towards the room." Stepping towards the other side of the room, he unlocks his armoire and pulls out a pair of gloves and a riding crop. Alex then walks back over to where I stand and first shows me the gloves. He explains, "These are called vampire gloves. Please, feel them." Reaching out I caress the softness of the leather and he turns them over, palm up, so that I see the small spikes across the fingers and palm. I glare back up at him with an appalled expression. Quickly, Alex speaks in a calming tone, "Ms. Winston, these gloves are typically used in punishment, but I have learned that when used in soft light strokes they can be quite pleasurable. Do not worry; you have not displeased me today, quite the opposite really. I took gratification in your enthusiasm today." He then shows me the riding crop. It is of dark brown leather and at the end, in the same leather, looks to be a woven rose.

"May I touch it, sir?" I ask quietly.

"Yes, Ms. Winston."

Stroking the fine leather, I find it is tougher than the glove, but equally as soft. The rose is so intricately woven it looks like a work of art.

"It is beautiful, sir."

"Yes, I purchased her with you in mind." Reaching up he caresses my shoulder than removes the straps from the gown and the material pools at my feet. "Please stand against the medallion, facing the wall,"

Alex says as he positions my legs much farther apart than last time. My arms aren't placed above me this time; Alex pulls them straight out from my shoulders. "Before I begin, Ms. Winston. I want to apologize to you again for my roughness these past few days. I would have done many things differently. I would have eased you into this, but I find myself lost in my need for control when you are submitting to me. I do not want to hurt you like last time. I know you are strong, but you must safe word if it becomes too much. Do you understand?" he explains.

"Yes, sir. Thank you, sir."

"Splendid."

Alex begins to move across my arms with the vampire gloves. The movement is so soft that it feels like a fur instead of spikes. His hands move down my sides and farther down my legs as he moves in tiny circles around my calves. When he moves back up and reaches behind my knees I can feel electricity shoot to my core. Little spikes travel up my inner thigh and then come around to stroke my behind. He alternates slapping each cheek lightly. After eight slaps my body is beyond hot, my breathing is faster, and my heart is pulsating. I can hear Alex remove his gloves and he slides a finger through my folds. A whimper buries in my throat from his touch and I pull on my restraints.

Removing his finger far too quickly he murmurs huskily, "Mmm. Ms. Winston, you are a delectable treat. Would you like a taste?"

Transfixed in this moment I reply, "Yes, sir." Skating his hand back through my folds, he causes another moan to escape from my mouth.

Slapping my behind again quickly, he admonishes, "Quiet."

Then he places his hand in front of my face so that I may lick his finger and I maneuver my head so that I can suck it into my mouth. Tasting myself on him, the flavor spreads more heat through my body.

"Enough," Alex shouts as he pulls his finger from my mouth and takes the crop into his hand.

My ribcage receives three sharp blows and though they are not painful, they continue to increase the pressure in my body. Using the crop to stroke along my arms and down my spine, Alex slaps each leg a few times and moves towards my inner thighs. The hits are so pleasurable that I find myself reaching my orgasm far too quickly.

As the crop slides through my center, Alex announces, "You may come, Ms. Winston."

He moves the crop down my body and then swats my core twice. The third hit pushes me over the edge and I come gloriously while chained to the medallion; my restrained position is barely keeping me standing.

"That was wonderful to witness, Ms. Winston," Alex praises as he quickly removes the cuffs on my wrists and ankles and lifts me into his arms.

Walking back to his bedroom, he places me onto his couch and steps away from the room, towards the bathroom, to return with my robe.

Smiling at his kind gesture I say, "Thank you."

"You're most welcome, Mallory. Did you enjoy our scene this evening?"

"Yes, sir. You were right; those gloves didn't hurt at all. They almost tickled."

"You can always trust me, Ms. Winston."

We sit on the couch together for a short amount of time as Alex reaches over and pulls my feet into his lap and starts massaging one of them.

"Oh goodness, that feels good," I moan.

He continues for a few minutes massaging each foot thoroughly; I hadn't realized he was using this as a distraction.

Soon Alex speaks up, "Mallory, I have to leave for a few days. My brother needs assistance with his campaign and there is an issue with one of my race teams."

"Oh," I pause, but continue, "I understand. When will you leave and return?"

"I will leave tomorrow morning and I plan on returning as soon as possible, but it seems like it may take a week or two to sort out."

My good mood vanishes. I have enjoyed sharing in his company for the past week; it will only feel worse when he leaves after two months.

Taking a few breaths to steady my voice I reveal, "Alex, I'll be here when you return."

"I know, darling. My hope is that this trouble back home won't mean I need to leave the states earlier."

"What will happen to our arrangement if that happens?"

"I'm sorry, Mallory, but if I have to leave earlier, then our arrangement will end as well."

The need to cry racks my body. How can he be so impervious to this situation? Abi mentioned that he is closed off and that he doesn't let people in, but I want so desperately to be loved by this man and I am determined to breakthrough to him. Hardening my resolve, I square my shoulders. If he is going to act so unaffected by leaving then so will I. Letting my emotions rule our conversation, I try to rile some conflict from Alex.

I say curtly, "That seems like a logical solution since what I want doesn't seem to be a priority."

"I know what you're doing, Mallory. I know you're upset."

I remove myself from the couch and stand before him annoyed that he would blatantly state my emotion.

"You know nothing. You don't know a damn thing about me!"

I storm over to the bed, remove the robe, and tuck myself into the sheets. Alex leaves the room and heads towards his office without saying a word more. There was no reason to act the way I did, but I can't seem to control myself when he is near. I don't want to see him leave; I only get him for such a short time. I don't understand why he isn't more upset about this.

Sleep doesn't find me during the night and I am awake as I hear both Alex and Abi get ready to leave for their flights. Before Alex heads out, he comes to crouch beside me while I lie in bed. My eyes are shut, but I am sure he knows I am awake.

"Mallory?" His voice carries a bit of hoarseness in it. "Mallory, please." I say nothing, but I open my eyes wide in acknowledgement. Skimming the back of his knuckles along my cheek he says, "I am sorry for how things ended last night. I know you are angry with me. Please, forgive me." He pauses, hoping for a response and then continues, "I have to leave now, but I hope you are waiting for me when I return. I'm not ready to lose you yet." He bends forward and kisses me softly on the lips before saying, "Goodbye, Mallory." A lone tear escapes from my eye and he wipes it away before standing and walking away from the bedroom.

Chapter Thirteen

GREGORY IS WAITING FOR me in the lobby as I exit the elevator on Monday morning. I feel disconnected from the world after watching Alex leave for a few days. He deserved to hear me forgive him and say goodbye, but my stupid pride got in the way. Now I dread that something is going to happen to him while he is gone or that he decides not to return.

"Good morning, Ms. Winston," Gregory sends as a greeting.

"Mornin' Gregory. Why didn't you leave with Alex?"

"Mr. Stone asked that I stay here to keep you safe and to assist you until he returns."

"That isn't necessary."

"He insisted, Ms. Winston."

"Well, am I allowed to stay at my house?"

RENEE HARLESS

"Mr. Stone suggested that you continue to reside at his home. He also recommended that I stay in the guest room if you felt unsafe."

"He is exasperating. I am going to work now."

"May I drive you miss?"

"Sure, I didn't get a lot of sleep last night. Oh, but only if we stop by Starbucks on the way in." My smile widens at the thought of caffeine.

I stroll into my office, with my coffee in hand, and it feels as if I haven't been here in ages, when in reality it has only been a weekend. Stopping at Annie's office, I plop into a chair in front of her desk. Looking up at me wide eyed, I hand off her coffee.

"Mmm. I love you. You're the best boss," she moans through sips of coffee.

"Bribes to make you work hard, Annie. How was your weekend?"

"Boring, we picked out flowers for the wedding. My mother-in-law loved it. Me? Not so much."

"You should have brought me, I love flowers."

"I know you do. I'll remember that if we can't make a decision. What did you do this weekend?"

"Well, will the summarized version of my weekend do?" With the nod of her head I proceed. "I went out with Madison and Mika on Friday. Mika lied. They ditched me. I wound up at Alex's. He had two beautiful women staying with him. One was his sister. The other is his now married, ex lover. But they were both sweet as pie. Saturday, we went to Cross St. Market. We went out for seafood that night. Ran into Mika and Madison. Alex told them off. Seriously, I think Madison was going to cry. Sunday, they took me to Camden yards. All in all, best weekend of my life so far, until Alex left this morning. Some issue at home," I finish and gasp for breath.

"Wow, sounds like a soap opera."

"Oh, it was. You should have been there. So, what's on the agenda today?"

"You have a director's meeting at 9:00am and then a lunch meeting with Kyle and Lily Johnson."

"Lunch meeting? I never schedule lunch meetings."

"Well," she pauses, "You didn't. I did. He called and tricked me into setting one up. He is just so damn charismatic. I'm sorry. Do you want me to cancel?"

"No, it's fine. He won't be nearly as bad if his sister is there. Plus, Seth hasn't eaten lunch with me in forever. So, it won't be a problem."

"Oh, and there is a beautiful rose on your desk," Annie shouts as I head back towards my office.

Scrambling to open the door to my office, I hope to find Alex sitting there. I am only mildly disappointed to find a single purple rose placed on my desk. Goodness how my body yearns for him. Just the thought of him being close to me is enough to cause my belly to clench tight. His possession has quickly wiggled and squirmed its way around my heart.

As I sit in my chair, I glance down to see a small envelope tied to the stem of the rose.

To my beloved, Ms. Winston,

Please see this rose as a request for forgiveness. My soul was tormented at my departure this morning. You have captivated me, Ms. Winston, and I hope to come back home into your arms soon. I haven't begun to explore you, or us, yet.

Yours,
Alex Stone

Things I know: You clasp your hands together and look down when you're nervous.

My cheeks heat and my eyes pool with moisture as I ponder what he means with the "Things I know" add on and then I realize he is referring to my comment that he didn't know anything about me. He really does pay attention to everything I say. As I read the letter a third time and sniff the rose, I hear a cough at the door and I look up to find Seth standing in my doorway.

"Hey Seth, what's up?" I ask.

Without a response, he turns around and walks away. I was sure he understood that I wasn't attracted to him that way and hopefully his jealousy will wear off soon so he can focus on his relationship with Stephanie.

When I return to my office after my Directors meeting, I see both Johnson siblings perched on my love seat.

"Ms. Winston, thanks for agreeing to join us for lunch today. We apologize for waiting in your office. Your assistant Annie allowed us to wait in here," Lily states somewhat embarrassed.

"No problem, Lily. It is great to see you. You as well, Kyle."

Grabbing my hand, Kyle kisses my knuckles saying, "It is always a pleasure, Ms. Winston."

"Please both of you call me Mallory. Where would you all like to go to lunch today?"

Lily speaks up, "There is a deli a few blocks away and they have the best sandwiches."

"That sounds great. Let me grab my bag."

As I move over to my desk, Kyle asks a question. "That is a beautiful rose, Mallory. From your boyfriend?"

"Um, yes, Kyle. It is from Alex."

"Won't he be jealous that you are joining me for lunch?"

"No. One, because I am joining you and Lily and two, because he trusts me."

"Lucky S.O.B.," he grunts under his breath causing me to laugh at his statement as we continue to the elevators.

Lunch was fantastic and the deli really did boast one of the best sandwiches I had ever eaten. Kyle, Lily, and I find ourselves in an enjoyable conversation. All three of us enjoy the same things and we make it a point to get together again soon outside of work. Lily returns to their loft after our meal and Kyle walks back with me to my office.

"I'm glad we could get together for lunch today, Mallory," he says.

"I am too. You all are now my favorite clients."

"Can I ask you a question?"

"Sure."

"I don't make you uncomfortable, do I? Lily tells me I have a tendency to flirt and I'd really like for you to be our friend."

"Your flirting doesn't have near the effect on me that it probably should. I am very happy in my relationship. But even so, you and Lily remind me of my twin brothers so it is a bit difficult to see you both in any light other than that."

Kyle and Lily are both equally beautiful with their beach blonde good looks. I bet Madison would like Kyle. Just thinking about Madison has me seeing red in fury. I'm not sure what is happening between us; we were always so close growing up.

"You ok there, Sparky?" he asks knocking me from my daydream.

"Uh, yes I'm fine, sorry. I was just thinking to myself that my friend Madison would like you."

"Ooohhh, do tell. Is she has stunning as you?"

"She is beyond stunning. Madison just got out of a serious relationship a few months ago and hasn't really started dating yet. She is barely over five feet tall and is 100 pounds of pure spunk. She has long brown hair, tan skin, and blue eyes. Oh, wait I have a picture on my phone." The digital image of the three of us from the night at Lucky 21 is set as my wallpaper on the phone. "Here," I say holding out my phone. "She is the one on the left, in the gold. My other housemate is Mika, in the silver."

"Well, she is as lovely as you described. Too bad you're taken though. You are definitely the most beautiful out of the bunch."

"Seriously? You and Alex both need to have your eyes checked."

"Men always see things differently than women."

"Whatever you say, Kyle," I joke as I take my phone back. "Can I get you anything before you head out?"

"No thanks, I'm good. Please call us this weekend if you want to hang out. We typically chill out at the loft, but we can venture out if you want."

"Sure, Kyle. I'll let you know."

The rest of my day passes at a snail's pace while I finish up the rest of the Johnson paperwork. The new vodka campaign will begin next week so I make sure to schedule all of the necessary team meetings. Steven pops in a few times to check on the upcoming campaign and he seems thrilled with my gaining of the vodka client. He says it was a very lucrative deal to make.

I wave goodbye to Stephanie on my way out, but she makes no attempt to address me. I'm a bit hurt at her dismissal of me.

Walking out of the lobby, I don't notice Gregory waiting. "Should I call him?" I ask myself. "He isn't my personal driver and I would feel bad if he was in the middle of something personal.

Turning to walk down the sidewalk, I decide to head towards my home. Even if I plan on staying at Alex's I would like to bring some lounging clothes with me and I need to water my plants and check my mail. As I get closer to my building, I can hear police sirens in the distance. This is a safe area and I hope something hasn't happened to one of my neighbors.

Suddenly, Gregory pulls up beside me and jumps out of his car shouting, "Ms. Winston, I apologize for running late this evening. Please let me take you back to Mr. Stone's."
He sounds hurried and out of breath.

"It isn't a problem, Gregory. The weather is lovely today. Why are you out of breath?"

"Please, miss. Let's head back and we can discuss it at Mr. Stone's home."

"I want to go to my home. I have a few things I need to do."

"Ms. Winston, I must advise against you going home."

"Why? What is going on? Why can't I go home?"

"Miss, please," Gregory insists.

"Well, Gregory, I suggest you either escort me to my home or I will walk alone. It's your choice."

"Yes, miss. I will escort you to your home," he relents defeated.

As we approach my row home, I see that the police cars are blocking off the road. Gregory parks along an adjoining street and we rush towards the police tape.

"Sir, I live here. What is going on? Is anyone hurt?" I ask urgently.

"Your name, please?"

 "Mallory Winston"

"Ms. Winston, please follow me. Your boyfriend can join us."
I look back at Gregory and smirk at the blush on his face, but I don't correct the officer.

"Ms. Winston, you were lucky that no one was home, but it seems that the perpetrator only targeted the lower apartment," the officer mentions.

"I live in the lower apartment."

"That's what I thought. We were alerted, through your security system on the apartment door that someone had entered the main house, but picked the lock to your door."

Walking through the main door to my home, SLUT has been painted in bright red across my door and WHORE has been painted on the hallway walls. I notice Gregory has pulled out a small camera and is taking pictures. I'm glad he is here with me because I am a bit frightened to see anymore.

"Ma'am, are you ok for me to open to door now?" the kind officer inquires as his hand rests on the knob.

"Yes, sorry," I answer shyly.

The officer opens my living room door and we step inside slowly. Piercing every wall and section of furniture are thousands of razor sharp cutting knives. I think I am more shocked that someone could so easily carry that many knives around with them, than the fact that someone wanted to harm me at my apartment. The officer guides me to the kitchen where I find the word TRASH painted onto my counter top. Glancing back at the living room, I take a deep breath.

"There is more, Ms. Winston," the officer says. Guiding me towards the extra bathroom, I see the bathtub full of blood.

"It seems to be animal blood," he acknowledges. "We don't believe it is human. The other bathroom looks the same. Strangely, the only room he or she didn't touch is the guest bedroom."

We continue to the master bedroom and I tighten my gut as we enter. Every piece of fabric, from my bedding to my clothes, has been cut up into shreds. None of it is even remotely salvageable.

"Why would someone do this to me?" I ask bewildered and in shock.

"Well, ma'am, that's what we'd like to ask you. If you don't mind, I have a handful of questions. I know you're probably uneasy right now, but we want to catch this person."

I glance around at my room again, looking for any clues that may help to point out the person responsible, but nothing jumps out at me. Searching for one piece of clothing I had hidden away, I reach under my bed to find the bronze dress still in its bag from the store. This is the dress I wore when I met Alex. Even when he isn't physically here, seeing this dress brings me peace and solace.

Gregory drives me to the police station so I can give my statement and answer a few questions.

The officer begins, "Ms. Winston, we are going to get started. This is not an interrogation so there is no need to be nervous."

Looking down at my hands, a giggle escapes thinking about the card earlier I received from Alex where he mentioned I clasp my hands together when I'm nervous.

"Yes, sir. Please go ahead," I say.

"The perpetrator entered your home at 2:00pm this afternoon. Where were you at 2:00pm?"

"I was back at my office finishing a campaign. My lunch meeting ended at 1:00pm."

"Is there anyone that would want to harm you? Can you give us a list of your close friends or acquaintances?"

"No, sir. I don't have any enemies that I am aware of. My other house mates aren't speaking to me right now, but we've been friends for a very long time. This isn't something they would do. My other friend, Seth, works in my building and he was at the office today. I saw him this morning. His girlfriend doesn't like me much either, she is our receptionist, but she is too innocent for something like this. My co-workers, Annie and Steven, were also both at the office today. The two clients I had lunch with both had meetings across town this afternoon."

Glancing in Gregory's direction the officer inquires, "Where was your boyfriend, Ms. Winston?"

"He left for England early this morning. Gregory," I say nodding in his direction, "was the one to take him and his sister to the airport." I start to ask myself, *where was Gregory this afternoon?*

He must be able to sense my thoughts because he speaks to me and the police officers, "Ms. Winston, I didn't want to alarm you earlier, but I have been allowed to tap into your security system at your home as a precautionary measure per Mr. Stone's request. I arrived at the scene the same time as the police. When the incident occurred, I was at my home talking to Mr. Stone about some matters in England."

I turn away from Gregory, appalled at this knowledge. I understand Alex wants to protect me, but hacking into my system is taking it a bit far. My fists clench and unclench as I try to control my anger.

Before I have a chance to unleash my fury onto Gregory, the officer speaks up, "Ms. Winston, you have given us a great deal of information and quite a few leads. I'd like to answer any questions you may have."

With the opportunity at my grasp I start, "Were there any witnesses? How much do you know?"

"No, ma'am. No witnesses have come forward as of yet. The perpetrator had a window of fifteen minutes before the police arrived, so we believe he worked with an accomplice. He also didn't seem to notice that you had installed a security system, so we don't believe he could be one of your close friends."

I quickly correct him, "Actually, when I bought the home I had it installed on closing day. No one knows about the system, not even my roommates. I'm surprised Gregory discovered it."

Gregory chirps in, embarrassed, "Sorry, miss. I have a device on my phone to recognize the electrical output of security systems and bugs."

The officer addresses me again, "I'm sorry I don't have more information for you currently, but we will be in contact as we learn more. The area has never experienced vandalism so the neighbors are very upset. We will be gathering statements from your roommates this evening and asking them to stay somewhere else while we clean up the debris. Do you have somewhere you could stay, Ms. Winston?"

"Yes, sir. I had planned on staying at my boyfriend's place while he was away."

"Great. Here is my card, Ms. Winston. Please call me if you think of anything that may help the case."

As we walk back to the car, Gregory turns to me and asks, "Are you ok, miss?"

"I think so. Does Alex know?"

"Yes, ma'am. He is angry that he isn't here. Are you hungry, Ms. Winston?"

"Starving!" I exclaim.

"I know just the place."

We are seated at this cozy, little, Italian diner where Gregory promised the best pizza in Baltimore. We both order a beer to help unwind from the afternoon.

"I'm sorry this has happened to you, Ms. Winston."

"It's alright. I just feel like I'm missing some piece of the puzzle. How could I not know that someone was planning this? I don't even know who to trust anymore."

"I'm sorry, miss. But you are correct in thinking there is a piece missing," he says as he reaches into his pocket for his phone. Continuing he states, "There were a few items sent to you in the mail that were taken away as evidence. I was lucky enough to take photos of them earlier. Would you like to see them now or wait until we return home?"

Stunned that I received threatening letters in the mail and left in the dark, I say coldly, "Uh, I'd like to see them now, please."

"Yes, miss."

Gregory holds out his phone and shows me picture after picture of threats written out in red ink. Some threats calling me the same names that were written out on the walls, doors, and countertop, while others were more descriptive. The final and more recent note made vomit form in my stomach and push up my throat. It said, *I will slit you mouth to core before you will end up with him.* I swallow heavily to keep the bile at bay and try to catch a breath.

"Is this why you are so worried, because someone may be targeting Alex as well?"

Gregory reaches across and grabs my hand saying, "Ms. Winston, never underestimate your importance to Alex, myself, or the world. Whether these notes were involved or not, Alex and I would be equally as concerned about your well-being."

Letting his words sink in I ponder; *will Alex still care about me when he returns to England in a few months?*

Thanking Gregory, he answers, "You're most welcome, Ms. Winston. Also, the police department has asked that you not return to work for a few days. They are afraid that the perpetrator may target you there. I spoke with your Vice President and he said you would have the next three days off with pay. They are glad you are ok and no one was hurt."

"What am I supposed to do in the mean time? My two closest friends are suspects," I say with my voice rising to a shout, and I have nowhere to go."

"Well, Ms. Winston, I can help with both of those. First, you will be staying at Mr. Stone's home at his request. Second, I have made a phone call and I believe you will have a visitor tomorrow morning. Unfortunately, that visitor will not be Mr. Stone. His brother has him tied up with some domestic issues."

Letting his words sink in, I calm down and utter, "Oh, ok. At least I will have clothes at Alex's. I don't seem to have any left at my home."

We settle into silence as our pizza arrives, both deciding to take in the events that happened today.

Entering Alex's home, Gregory sweeps the premises first as a precaution before allowing me to proceed. I'm not sure it is necessary, but I wait for him to finish before I enter the rest of the apartment.

"Ms. Winston," Gregory starts, "Alex has requested that I turn on the video surveillance in his home while he is away. Are you ok with this?"

"Um…" murmuring as I clasp my fingers and look down, blush sprinting across my cheeks.

"I'm sorry, miss, let me explain. There is no surveillance in the bedrooms, bathrooms, or closet; only the main rooms have the cameras, but I can hear you if something happens."

"Oh, ok. Thanks for clearing that up," I say through a chuckle.

"I will head back down to my place, but please call Mr. Stone once you get settled."

"Thank you, Gregory."

"It is my pleasure, Ms. Winston. I'm here to look after you."

Hoping that Alex isn't asleep, I quickly dial his number and he picks up after the first ring.

"Mallory? Oh, sweetheart. I am so sorry I cannot be there. Are you ok?"

"I'm fine, Alex. No need to worry."

"I am always worried where you are concerned."

"Maybe so, but it is unnecessary. Anyways, I'm here at your place lonely and wishing you hadn't left. I'm sorry at how stubborn I was this morning."

"I know, darling. I'm sorry this has cut into our time together. I do find it a bit interesting that this has occurred while I am gone, considering the letters you have received."

Breaching a darker level of the crime I ask Alex, "Do you think someone is after me to get to you?"

"I hope not, but I can't rule it out. I'm not sure how anyone would find out about you, though. I keep my personal life extremely private. No one at home even knew about Vanessa when we dated and that lasted off and on for four years."

Ignoring the comment about Vanessa I say, "I haven't a clue why anyone would want to target me. But I am safe now and hopefully the culprit has been spooked with the police's involvement."

"One can only hope, love."

Safely changing topics, I ask, "How was your flight? Were you able to get things situated with your brother and formula one team?"

"My flight was most unpleasant. I plan on bringing my private jet back so I don't have to sit next to some snot nosed, little, bugger again. Furthermore, my brother has no clue what he is doing. He should really hire a political advisor. I won't meet with my driving teams for two more days, so I can fill you in then."

"What does your brother do?"

Seeming to catch his mistake, Alex quickly covers up by saying, "Oh, he, uh, is campaigning to take the parliament seat from my father. Since my father hasn't passed yet, but wants to retire, my brother feels he should create a campaign for entry into the parliament."

"Alex, I have no clue what you're talking about. No need to fret."

"I forget, darling, that you American's have your own twisted sense of politics." I giggle over the phone line and he declares, "Lord, how I miss that sound. I pray that I get everything tied up quickly so that I may return to you."

"That's sweet, Alex, but I'll be here when you return." Regretfully I cry, "I'm sorry again that I didn't say goodbye to you this morning. I know you didn't mean what you said last night."

"Thank you, sweetheart. It has been torturing me all day."
There are a few seconds of awkward silence between the two of us, both comprehending the situation we are currently in.

"Alex?" I ask timidly.

"Yes, love?"

"Are you going to see anyone else while you are home?"

Taken aback Alex responds immediately, "No, Mallory. I have no intentions of sharing you, so don't plan on sharing me. Do you trust me so little?"
I can hear the anger in his voice at his question.

Speaking up quickly, I try to explain to him why I asked. "Alex, of course I trust you; more than anyone, if I am being honest. I'm sorry to anger you. I only wanted clarification. I most definitely do not want to share you either."

Contemplating my anxiety Alex chimes in, "I understand your concern, Mallory, and I am sorry I jumped to conclusions. I'm sure it is because I am tired and need you."

"Well I am tired too so I will probably head to bed soon. Maybe we can indulge in some phone indiscretions later."

"Are you asking me to have phone sex with you, Ms. Winston?"

My cheeks redden from his question and I replay bashfully, "Only if you want to, sir."

"We will have to see. It may only make matters worse since I won't have you in front of me to touch, to smell, to taste. But it may hold me over until my return." At his words, I can already feel myself beginning to soak through my panties. He continues, "Ms. Winston, I have one last request before I leave you tonight."

"Yes, sir?"

"Do not touch yourself while I am gone."
What? Can I do that considering my clit is already
throbbing from this conversation.

"Do you understand, Mallory?"

"Yes, sir."

"Good, I hope to see you sooner, rather than
later."

"Me too."

 "Sleep well, beautiful girl."

"You too, Alex."

Ending the call, I walk to the bedroom and strip
off my clothes. On Alex's side of the bed, I tuck myself
into the luxurious sheets. I can smell his clean scent on
the pillow and I am lost for the night; dreaming of dark
hair, tanned skin, and sultry golden eyes.

RENEE HARLESS

Chapter Fourteen

I WAKE LATE IN the morning to pounding and yelling on the apartment door.

The voice shrills, "Dammit, Mallory. If I have to knock one more time I am going to call Gregory and he will not be happy about that!"

Rushing out of bed, I throw on my bathrobe and run over to the foyer door, tripping over myself a few times. I throw open the door with a whoosh and grab Abi in a fierce hug.

"Oh my gosh. I am so glad you're here," I roar elatedly.

Continuing to hold me in a forceful hug, Abi says, "Goodness, after Alex told me what had happened I jumped on the first flight back here. I wasn't about to let you stay here alone."

"Gosh, look at me. Please come in. Why didn't you use your key?"

She pouts and replies, "Alex took it from me. He said he didn't want any more unexpected visits." She huffs and looks me over as she asks, "Oh, bugger, were you still sleeping?"

"I was. I had a long day yesterday."

"Well hey, that works for me. That flight wore me out. Why don't we both go back to bed for a bit?"

"You won't hear any arguing from me. That sounds fantastic."

As I turn to close the front door, I spy another purple rose lying on the vestibule table. I wait for Abi to make her way back to her bedroom before I pick it up and take it to the bedroom with me. Placing it in the vase on the coffee table with the white peonies, I untie the note from the stem and open the tiny envelope.

Things I know: Your eyes shine like the emerald. Never have I ever seen eyes as beautiful as yours. Emeralds hold several meanings, but many believe it is a gift from Venus, to preserve love and symbolize hope. Emeralds are also used as a healing stone to help heal the heart. You, Mallory Winston, are a healer and my symbol of hope.

His words are beautiful and even as a tear streams down my cheek, I can't help but giggle at his use of *never have I ever*, our popular drinking game. I place the note in my nightstand drawer and lie back in bed, falling asleep quickly so that I may dream of golden eyes.

Abi and I both wake around noon, feeling more revived than we expected.

"Mal, what do you want to do today?" Abi asks.

"Well, I was told it is in my best interest to stay inside today and tomorrow."

"Oh, I know what we can do. This building has a spa. We can go get some massages. That is just what you need."

"That sounds fantastic. Let me message your brother and Gregory to tell them where we are headed."

"Okay, I'll make the reservations."

The boys are glad to see us not cause a fuss about staying inside and Alex even phoned in his credit card information to the spa so that we could have the full works.

Abi and I leave the spa four hours later after being buffed, polished, and rubbed in every nook and cranny.

"Wow, Abi," I say. "I will have to have this done again when your brother returns. I have never felt so relaxed in my life."

"Same here, I love getting a good massage. What would you like to do tonight?"

"How about I order us some dinner and we can drink out on the balcony?"

"That sounds perfect." Gazing in my direction Abi studies me then says, "You seem pretty calm after everything that has happened."

"I know. I'm trying not to let it get to me. Your brother and Gregory will keep me safe until they catch this person."

As we enter the apartment, I shoot Alex a text thanking him for the treatment. I notice I don't have any messages from Madison or Mika. "Aren't they worried about what happened?" I muse. Dialing Madison's number, I wait for her to pick up.

"What do you want?" are the words spoken by the voice on the end.
Looking down at my screen, I verify that I dialed the correct number.

"Um, Madison?"

"Yea?"

Stuttering I say, "I, uh, I was just checking on you. After, you know, yesterday and all."

"Well, obviously I'm fine. I figured you were too after the cops said you gave a statement."

"Oh, okay, well I am staying at Alex's for a while so if you need me you can reach me here."

"Look, don't play all innocent Mal; I'm furious right now. I know what you did with David."

"Madison, I have no idea what you're talking about. Care to fill me in?" I ask confused.

"Don't lie, Mallory. Karma is a bitch you know."
Then she promptly hangs up.
I stare at the phone screen for an unknown amount of time trying to determine what happened to my best friend.

Abi comes around and sits at a bar stool asking, "Who was that bitch on the phone?"

"That was my best friend Madison; we grew up together."

"Well, what did you do?"

"Nothing. The only time I ever saw her ex David was when she was around. I haven't the slightest clue what she is talking about."

"Does she think you're the reason they broke up?"

"I guess. I don't know how though, unless he lied to her."

"Well, I'm glad I'm here, Mal. It seems to me like you need some new friends."

"Agreed. Hey, do you want to go out this weekend? I have two new clients that are pretty outrageous and they want me to meet up with them."

"Sounds great. I'm here for as long as you need me."

"Thanks, Abi. Grilled chicken salad sound good for dinner?"

"Yep. I'll get the wine while you order."

Lounging on the balcony, Abi and I face the harbor watching the setting sun. We have already finished off one bottle of wine and start on a second.

"Hey, do you think my brother would let us go shopping tomorrow?" Abi queries with a large smile on her face.

"I doubt it, Abi. The police specified that I needed to stay indoors until at least Thursday."

"I don't know. I think it would be ok if Gregory went with us."

Rolling my eyes, I state through a chuckle, "I could never do that to Gregory. He would be bored out of his mind. We can do some online shopping though. I have a new paycheck to spend."

"I can one better you. I bet my brother would pay. He has internet TV and that screen is so big, it will be like shopping in the store."

"I need to call him real quick before we start playing a game."

"A game?"

"Yep, you just sit tight," I say winking in her direction.

Wandering inside, I start to dial Alex's number and begin searching through his cabinets for two shot glasses and some liquor. Only finding the glasses, it looks like we will be taking shots of wine, but that doesn't hasten my excitement.

"Stone," a cold voice says over the receiver.

"Alex?"

Instantly changing his tone to one of delight, my mercurial man decrees, "Mallory! I'm sorry. I didn't see the screen before I picked up. How are you, darling?"

"I'm great. Thank you for the spa treatment earlier. It was exactly what I needed. You and I will have to go together when you get back."

"That sounds wonderful, love. How is my sister?"

"She is fantastic. Thank you for sending her; I enjoy her company, though I still wish you were here."

"As do I. I'm sorry, Mallory, but I must go. I have a sponsor on the other line that I need to finish up with."

"It's not a problem, Alex. I am about to play a drinking game with Abi."

"Do be careful."

"I always am. Miss you, Alex."

"I miss you too, Mallory. Sleep well."

Alex hangs up and I head back out to the balcony.

"Did he agree to use his credit card?" Abi inquires.

"I'm sorry, I forgot to ask."

"Don't worry about it. I'll text him in the morning. So what game are we playing?"

"This game is called, *never have I ever*. My friends and I always played it before we went out for the night."

"How do you play?"

"Well, I will say something like, 'Never have I ever met a celebrity.' If you have, then you take your shot. I'm not sure there is ever truly a winner because either you're embarrassed you've done everything or your stone cold sober."

"Oh, this sounds like fun. Can I start?"

"Sure. Let me pour out the shots. By the way, I couldn't find any liquor, so wine will have to do."

Beginning the game Abi shouts, "Never have I ever swum naked."

After tossing back my shot, I take my turn stating, "Never have I ever kissed in the rain."

Abi drinks her shot. Jealous, I immediately add that to my bucket list.

"Never have I ever had sex in a car," Abi shouts through a giggle then takes another shot. Apparently, she hasn't realized that she isn't supposed to do the things she says.

"Never have I ever…," I begin and then pause to contemplate, "…dated a celebrity."

I hear Abi sigh, "Shit" before taking her shot then she smirks at my still filled shot glass and me. "Really, Mal?" she asks with a crooked brow.

"Am I sure about dating a celebrity?" I question in my mind. Envisioning Alex, I don't think having money constitutes someone as a celebrity. With my resolve I answer, "Yep, I'm sure. I don't keep up with entertainment gossip, so I wouldn't know one if they slapped me on the ass." As Abi falls into a burst of laughter I exclaim, "You're turn, Abi."

"Ok, Ok. Hm… you need a shot. Never have I ever fallen in love."

"Damn," I say to myself as I toss back my glass. She knows I'm in love with her brother and I see that she still holds her glass.

"Really, Abi?" I ask.

"Really," she replies in a depressed sounding voice.

Trying to liven up her mood, I jokingly say, "Ok. Never have I ever been to a wedding."

"What? That is rubbish. Do I have to take a shot for every wedding I've been to? We'll be here all night."

Cracking up at her slurred words I respond, "No, just one shot. Final round?"

"Yes, please. Ok my turn. Never have I ever had sex on an airplane."
We both keep our shots.

"Last question and with this one we will just split the rest of the wine into our glasses. You ready?"

"Yep."

"Never have I ever done something I regret." We both stare at the glasses for a moment then glance at each other. A fit of giggles explodes from each of us and we each drink our glass of wine.

Abi yells, "That was fun, Mallory. We will have to play this with your friends over the weekend."

"Maybe."

Abi and I sit in silence while we both watch the night sky over the ocean.

"Abi, is everything ok? I know we don't know each other well, but it seems strange that you would have a great career opportunity with your brother, yet you choose to come to the states to visit friends for the next few weeks," I inquire.

"You're very perceptive, Mal. And you're right; it is bizarre that I'm here in the states right now. Maybe when I sort out things in my head we can talk about it."

"Fair deal."

Listening to the boats pulling into the harbor, Abi and I sit in companionable silence before she decides to inquire about my romance with her brother.

"Do you want this relationship with my brother to last longer than the next month?"

"More than anything," I whisper.

"That's what I thought. He'll come around, Mal."

"I don't think so, Abi, but that's ok. I know what I signed up for."

She takes a sip of her wine and huffs, "He's a hard-headed bastard most of the time, but he does have good heart. I promise you that."

"I know he does. He shows me every day without even realizing it."

"I'm heading to bed," Abi states, "but I want you to know that I don't think this will be the end for the two of you. I just a have a good feeling and my instincts are always right. Plus, I actually like you. With his other girls, I wasn't nearly so fond of them. Not even Vanessa. It took her getting married and knocked up before I would come around."

"What makes me different?"

"Well, one, you're not a gold digging whore and two, you have a good heart."

"Thanks Abi. I'll see you in the morning."

Abi and I wake to some French toast that Gregory had sent up for us. During breakfast, Abi sends a text to Alex asking to use his card for some purchases, to which he replies that we don't need to ask. After finishing our breakfast, we stand in front of the television holding the remote.

"How do you turn this bugger on?" Abi ponders out loud.

"No clue. I don't even see a red power button."

Walking over to my phone, I dial Gregory's number and he answers, "Yes miss?"

"Help us," I scream into the phone then end the call.

Obviously in panic mode, Gregory runs into the family room a minute later shouting, "God save me ladies, I thought you were hurt."

With her hands sitting on her cocked hips Abi rebukes, "Gosh, Gregory, don't be so dramatic. Mal and I couldn't figure out the TV. We want to do some shopping. This is an Emergency!"

Bending over trying to catch his breath, he wheezes, "Just so you know, Abi, it is my job to worry. I just ran up twelve flights of stairs at record speed. I won't even need to go to the gym today."

I giggle in the background as I envisage him running up the steps in panic.

Walking over to Abi, he grabs the remote from her hand and tosses it aside saying, "It would help if you used the correct remote. This one is for the DVD player." He moves to the coffee table and grabs the bulky gray remote. "This one works the TV. When you want to use the internet place the remote on the coffee table or a flat surface, press the blue button and a laser keyboard will show," he explains.

"Holy shit, ain't that fancy," I declare.

"Yes, Ms. Winston. It is fancy. Can I do anything else for you all?"

"No, Gregory. I think we're good. Sorry for scaring you."

"It's not a problem, Ms. Winston. You all enjoy your day."

One hour later, Abi and I have purchased a handful of designer clothes. I tried using my own money, but Abi smacked me and said she would tell Alex if I did.

"Do you go back to work tomorrow?" she asks as we vegetate on the couch.

"Yes, I do. I am not exactly sure what to do about the security situation though. What will you do while I'm at work?"

"Oh, I have a few friends in town I can catch up with or I may continue to shop."

"You're ridiculous."

"I know."

After showering, we decide to have a Disney movie marathon, because every girl loves a fairy tale happy ending. When Abi heads off to get something from her room, I sneak into the foyer. There I find what I was hoping for, another single purple rose. Racing back to my room with the flower, I tear open in the envelope.

Things I know: You are addicted to peanut M&M's. P.S. I saw them on your desk, in your living room, in your bedroom, and you carry a bag in your purse. We may need to schedule an intervention. Have you even tried the peanut butter M&M's? And how is it you have no cavities?

Smiling again at my two roses, I dial Alex's number.

"Hello, Ms. Winston."

"Thank you for the roses, Alex."

"You're most certainly welcome. Did you and Abi enjoy your evening and morning?"

"We did, thank you. We both purchased an obscene amount of clothing. I hope you don't mind."

"Don't be silly. I am glad to see someone use that money. It just sits in a bank account all day."

"I suppose you won't let me pay you back."

"Don't even think about it." I laugh at is quick change of attitude. Breaking me from my amusement Alex asks, "Mallory, are you returning to work tomorrow?"

"Yes. I need to finish up the Johnson campaign and begin some ideas for my new vodka client."

"I see. Well, I believe I will have Gregory drive you until the person threatening you is caught."

"Ok, I understand. My poor car is probably feeling neglected though."

He chuckles and says, "You can always ask Gregory to drive her, though I am not sure he would fit comfortably." I laugh heartily at that vision. "I miss your laughter, Ms. Winston."

"Any idea when you are coming back?"

"No, not yet."

"Well, would you like me to call you later for some fun?"

"I think that sounds marvelous, Ms. Winston. Say 9:00pm your time?"

"Yes, sir."

"Until then, Ms. Winston."

"Bye, Alex."

Swiftly, I hop off the bed and join Abi on the couch in the family room. She has laid out a buffet of popcorn, nachos, soda, and candy.

"How did you get all this?"

"I told the concierge we were having a movie day and he sent all this up. Pretty awesome, right?"

"It is divine."

Indulging in our calorie loaded feast, we watch a handful of classic Disney princess movies. When I notice it is close to 9:00pm, I slip away from the family room and start a bath for my phone call with Alex.

As I rest my head against the back of Alex's tub, I envision that he is there with me. I want to feel his hands and mouth everywhere. Just imagining him here in this room with me is enough to get me hot. Once I'm settled, I pull up Alex's number and call him.

"Ms. Winston."

"Mr. Stone."

"Where are you?"

"I am sitting in your tub."

"Good, place the phone on the counter and set it to speaker."

"Yes, sir." I follow his instructions and place the phone on the counter near my head. When I am positioned in the water, I announce, "Ready."

"Good, now I want you to envision me in that tub with you; that your hands are my hands and that you can feel my mouth on you. Can you do that?"
I am already starting to pant as my breath quickens and releases in quick successions. His voice is enough for me.

"Yes, sir," I reply as I sit back and close my eyes, waiting for him to take me away.

"You are resting in the tub with your back against my chest. I have your legs pinned open with my own. My hands lightly caress your shoulders, stroking back and forth along your collar bone." My hands mimic his words as my fingertips glide along heated skin. "You rest your head back against my shoulder and I kiss along your neck. My hands travel down to your breasts and I begin by massaging them both, rolling your nipples between my fingers." I let out a moan as I act out this scene. I can vaguely hear him moan in return, "Baby, you are getting me so hot when you make those noises." He pauses for a few seconds and I can hear the telltale sound of a zipper coming undone. I take a moment to envision him taking out his massive cock and stroking it with his hands. Adding to my image he whispers, "One of my hands snake down to your pussy, rubbing your clit." A whimper escapes from my mouth as my hands follow Alex's lead. "I stoke back and forth across your folds and clit. You're so wet and hot, that even in the tub, I can feel your juices on my fingers. You turn your head towards me as I tease your entrance with the tip of my finger. Your hands tug me into a kiss filled with passion and I insert another finger into your core. I pulse my hand back and forth, as your tongue massages my own. I can feel your core start to contract so I crook my fingers to rub your spot and my thumb presses harder circles onto your clit. Your body convulses moments later and we both tumble into our climax." At the same moment he speaks of the imaginary orgasm, I reach mine with my own hands.

Coming back to reality Alex says, "Next time, darling, we will need to Skype. I want to see you come with my own eyes. You're beautiful when you let go."

"I prefer your hands, Alex."

"I know, love." As I sigh at his terminology Alex inquires, "Are you alright, Mallory?"

"Yes, sir. I am just tired. I have a busy day tomorrow."

"I understand. I will phone you tomorrow. Sweet dreams, Mallory."

"Goodnight, Alex."

We end our conversation and I spend another 15 minutes in the tub hoping to relax from my orgasm, but all it seems to do is make me want another. Alex is turning me insatiable as well.

Chapter Fifteen

THE NEXT TWO DAYS at work pass quickly as I am bombarded with items to catch up on. My meeting at the end of the day is scheduled with Kyle and Lily to finalize the last leg of their campaign. Sitting at my desk admiring the two additional roses I have received, I accept a call from Gregory.

"Ms. Winston?" he solicits.

"Yes, Gregory?"

"I intercepted another piece of mail today and it is similar to the last. I will be taking it to the police station in a few moments."

"Ok, thank you."

"My pleasure, miss."

Kyle and Lily arrive shortly after the call and I discuss with them the bits and pieces I know about the case. They mention that they have both given statements and alibis to the police.

"Are you still coming over tonight?" Lily questions.

"I think so. Do you mind if I bring Alex's sister Abi? She is great and has been keeping me company."

"Of course. We will order a smorgasbord of Chinese. How does that sound?" Kyle replies.

"Sounds perfect. Now let's finish up this campaign so I can get you two crazy people out of my hair."

At 5:00pm, I walk out of my building and run into Seth.

Surprised at my appearance, Seth exclaims, "Hey, Mal, how are things going? I wasn't sure if you were here or not. I didn't see your car."

"Oh, that's because Alex has his security guy bring me. Doesn't want to take any chances I guess."

"I get that. I mean if you were my girl I'd do the same."
I shoot him a look conveying to him that I didn't appreciate his comment.

Noticing my alarmed façade Seth apologizes, "I'm sorry, really. I know you're with someone, I have Stephanie and I know that you don't feel that way. I was just joking, really."

"It's ok, Seth. How are things with you? I haven't seen you at lunch."

"Things are good. I've been taking an earlier lunch with Steph and I've had a new project placed in my lap, so I'm pretty busy. Oh hey, are you coming out with the girls tonight?"

"No, I wasn't invited. They seem to all hate me for some reason. Madison even thinks I'm the reason David broke up with her. I think everyone has taken a crazy pill."

"Seriously? He won't tell her the truth? She shouldn't be blaming you at all. But I guess that is her story to find out. Anyways, sorry things are falling through. I've got to head over to Steph's. Call me later."

"Will do." I lean in and give him a hug. "It was good to see you, Seth. Don't be a stranger."

"Goes both ways, Mal."

He's right. I have been neglecting everyone, but I only have Alex for a short time. I never thought I'd be that girl, but I'm so wrapped up in us that I don't even realize I'm ignoring everyone else.

Waving goodbye to Seth, I notice Gregory waiting for me.

"Who was that, Ms. Winston?" he asks curiously.

"Oh, that was Seth. We started here at the same time. We've been good friends for about seven years."

"Can you trust him?"

"Can I really trust anyone right now?"

"Touché, Ms. Winston."

Ushering me into the car, we head back towards Alex's apartment. As I enter the home, I head back into the bedroom while shouting out to Abi that I was going to change and then we can leave.

She follows me into the bedroom a few seconds later asking, "Hey, do I need to dress up tonight?"

"No, not at all. They are ordering Chinese and then I suppose we will drink a bit. Oh shit, I need to ask Gregory if it's ok that I drive."

"I don't think it will be a problem, Mal."

"Alright, well I'm just going to throw on some jeans. You're fine in what you're wearing."

"Cool. So…is Kyle hot?"

"Well, most of the staff thinks so. I don't quite get it though. He is what you would expect an American surfer to look like. Your brother is much more my type."

"Eh, I'd probably agree with you if he wasn't my brother. I tend to lean towards the bad boy types myself." Finishing our conversation, I walk out of the closet and follow Abi towards the door.

We stand by the valet waiting for my Mini to pull up as my phone rings. Alex's name flashes across the screen and a smile crosses my face since I haven't spoken with him today.

As I am about to say hello he interrupts my sweet revelries, "Mallory, where the fuck do you think you are going?"

"Excuse me?"

"Why aren't you in the apartment? Gregory doesn't know where you've gone."

At this point Abi and I are seated in my car and I am about to turn out of the parking lot.

In a spurt of irritation, I reply, "Well seeing that I am an adult, I have decided to take your sister to dinner with two clients this evening. I also have a valid driver's license and am driving myself. I assure you, I am most capable."

Noticing Abi has fallen into a fitful of laughter, I barely hear Alex chime in, "Mallory, so help me, if I was there right now your sweet arse wouldn't be able to sit for the next year."

"Well, Mr. Stone, you are not here. Nor are you my keeper. And while I appreciate yours and Gregory's overzealous need to protect me, I guarantee that I am capable of taking care of myself. I have done so for the last seven years that I have lived on my own."

"Ms. Winston, do not push me."

"I am not pushing, Mr. Stone. I am proclaiming."

With a bit of defeat in his tone, Alex says, "You are not nearly so judicial in the bedroom, Ms. Winston. I can see how you have risen to senior level at your job so quickly."

"Is this the reason for your call, Alex; to try to manipulate me to stay indoors?"

"Indeed, it was. I do not like being undermined, Ms. Winston."

"There was no undermining involved. I stayed indoors when instructed by the police and I am only venturing to a client's home, to also stay indoors, and to enjoy myself for the evening in your absence."

"Obviously, there will be no changing your mind. Please keep an eye on my sister as well as yourself. I would hate to have the both of you in some sort of trouble while I am away. Also keep in mind that there will be some form of punishment at my return, Ms. Winston."

"Looking forward to it, Alex. Goodbye."

I abruptly end the call, as I have no plans on relinquishing my control to him 24/7. Is he really that worried about me and Abi? I don't find Kyle or Lily harmful in the slightest. Perhaps he would have thought differently if he had met them prior to his departure.

Snapping my mind from endless wandering Abi says, "Mallory, I have never, ever, seen someone hold their own against Alex. That was one of the single greatest moments of my life."

"Glad I could offer you a form of entertainment. We're here by the way."

Both scrambling out of the car, we stare up at the new building housing the Johnson's loft.

Lily answers the door and pulls both Abi and myself into a hug.

"I am so glad you are both here. I am starving and the Chinese smells so good," she cries.

Astonished I say, "Oh, you both didn't have to wait for us."

Tugging us into the open spaced living room, we both look around the loft. The first floor is completely open while there is a staircase on the left and the right, each leading to a bedroom.

"This is a really nice space, Lily," I say and then pull Abi close. "By the way this is my boyfriend's sister, Abigail. Abi, this is Lily."

They each say hello while I look around for Kyle.

Noticing my traveling gaze Lily interrupts me, "Kyle went to go help our neighbor with her groceries. Poor little thing can't ever make it up all those flights of stairs."

"That's sweet of him," Abi says.

An instant later Kyle comes strutting into the loft and pulls me into a hug.

Stepping aside, I gesture towards Abi and say, "Kyle, this is Abigail Stone, my boyfriend's sister. Abi, this is Kyle Johnson."

They both shake hands and exchange pleasantries. Seeming more shy than normal, I consider that Abi may instantly have a thing for Kyle. As Kyle goes to spread out the Chinese onto an industrial coffee table, I notice he has two, full, arm sleeves of tattoos. I have only ever seen him in dressy attire for our meetings, so it is no wonder Abi is smitten; he is a pretty boy and bad boy all in one. I giggle at my inward reflection just as Kyle catches me.

"Something funny, Mallory?" he asks.

"Nope, I'm just thinking about something. This food looks awesome by the way."

Digging into the meal, Lily and Kyle discuss their fashion line and Abi points out how they could start to brand their new line a bit differently than their celebrity line. If Abi lived in the states, and I had the money, I would love to open my own agency with her. We have a similar creative mind set for campaigns.

As Lily and I clean up the mess of food on the table, she says, "They seem pretty into each other."

"I know, right?"

"She isn't his usual type. He usually dates those stick, thin, blonde bimbos."

"Abi is a doll. Too bad I don't think she will be staying here long. She is only in the states to catch up with some friends."

"Shame. Does she have a boyfriend back home?"

"I don't think so. She hasn't mentioned anyone. Her brother hasn't either."

Switching gears Lily focuses on me inquiring, "So, you and her brother are pretty serious?"

"For now, until he returns to England in a month and a half."

"Why? What happens when he leaves?"

"I'm not sure. That's just what we agreed on."

"Fair enough. Do you want to grab the Moscato out of the fridge and we can all veg on the couch?"

"Sure thing."

The rest of the night Lily and I pretend to watch television, but we really watch the scene unfold between Kyle and Abi. He has his arm around her shoulders and is rubbing her arm while Abi is cuddled up into his side. They look like they have known each other for years, not a couple of hours. Kyle is being incredibly sweet with her. I think this is what she needs right now, someone to take care of her. I may even pat myself on the back for this unintentional hookup.

It is getting a bit late and the exhaustion from the week is starting to hit me.

Breaking the silence, I speak up, "Hey Abi, I am a bit tired so I am going to head back. I'll come get you tomorrow if you want to stay."

"No, No. I'll come back with you."

Thanking Kyle and Lily I say, "Thanks guys for having us over. I'll call you soon."

"Alright. Thanks, Mallory, for hanging out. Let us know if you need anything with this whole stalker business."

"Sure thing. Have a good night.

As we ride the elevator up to Alex's apartment, I stare at Abi, waiting for her to crack.

"You like him," I begin but she doesn't say anything so I continue, "He likes you too, you know."

"I know."

"Then what's the matter?"

She huffs then turns to face me saying, "I'm not my brother. I have no intentions to ruin someone's life and make them miserable when I have to leave. I see what Alex is doing to you; I'm not going to do that to Kyle."

Considering her words, I articulate, "I see. Don't you think that it is a decision he should get to make?"

"What do you mean?"

"Shouldn't he get to decide if spending however much time you can give, is worth the pain? If Kyle is like me, he will jump at the chance to be with you while you're here. I'd rather feel passion and pleasure at some point in my life, than regret the decision to not feel it at all."

Seeming to ponder this for a while, Abi stays silent until we enter Alex's home.

"You're right," she exclaims. "He asked me to go out with him on a date tomorrow. I've never been on an actual date."

"Don't worry you'll be fine. You're brother took me on my first actual date as well."

"I'm glad we're here like this, Mal. I've always wanted a sister."

With a saddened voice I say, "Me too. Good night, Abi."

After sending both Alex and Gregory a text to let them know we're home, I remove my clothing and slide into the bed. The sheets feel unbearably cold without Alex lying next to me. Staring at the alarm clock for an hour before grabbing my phone, I see that I haven't received any messages from Alex. Contemplating that he must still be annoyed with me, I toss and turn throughout the night, not ever falling into a restful slumber.

As the weekend creeps by, I still find a rose on the vestibule table daily. Each rose containing a note discussing my family, loyalty, and my intelligence. Yet I haven't received any messages or calls from Alex and he won't return my attempts.

*   *   *

As each day passes without Alex, I seem to slip farther into a robotic mode. I come into work my shift from 9:00 am-5:00 pm, collect my rose, make dinner at home, take a bath, and go straight to bed. It is the same routine I had before I met Alex, but now it seems extremely mundane. His presence brought color into my life.

How will I ever survive this without him? I ask myself.

Chapter Sixteen

FRIDAY MORNING, A WEEK later, Gregory allows me to drive myself since I need to meet my clients at their office at 9:00 am. During the presentation, I muster up just enough enthusiasm for the campaign to highlight my skills. I must have done a significantly good job because they were very pleased with the production. After finalizing the paperwork, I drive back to my office smiling at myself. It feels good to have an approved campaign the first go-round since it doesn't happen very often. With the high from the presentation, I am tempted to give Annie and myself a half day from work. She worked tremendously hard to pull the figures and specs that I needed this week.

I wave to Stephanie as I walk in, ignoring her glare, and burst into Annie's office.   Startling her I announce, "Annie, if your schedule allows, please take the afternoon off."

"What? Really?"

"Yes, really. The vodka clients approved the campaign the first go-round so we don't need to make any revisions."

"Holy shit, Mal. That's freaking amazing. That never happens. You are so good at this."

"Thanks, it feels pretty amazing. I will probably take the afternoon off too."

"You never take days off, except last week. I bet you've maxed out your vacation build up and everything. Good for you."

I laugh and embarrassingly shrug my shoulders, "You're right. I think I have accumulated three months of paid time off. I may need to start taking vacations before the company starts to deduct days. And now I won't feel so worried to leave since it will all be in your capable hands."

"You're too sweet."

I sigh dramatically, "I know. Anyway, take the afternoon off and finish up those wedding plans."

Laughing heartily, she adds, "Yes, Ms. Winston."

I finish my morning by sorting through some e-mails that need a response and revising my calendar for next week. The following week is Fourth of July and I consider taking few days to visit with my family at the beach. I glance back and forth between my computerized calendar, my personal calendar, and the timeline for my campaigns so that I can mesh the calendar dates. Spending ten minutes shifting notes back and forth I place my request for a week off to visit my family and move a few more notes on my personal calendar.

"Beautiful girl," a dark silky voice says, "I have missed you."

Gazing up from my calendar, my heart stops when I see Alex standing in my doorway, looking more handsome than I remember. He is here, in my office, with another single purple rose. Jumping out of my chair, I rush into his waiting arms and he wraps them around me tightly as I pull his head down into a smoldering kiss. His mouth tastes of mint and coffee and his masculine scent engulfs my senses.

Halting our reunion Alex whispers, "I believe we have an audience, Ms. Winston. Care to take this inside?"

Peeking around him, I laugh at the faces of all my female co-workers, including Annie and Stephanie, gawking at Alex. I can't blame them he is quite a sight.

As I take a few steps back into my office, I stand against the front of my desk. Closing and locking the door, Alex turns and struts toward me. I am so thrilled to see him here that I hadn't realized that tears were pooling in my eyes and a few had spilled over. Placing the rose on my desk, he reaches up to wipe away the tears.

"Why are you crying, beautiful girl?" he asks.

"I hadn't realized I was. I missed you is all."

"Oh, love. I missed you as well. These past two weeks have been unbearable," he says as he bends forward to clasp my lips in another heated kiss.

My arms wrap around his hips and I pull him against me. It has been too long since I have felt him against my body. Alex must feel the same desire as I do because his hands snake down my arms and grab my waist. Swiftly, he lifts me onto the desk and tugs me towards him, aligning my center with his growing erection. His hands trail up my skirt, sliding it up as he goes and when he reaches the top of my silk stockings and garter clasps, he halts the kiss.

"Fuck. When did you get these?" he says after taking a sharp intake of breath.

Breathing so heavy I can barely speak I whisper, "I bought them with your money." Staring at the mesmerized look on his face I proclaim, "Alex, kiss me, please."

He peeks up from his lashes and dives back into our kiss, pushing up my skirt up to my waist. His finger moves to the waistband of my panties and tears them on both sides.

"I'm sorry, baby. I'll buy you more."
Shoving the panties into his pockets, he continues to kiss me, nipping at my bottom lip. One of his hands slides across my mound and he delves a finger into my core.

"Damn, you're so wet already. I need you now, baby. It's been too long"
As he inserts another finger, I moan and move my hands to the buttons on his jeans, undoing them as best I can.

"Yes. Please, Alex. I can't wait," I whimper.

With the absence of underwear, I tug out his cock and begin to stroke him using my thumb to spread the drop of moisture across the head. Groaning into my mouth, Alex tilts me back onto the desk as I remove my hands and rest them behind me, wrapping my legs around his waist. As he glides into me, I whimper at the sensation of feeling full.

"I won't last long baby," he divulges, "you feel too good, so tight."

"Me either."

At that declaration, Alex begins to pound into me. I am so close to my orgasm that I have to bite my lip to hold it in; I want to come with him. Feeling him starting to get close, I raise my hips and he begins moving in circles with his pelvis between thrusts, rubbing against my clit. Each circle causes me to gasp at the feeling.

"Come now," he commands.

Instigating my body to explode and he follows behind me.

Lying against my desk with Alex pressed against me we both work at filling our lungs with air.

Alex breaths deep, his chest heaving, "Holy shit."

"Yea."

"I would apologize for taking you like this at your place of work, Ms. Winston, but that was too incredible to feel remorseful."

"Yea."

Leaning up from me slightly Alex asks, "Can you say anything else, Ms. Winston?"

I laugh and respond, "Yea."

He chuckles along with me causing him to slip out of me and I instantly feel hollow from his exit. Standing from the desk, Alex bends down with a tissue in hand and helps to clean me up. I should be embarrassed by this gesture, but I find it incredibly sweet.

"I'm sorry to barge into your office like this, Mallory," Alex discloses. "Once the plane landed I had Gregory bring me straight here. I couldn't wait any longer to see you." His words melt the walls I had only begun to build around my heart in the hopes to preserve any part of me that I have left once he leaves for good. With a sweet smile plastered onto my face, I wrap my arms around his neck.

"I'm glad you came here first, Alex. You caught me just in time. I was planning to take the afternoon off. My meeting this morning went so well that I felt like enjoying my weekend."

"That sounds marvelous. What would you like to do?"

"Honestly? I just want to be where you are."

Bending down to kiss the tip of my nose he says, "Music to my ears. Let's grab your things and head back to my place."

"Yes sir."

Once in the car, I remember my vacation plans with my family and broach the topic.

"Alex, I was thinking of visiting my parents when they travel to the beach in a week. Would you like to join me?"

Excitedly Alex answers, "I would love nothing more, darling. Right now a vacation sounds splendid."

"Fantastic! I will call and let them know we are coming along."

"I don't want to be an intrusion, so if it's a bother I will understand."

"Alex, you will not be a bother. And if you can't go, then I won't go."

I dial my mom's number while we walk through the lobby of The Braxton and she answers on the first ring.

"Mallory, how are you dear?"

"I'm great mom. I just had a quick question."

"Shoot, baby girl."

"Can I join you at the beach and bring a guest?"

"We would love to have you, sweetie. Are you bringing Madison?"

"No, she isn't speaking to me right now. I will tell you about all of that another time, but I will be bringing my boyfriend Alex."

At the term boyfriend, Alex squeezes my hand while we stand in the elevator.

"It must be serious if you want to bring a boyfriend, Mal. Your dad, brothers, and I would love to meet him."

"Great. We're excited! I love you, mom."

"Love you too, sweet cheeks."

I end the call and smile at Alex as he ushers me through the door. Glancing over the vestibule table, where I have been finding the single rose daily, I am greeted with a large vase holding two dozen purple roses with a mixture of lavender calla lilies.

Shocked by seeing the exquisite array of flowers in the hall I cry out, "Alex, these are beautiful."

He intertwines our fingers and pulls me with him towards his bedroom while saying, "Not as beautiful as you, Ms. Winston."

"Isn't Abi home?" I ask.

"She has gone to spend the weekend with a Kyle Johnson. Apparently, I have you to thank for that."

"They really like each other. I think she is considering moving here for him," I say imploringly.

"Do you really like me, Ms. Winston?" Alex asks. Is he generally asking or is he referring to my comment about Abi?

Pondering I announce, "I do, Mr. Stone."

"Good." Swooping in, he places a fiery kiss on my lips, hands gripping my hips, but pulls away quickly.

"Please get into position; I believe we have a punishment to take care of. Though, my anger has dissipated immensely, I still feel you should be taught a lesson about safety."

"Yes, sir."

As Alex leaves the bedroom, I get myself into position for the scene. I don't have to wait long for Alex to return. Wearing only his gray gym shorts, I find myself trying not to be caught glancing at him.

"Lovely, Ms. Winston. You may look up." Following his command, I do as he says. "Did you wear my collar everyday in my absence?" he inquires.

"Yes, sir."

"Good. Do you understand why you are being punished today, Ms. Winston?"

"Yes, sir."

"Your punishment runs a very fine line between pleasure and pain. You may feel only a little pain once we begin. Please remember your safe word. Do you understand?"

"Yes, sir."

"Good, come with me."

I follow Alex to the media room and he guides me to the ottoman, which has been lowered to a sitting height. Behind the ottoman is a long table full of different colored candles and a bottle of oil.

"Do not be nervous, my dear," Alex comforts.

Noticing that I am ringing my hands I glance up at him and apologize with my eyes. I know not to speak in this room unless he asks me a question.

"Ms. Winston, please lay across the entire ottoman," Alex indicates, "You may face your head to the right, towards the table."

Doing as he says, I begin by pressing the front of my body against the smooth leather. The table is longer than I thought and I place my stretched arms above my head. Alex then pulls two leather straps from his armoire, securing them around the ottoman and across my ankles and wrists. Fastened to the furniture, I feel cool droplets of oil splatter onto my skin, gently rubbed by Alex over my exposed limbs and back. My body glistens from the oil in the dim light of the room. Departing the room for a few minutes, he leaves my body to sizzle in its restraints. I'm not sure what to expect as my punishment, but the writhing of my body against the leather is quickly burning a fire in my core. Strolling back into the room, Alex stands over me examining my body.

With an authoritative voice Alex directs, "Do not move or make any noise unless it is your safe word. Understand?"

I nod in response.

"Good."

As he reaches across me, only then do I realize his intentions. Searing pain, like the kiss of a flame, splashes across my flesh. The burning wax pours onto my body and he switches back and forth between different candles, spilling the wax in erratic spurts. The hot wax covers my skin and as it cools, it creates a hard shell over my body. Fifteen minutes have passed and reaching for one last candle that burns bright red, Alex trails the wax from the nape of my neck down to each instep. On his final way back up my left leg, Alex watches the wax pour over the crack of my behind into the crevice of my center. My entire body wants to curl into itself from the heat on my folds. After a minute or two, the wax has hardened into a stiff casing.

"How does that feel, Ms. Winston? Do you feel trapped?" he asks and then continues, "That's how you made me feel when I was away in England. When you felt it necessary to take your security into your own hands. You didn't trust me enough to protect you from a distance. You made me feel mentally and emotionally confined as you are now physically. Do you understand now, Ms. Winston.?"

I nod my head in response.

"Good. The wax is still slightly warmed from your body and the oil will help it come off, but as part of your punishment I will be taking off to my liking."

The curiosity thrills me as I wonder how he will remove the wax since it covers the entire back of my body. The dripping of the wax was very erotic and the fire that had been building inside me continues to smolder.

Snapped from my revelries, I cringe when a loud crack lands on my thigh and I clinch my hands in pain. It's quick, but is followed up by another smack on the opposite leg. The nips continue across my body and the pain has me digging my nails into the palms of my hands, certain that I am drawing blood. As he works his way up my arms, I see that he has been using a plastic cane to inflict his punishment. He snaps the rod at each of my hands when he sees they are clinched.

"I told you not to move, Ms. Winston," he exclaims. Trailing the tip of the cane over some of the broken wax, he chips pieces away. Alex asks, "Do you think you have learned your lesson?" Closing my eyes, I hold back my moan as he trails the cane around my inner thighs. He orders, "You are not allowed to come."

Sending little nips at my center with the cane the fire ignites in my belly again. To hold back my orgasm, I grind my teeth together as the cane Alex commands bites at my folds ten times before he tosses it aside and slides his finger inside me.

"I think you have learned your lesson, Ms. Winston," Alex says in a husky voice, removing his finger. "Stay still and I will peel the remaining wax away." Pouring some oil into his hands, he slides pieces of the hardened wax away from my skin and places it into a large bowl. A few minutes later, he has removed every sliver of wax. Reaching down, Alex unlatches both straps and rubs the area the leather had rested against my skin.

Concerned he asks, "How are you feeling, Ms. Winston? You may answer."

My muscles are stiff and I am a bit numb as I struggle to answer, "I, uh, don't want to do that again."

"I understand. It was along scene for a punishment, but I felt it was necessary for your lesson. I am proud you didn't safe word. I enjoyed both pouring the wax onto your fevered body and seeing the hardened shell crack from the cane."At his words, I bite my lip as I am still burning throughout my body. "Can you walk or do you need help?"
My muscles seem frozen in place as I try to move my limbs.

"I'm sorry, sir," I say apologetically.

He leans down and lifts me up so that I am sitting on the ottoman.

"I will let your body adjust for a moment and then I will give you a bath and a massage. How does that sound?" he questions.

"Good, thank you, sir." His oiled hand glide across my cheek and his thumb tugs my lip away from my teeth.

"You have pleased me very much, Ms. Winston. You did a marvelous job. I am awestruck that you were able to hold back your pleasure; many take years of practice to learn that skill. Even when you were dripping wet and one crook of my finger would have pushed you over the edge, you held back. I am very impressed."

Sounded defeated I answer, "Thank you, sir."
He furrows his brows at my tone and expression.

"Come."

As Alex helps me walk into the bedroom, my body feels confused by his denial. My brain understands why he must keep me from orgasm, but my body is too heated to comprehend. Unsure of what is next to come, I stand by the door as he strolls into the bathroom. The scent of lavender engulfs my senses and I immediately relax from the sensual fragrance. Alex stalks back over to me and lifts my head into his hands, searching my eyes for something, but I am not sure what he hopes to find. Bending he kisses my forehead and leads me into the tub.

"The cane didn't leave any welts on your skin, that's good," he says as he examines my body in the water. "You shouldn't feel too sore tomorrow."

Saying nothing, I stare down at my hands in the water. The tiny crescent shapes along my palms are proof enough that the cane did its damage. Noticing my shiver in the warm water, Alex's fingers glide down my arms to grasp my hands. The burn he usually leaves on my skin at his touch doesn't do anything to warm me. As he reaches my hands, I whimper in pain and he swiftly grabs my wrists turning me in his direction, analyzing my self-infliction.

"Goodness, Mallory, why did you do this? Why didn't you stop me?" he shouts continuing to glance between my palms and eyes.

Staring into his face, I don't immediately respond to his words.

Seconds later I stutter, "I, uh, I don't know."

"You don't know!" he shouts back at me.

Tossing my hands back in the water, he stumbles out of the tub and grabs a towel along the way, leaving me in the bathroom alone. I try to hold back my sob, but it is no use as one single tear falls from my eye. The rest escape shortly after.

A few minutes later, I rest back into the cooling water and reflect on the scenario that just occurred. I don't believe Alex is mad at me. He is concerned that I didn't take my wellbeing into account during our scene. I should have safe worded or at least dug into the furniture, not my hand. Stepping out of the tub, I gingerly grab a towel to dry off and then I throw on my bathrobe, hoping to search for Alex. Exploring the home, I can't find any signs of him and as I am about to call Gregory I notice that the balcony door is open off of the living room. I step outside into the afternoon sun and find Alex leaned over in a patio chair. His hair has a messy look to it as though he must have been running his fingers through the wet strands. He looks so sexy sitting there that I itch to touch him.

Walking slowly towards him, I sense that he is lost in thought and he doesn't seem to notice me. Crouching down, I kneel beside his leg. When I look up at him, I am startled. Alex's eyes are wet with tears. I reach my hand forward, but quickly bring it back to my lap. I am afraid to touch him.

Whispered words release from my lips, "Alex? Alex, I am so so so very sorry. I won't do it again. I promise. Please don't be angry with me." I wait for a response, a grunt, a sound, anything, but he gives nothing away. His body is at statue stillness and his breathing is the only clue that he is a living being. When I am about to lose hope, and go inside to leave the house,

Alex turns his head to me. I search his eyes and all I find is torment. He is at war with himself.

"Alex, please," I whisper again.

He continues to hold his tongue. When my hope has vanished, I break the contact with Alex and look down at my clasped hands. Abruptly, both of Alex's hands snake into my hair and tilt my head towards him. He leans towards me and presses his forehead against mine.

Alex speaks in a hushed chopped tone as if he is clenching his teeth, "Mallory, you mean the world to me. I am the one that should be sorry. My behavior is inexcusable."

I reach my hands up to grab his forearms and speak, "I don't understand."

Untangling his fingers from my hair, he pulls me up towards him and leans back into his Adirondack chair tugging me onto his lap. I curl into him, resting along his chest.

With a sigh Alex explains, "It is my duty to know your limits and to only push those limits with your consent. I am sorry that I caused you enough pain to hurt yourself, but more than that, you didn't trust me enough to think I would stop. What can I do to make you trust me, Mallory?"

Sitting up, I grasp his face in my hands.

"I do trust you, Alex, but I'm not sorry I didn't stop you. I know what a punishment entails. I should have dealt with the pain in a different manner; it was my own fault for clenching my fists. I want to make you happy, Alex. I want to please you. I am only sorry that I have upset you instead."

Tightening his arms around me, Alex and I both relax onto the chair and contemplate what may have changed in our relationship.

*   *   *

I wake to find myself on Alex's bed and realize I must have fallen asleep outside. Glancing towards my nightstand, I see that I have only slept for forty-five minutes. A glass of water and aspirin are sitting beside the clock and I reach over to take them. The water is still very cold and tastes wonderful against my dry mouth.

Once stepping out of bed, I put on jeans and a t-shirt and go in search of Alex. I find him in the family room using the large internet television to video chat with someone. She sounds a bit older and has a strong English accent.

The unfamiliar voice asks, "Alexander, haven't you taken a long enough vacation? I enjoyed having you here the past two weeks. I think you should come back home as soon as possible."

"Mother, I am not ready to return yet and if you keep badgering me I will extend my vacation."

As I step in the room, my movements alert Alex of my presence and he grins widely in my direction. I glance at the screen and I notice that a lovely older woman is looking at me as well. She has Alex's golden eyes and both Abi and Alex's dark hair; this must be their mother.

I look back at Alex with a startled expression and apologize, "I'm sorry, I didn't mean to interrupt."

"No worries, darling. Please, come join me," he says as he turns his attention back to the screen.

"Mother, please meet Mallory Winston. Mallory, this is my mother."

I respond nervously, not quite making eye contact with the screen, "It's a pleasure to meet you."

"You as well. I have heard an earful about you from my Abigail. Only good things of course. She mentioned that you are the youngest executive at your advertising agency. That is quite an accomplishment young lady."

Alex seems to be enjoying the blush that rises to my cheeks from her compliment.

"Thank you, ma'am," I reply. "I really enjoy what I do."

"Smart and beautiful; you have done well, Alex. Now I see why you won't return to us," the sophisticated older woman says jokingly. Noticing he redness across my cheeks she proclaims, "No need to feel embarrassed, dearie. Abi was right; I think Alex is head over heels for you too."

"Mother!" Alex shouts as he nervously adjusts his jeans.

"Oh hush, boy," his mother retorts. "So, Mallory, what are your plans when Alex returns to England?"

"Wow, Mrs. Stone you cut right to the chase," I tease.

As she bursts out into laughter, I glance over to Alex who looks somewhat eager to hear my answer.

Confused at his reaction I reply, "Ma'am I don't have any definite plans right now other than to continue with my new position at the agency. Alex and I have agreed to only see each other while he was here so, ma'am, if you don't mind, I'd like him to stay as long as he can." Alex's mother is shooting daggers in his direction and then I remember him mentioning her need to marry him off. I may have made it worse for him when he returns. I mouth to him, "I'm sorry," and look back at the screen to say, "Mrs. Stone, you must be very proud of your children. From what I know they have all achieved admirable goals."

"You are right, Mallory. I am beyond proud of my family. I just wish in their lives that they experience the sense of love and happiness that their father and I have."

"I believe all parents wish that, ma'am. Everyone finds their own happiness in time."

"Perhaps, but some need a little push," she says considering my words. "Alex, your father is calling for me. I will talk to you soon. Mallory, it was a pleasure to make your acquaintance."

"You as well, ma'am. You've raised a magnificent son."

"Thank you, dear." The screen turns black and I look back at Alex, who is sporting a wiry grin on his face.

"Something amusing you, Mr. Stone?" I inquire as I relax and wander closer into the room.

"Nope. It seems my mother is taken with you as well."

Crawling over to him on the couch I ask, "Taken? Well, sir, what does that mean for me?"

Grabbing my waist, he places me on his lap, straddling him. "It means everyone in my family that has met you loves you. Though that isn't very surprising; you're quite easy to love." His words stop my heart as I hope that he will utter those three magical words to me. "I'm sorry you won't get to meet her," he continues. "At least now she may hold off on her talks of marriage for a few more months."

And with those words my dreams are shattered. I need to remember where I stand with Alex.

Plastering a fake smile on my face I state, "I'm glad I could help."

He looks at me quizzically for a few moments causing me to squirm slightly on his lap and then I assume he gets the answer he was searching for when he says, "Would you like to go to dinner tonight or stay in?"

"Whatever you would like to do. I know you're probably tired from your flight."

"I am never too tired to spend time with you, darling. Let's head out for something light and then you can show me how much you missed me."

With that statement, he turns to lay on the couch pressing me into the cushions and wedges himself between my legs, planting kisses along my jaw line.

"Alex," I begin, "if you keep doing that we won't ever make it out for food."

Reaching down he pushes up on the hem of my shirt and slides his hand along my ribcage.

"But you taste so good, Ms. Winston," he declares huskily.

As he nibbles my ear, I release a moan and grind against his pelvis.

Tempting him I pose, "Maybe we can have dessert first?"

The hand on my ribcage travels down to the waist of my jeans and unhooks the buttons.

"I like your way of thinking," Alex responds and continues to tug my jeans down as he meets my lips in a scorching kiss, devouring me whole.

Quickly, he pulls my shirt off to join my jeans on the floor and Alex sits up to remove his shirt and jeans, tossing them next to mine. I sit up and reach behind me to unhook my bra, sliding each strap down my arms as Alex watches me mesmerized. His hand juts out and he pulls me towards him, my mouth meeting his. Our tongues dance choreography of their design. I let the bra fall from my hands and make swift work on the panties I am still wearing. Once I have removed all my clothing, I bend to place kisses along Alex's chest, hearing his breath catch as my mouth makes contact with his skin. My hands extend to the waistband of his boxer briefs and I slide them down to his folded knees. His erection springs forth and I instantly feel my mouth begin to water. I take his penis into my hands and lean down to lick along the sides. My tongue skates across the head and I grow wetter when I taste his salty bead of moisture. Guiding his erection into my mouth, I take him as far back in my throat as I can manage and I stroke the base using my saliva as a lubricant. When I reach forward and massage his sack, I hear a groan release from Alex's throat. Soon, I feel Alex place his hand on the back of my head and direct my movements.

"I am going to come, baby," Alex proclaims through a tight groan. "Swallow it."

I feel the hot liquid spurt into my throat moments later and I continue to suck, hoping to drain every drop. The flavor Alex expends is mouthwatering and I am addicted to the taste. When he releases me, and pulls me up his body I see that his erection still hard and throbbing. Pushing me back on the couch Alex grabs a hold of my wrists and places them above my head in one of his hands. He leans forward to take a nipple into his mouth and the pleasure sends a lightning strike to my core. Releasing my nipple with a pop, he makes work on the other breast. Alex is keeping my legs spread apart with his own so that I have nothing to release the tension and I can feel the surge building in my belly. Every time Alex bites at my nipples, I whimper at my proximity to release. Sensing my need, he trails his other hand down to my clit and flicks it once triggering me to explode as a kaleidoscope of colors pass before my eyes. I meet such an intense orgasm that I am afraid I will lose consciousness. He places sweet kisses on the corners of my mouth and I am immediately brought back to the moment.

My body is still yearning for him to be inside me, as I haven't gotten enough of him. Alex moves to the other side of the couch and tugs me along with him, straddling his lap. Lifting me slightly, he aligns my opening with his erection and teases my entrance with the head of his cock. Taunting my body, he moves little by little, only going an inch further every time. The hands that I had placed on his shoulders move up to his face, pulling him into another fiery kiss. Tugging me up at the waist so that his cock is barely inside me, he impales himself into my core with one thrust. The movement causes a moan to escape from my lips that he swallows greedily.

He begins to thrust while still holding me up and I move my hands back to his shoulders so that I can use them as leverage to meet him at every pound. With the sweat dripping from our bodies, Alex takes me by the shoulders and leans me back at a different angle. He begins rubbing the spot that will send me over the edge and I barely feel his hand move down the opening of my behind. Alex inserts a finger into my tight rosette and I reach another explosion. As I scream out Alex's name, he follows my orgasm with his own. Losing sense of reality, I recognize that I have never had such an incredible experience with a man.

Exhausted we both lay in a heap of sweaty limbs on the couch.

"I'm going to need another shower before we go out," I say through a laugh.

"You're probably right, why don't we order in and go out tomorrow."

"That's the best thing you've said all night."

Chapter Seventeen

DURING THE WEEK, ALEX and I develop a familiar routine. We both complete work during the same hours and use the evenings to explore more about each other. Alex spends time describing his childhood home and what it's like in England. I learn he has traveled to several countries around the globe, something I yearn to do. We have similar tastes in music and art and we both love to watch reruns of old comedies.

As I leave work Friday afternoon, Alex helps me to pack for our trip to the beach.

"Mallory, are you certain your parents are ok with my accompanying you?" he asks a bit apprehensive.

"Of course. Believe me, if they weren't ok with it, they would say so."

Alex and I chose to leave that evening and stop at my family's home along the way to shorten the trip a bit. My family always heads to Hatteras Island in North

Carolina and rent a cottage on the beach. From their home in Richmond it is only a 4-hour trip, so it is a relief we can stop along the way. I offered to drive, but Alex insisted.

Once the entire set of luggage is sitting out in the vestibule, I go in search of my charming boyfriend.

"Alex, are you ready?" I inquire.

"I am. I called the concierge to come grab our bags and pull my vehicle around."

"Are you sure you don't want me to drive?"

"I am very capable of following directions, Ms. Winston. I can even listen to a GPS," he says jokingly as grabs me around the waist and places a gentle tickle along my ribs.

Wrapping my arms around his neck, I lean in for a kiss and add, "You're very funny, Alex."

As we exit the elevator and walk through the lobby, Alex stops off at the security desk to let them know that he will be away for a week, but that his sister and Gregory are granted access to his home. Waiting outside, I see a brand-new Ford Raptor pull up to the curb and my Southern heart cries out in envy. Moments later, Alex steps out to join and whistles.

"She is much prettier than I imagined."

"What?" I exclaim. "This is yours?"

"Indeed, she is."

"Holy shit, Alex. Your sexiness factor just skyrocketed off the charts."

"You have a thing for utility vehicles?"

"I have a thing for sexy buff guys that drive a pickup. Every Southern girl does."

"Well then, I am happy I made this purchase."

Moving closer to the truck, I say enviously, "I am so jealous of you right now."

He smiles down at me and lifts me into the truck before placing a soft kiss on my lips.

"I know," he replies as he shuts the door and struts around to the driver's side.

After Alex climbs into the cab, we head towards my childhood home.

A three-and-a-half-hour drive later we arrive at my parent's modest home. It's a quant, bungalow style home located in the north side of the city. My mother runs out to the car to greet us, engulfing me in a giant hug.

"Baby girl, I have missed you. You need to come home more often."

"I know, mom, I will try. I promise."

"Now where is this gorgeous man you were talking about?"

Stepping around from the bed of the truck, Alex holds our overnight bag and introduces himself, "Thanks for having me, I'm Alex Stone. It's a pleasure to meet you, Mrs. Winston."

"Well slap me silly. You are a dazzling creature, aren't you?"

For the first time I see a slight blush cross Alex's cheek as he responds, "Thank you, miss."

"Mallory, you're here," my dad shouts as he strolls out and surrounds me in a hug.

"Hi, daddy," I whisper and then backing from my parents I announce, "Dad, mom, this is Alex Stone. Alex, these are my parents Chris and Sarah Winston." Alex reaches out to shake my dad's hand as my mom continues to stare at him. I must admit he is captivating to look at.

"I like your truck, Mr. Stone," my dad states.

"Thank you, sir. It is a new purchase."

Chirping in I reveal, "He enjoys his toys, daddy. Mom, why don't we all go inside and have some dinner? I cannot wait to put my toes in the sand tomorrow."

"Sounds great, dear," she answers as we follow her inside the small home.

While we are seated at dinner, the parental inquisition begins, mostly led by my father. I tried to explain to my mom that Alex and I are only together for a short time so the questioning wasn't necessary, but she said it was my dad's fatherly right to find out anything he wanted about someone I date. I relent and let them have their way.

"So, Alex, what is it you do?" my dad inquires.

"Well, I graduated from Oxford and I have Ph.D. This is why I am here, assisting the Institute. My real passion is for a few of my investments. I own two Formula One racing teams in England."

"That is very impressive. What do your parents do?"

Alex seems to hesitate at this question for a minute and then utters, "Well, they, uh, are both retired from the family business. My brother is working on that end currently."

As my father continues to grill Alex, I sit quietly trying to piece together information, but I get nowhere.

"Mom, what time are we leaving in the morning?" I ask.

"Your father and I would like to leave by 9:00 am, I'm sure we will hit traffic as always. Your brothers went down earlier in the week with some friends to surf, so they will grab the keys for the cottage."

"Good deal. Well if you all don't mind I am going to hit the hay. Staring at the road for three hours took its toll."

Gripping me in an embrace my mom says, "I love you, Mal. Sleep well."

"Alex, do I need to show you were you are sleeping?" I solicit before leaving the dining room.

He looks at me horrified like he hadn't thought we would be sleeping separately and answers, "Yes, please. Thank you for dinner, Mrs. Winston. Mr. Winston."

"Alex, you will be staying in the guest room across the way from me. My parents would have let you stay in my room," I say with a smirk, "but it is a twin sized bed. I don't think you would fit."

Chuckling Alex says, "I understand, Mallory. There is no need to explain. At least we will be sharing a room at the beach."

Snaking my arms around Alex's neck I lean into him and whisper, "I can always sneak in later if you're awake."

He leans down and sears me with a scorching kiss.

With a moan he expresses, "Mmm. That would be nice, but we both need our sleep, love." I pout at his denial and he chastises me, "Don't pout, little girl."

Then as I turn, he smacks my behind and closes the guest room door, leaving me in the hall. Situating myself in my old bedroom, I fall into a dreamless sleep.

*   *   *

Alex and I join my parents for breakfast in the morning and we head out shortly after, with hope to make it to Hatteras in five hours. After a few hours in the car listening to Alex's iPod, we make our way onto the island. My parents rented a cottage with a great view of the ocean and before Alex has even parked the truck, I jump out of the cab and make my way to the sand and water. By the time Alex reaches me, I am knee deep in the Atlantic. Chucking his shoes, he struts into the chilled water to reach me. Once he is close enough to make contact, Alex wraps his arms around me and I lean into him, both of us gazing into the water.

"It's beautiful. You love it here, don't you?"

"I do. It is the only place I truly relax. If I could live on the beach, any beach, I would."

"I could buy you an island you know. Name it Cape Mallory," he says as he nuzzles my neck.

Laughing I say, "You're crazy."

"So, I've been told."

We stand there for an untold amount of time before I say, "Alex?"

"Yes?"

"I can't feel my feet."

"Oh, thank goodness," he exclaims. "I think lost feeling in my toes ten minutes ago. This water is horribly cold." We laugh as we scamper out of the water trying to avoid the waves. Once we reach the shoreline, Alex stops, kneels slightly and turns his head, sending a wink at me.

Beckoning me forward he shouts, "Come on." I giddily jump onto his back and he bends to grabs our shoes before heading towards the house.

The week passes quickly as we spend our days resting on the sand or fishing. On the night of Independence Day, Alex and I drive onto the beach to enjoy the firework show over the ocean. In true romantic fashion, he puts a bunch of blankets in the bed of his truck and we watch the fireworks from there. We place light touches on each other during the show, causing the flame to build inside each of us. When the extravaganza is over, we find ourselves completely lost in each other, making love in the bed of his truck and creating a firework show of our own.

As Saturday morning arrives we all drive back to my parent's home, disappointed that our wonderful week together away has ended. Alex and I stop for only a short bit, but decide to head back to our home that day as well. He even lets me drive his truck part of the way while he selects the music.

We arrive at Alex's home in the early evening and as we board the elevator Alex pulls me into him.

"Mallory, I need to tell you something," he says urgently and I begin to worry from his tone of voice.

"Okay…" I say with apprehension lacing my voice.

"We received more letters while we were away. One was sent for you here at The Braxton, which Gregory apprehended and took to the police. The second was sent to the cottage we were staying at in North Carolina. I snatched it before your parents saw, but you may want to let them know what is going on. This perpetrator is following you and I'm afraid he may harm your family." I can feel a panic attack rising in my body and I can't seem to bring air into my lungs.

Alarmed at my oncoming panic attach Alex cries, "Baby, breathe, please. Follow me. In and out." I try to mimic his breathing, but after a few minutes, I still can't seem to calm down.

"Please breathe, Mallory, you're worrying me. Are you prone to panic attacks? Keep following my breaths" I shake my head not able to respond.

With a calming voice Alex says, "I understand, darling. If you'd like, I can be the one to tell them and assure them that I have security protecting you." Knowing that Alex will do everything in his power to protect me, I am finally able to breathe.

"Thank you, Alex," I say through a wheezing voice once I calm down.

"Anything, love. Please don't scare me like that," he answers, kissing my head and leading me towards the bedroom.

Alex's nimble fingers peel off my clothing and he asks me to lie on the bed face down. He exits the room for a moment and returns with a bottle in his hand.

"Baby, I am sorry that all of this is happening. I hope that a massage will help you relax."

"That would be lovely. Thank you."

He begins at my neck and works over every inch of my arms and back. The contact from Alex's hands on me has left my skin on fire. He isn't unaffected from the touch either as he is now sporting a large tent in his pants.

"Mallory, flip over and I will massage your legs." Beginning at my feet, he pays close attention to each toe and then the instep. When he places a slight bit of pressure on the sensitive area, I can feel the heat engulf in my groin. In an attempt to hold back my groan, my body squirms under his hands.

"Do you like that darling?" Alex asks intrigued.

"Yes, I would pay you to do this every day."

"That could be arranged, you know. I may even give you a discount."

I chuckle at his bit of humor and Alex continues to massage my legs making small, gentle circles with his fingers and hands. Soon his fingers reach the apex of my thighs and I whimper at the sensation. His fingers tenderly slide back and forth along my center and folds, leaving my skin seared from the touch.

"Mallory, reach above you and hold onto the headboard," Alex demands.

Following his command, I position myself the way he requested and he moves his head down to my center. Alex's tongue slides along my folds and then dives into my core, his hands resting on my hips to steady my movements. The attention he is paying to my core is causing my breasts to flame. With an understanding of my needs, one of his hands move towards my nipple and rubs it between his fingers.

"Oh, Alex," I moan. "I'm so close."

The tongue pressed against my core is removed and replaced with his finger as he moves up my body and tilts my head, thrusting his tongue in my mouth. I meet him in our tango and I reciprocate the desire in his kiss. With a small maneuver, Alex moves his body over me and inserts himself quickly into my core. He thrusts a few times while continuing to probe my mouth and then leans back onto his knees positioning my legs onto his shoulders. His movements become more fierce and powerful as he circles his hips between thrusts pushing me closer to my orgasm. The explosion is nearing for both of us and I can feel his erection grow within me.

"Come. Now," Alex decrees and I unleash my energy as Alex joins me.
Continuing with small thrusts, I hope to milk him completely of his climax.

Lying across my body, he leans up on one of his elbows and pushes the hair from my face.

"You are beautiful, Ms. Winston," he states.

Looking into his eyes, I smile at his sincerity. "You are too, Mr. Stone."

*   *   *

Alex and I return to work and we both message back and forth that we miss lying on the beach in each other's company. Around 2:00pm in the afternoon, I hear a knock at my door and I instruct them to enter. My remarkable boyfriend waits against the doorjamb with his sexy smile. Taking my time to eye his body from head to toe I lick my lips taking in my fill. He looks delectable in a tailored suit He chuckles when he catches my ogling.

"Good afternoon, Ms. Winston. I have a surprise for you."

Getting up from my chair, I walk over to where Alex stands and I shut the door behind him before wrapping my arms around his neck.

"Do you now?" I ask sultrily.
Alex places a soft kiss on my lips and then reaches around to remove my arms.

"I do," he replies.
As he walks over to my couch, a pout embellishes across my face at his rejection.

"Come here, beautiful," he orders. "Sit on the couch."

With a sway in my step I make my way over to where he is perched on the armrest and sit on the couch facing in his direction. Reaching into his pocket, Alex pulls a small remote control, followed by a small bullet, and two tiny balls connected by a string. He situates all of the devices on to the coffee table and then reaches into his suit pocket to pull out a pair of hard leather looking straps connected by a lock.

Quickly turning into dominating Alex, he commands, "Ms. Winston, please remove your panties and hand them to me."
Standing, I remove the panties from beneath my skirt and I hand him the scrap of bright pink lace.

As he takes the material from my hand, he brings it to his nose and with a sniff exclaims, "Divine. Now kneel beside me."

Again, I do as he says and sit back on my heels beside his legs.

"Good."

With a caring touch he strokes his hand through my hair; caressing my head and face.

"I have missed you, darling," Alex reveals with softness in his eyes. "I grew fond of our companionship this past week." I nod in agreement as he continues, "I want to play with you now. You see the bullet and balls on the table?"

Looking towards the table, I nod.

"Those are remote controlled by the device in my hand," he explains. "The other contraption is called a chastity belt. Do you need to use the restroom?"

I shake my head.

"No, sir," I whisper.

"Good. It will be difficult with the belt. What I plan to do is place the small bullet against your clit, one of the balls inside your pussy, and the last ball will rest against your perineum. It will be a different but pleasurable feeling and will quickly trigger an orgasm. I will control your release with this device for the time I decide to relax here in your office. When I decide to leave, I will exchange your panties for the chastity belt. You won't be able to reach your release until I deem it so. Understand?"

Distressed I ask, "Am I being punished, sir?"

Astonished at my question, Alex has the decency to look embarrassed and quickly corrects himself, "Oh no, sweet girl; I may allow you to reach a climax or two while we play, but once I leave I will keep your orgasms at bay. It will make our time together this evening much more pleasurable."

I nod my head in understanding.

"Please stand, Mallory, and step into your panties."

Holding the lace out for me to step into, he rests them above my knees.

Without hesitation he commands, "Turn around and bend over."

Carefully turning with my restricted legs, I bend over placing my hands onto my ankles. Alex rubs his fingers back and forth along my center and I moan at his touch.

"You're so wet for me, baby. You've missed me too, haven't you?"

"More than you know, sir. I want you more than anything." Leaning forward, he directs his tongue to lick from my clitoris to my rosette.

"So divine, Ms. Winston."

Suddenly, I feel his finger thrust into my core and stroke back and forth causing a moan to release from deep in my throat.

At my desire Alex adds, "Soon darling, you will have all of me tonight. For now, this will have to do."

After a few tantalizing strokes Alex inserts the first ball into my pussy. It doesn't feel too intrusive, but the chill of the ball is enough to awaken the fire in my belly.

"Stand and turn back around," he demands and as I follow his instruction I can feel the ball resting along the walls of my womb. It feels heavy, but soft. Alex quickly tugs up my panties and reaches his hand into the center to place the outer ball and bullet into his chosen location.

"How does that feel, Mallory?" he asks.

Twisting my body to feel the devices, I utter, "Um, so far so good."

A wicked smile spreads across his face as he says, "Splendid. Please continue your work and pretend that I am no longer here."

Nodding in his direction I make my way over to my desk and out of the corner of my eye I watch Alex relax onto my sofa, propping his feet onto the cushions.

I spend thirty minutes working on my vodka campaign before I have my final meeting with the clients in an hour. After a while, I begin to think that the remotes batteries aren't working, as I haven't felt any movement. When Annie walks into my office a few moments after I make my final change to the presentation, the torment begins.

"Mallory, do you have the story board ready for the clients today?" my Junior Executive asks.

Taking a deep breath, I try to control my voice, "It's ready to go, Annie."
I keep my words short and crisp.

Annie tilts her head to study me, inquiring, "Are you sure you don't need me to add anything?"
My knuckles whiten as I grip the corners of my desk when Alex intensifies the vibration.

Closing my eyes, I tilt my head towards my desk. "No," I reply.

"Mal, are you ok?" she asks just before she notices Alex sitting in my office.

"Oh, my goodness. How rude of me," she proclaims. "Mallory, you could have said you had a guest. Goodness. I will see you upstairs in half an hour."

"Ok," I respond rudely.

The instant Annie leaves the room I reach my climax and the vibrations stop.

Resting my head onto my desk I hear Alex speak, "You did very well, Ms. Winston. For your sake, I hope you don't receive any more visitors."

I send a glare over in Alex's direction and he responds with a sexy smirk. Ten minutes prior to my meeting, as I am gathering my paperwork, Alex begins the vibrations again. I lean over my filing cabinet and let the pleasure take over.

As I come close to the pinnacle, I release Alex's name as a moan.

Not realizing he had stalked up behind me, I am startled to feel his hand skim across my waist. Whispering in my ear Alex says, "Let go."

I release my second climax and fall back against his chest and rest against him. As Alex holds me close and nibbles along my neck, I grab hold of my surroundings and recover from my explosion. Once Alex realizes I have come back to earth, he kneels down and jerks my panties, grabbing the bullet. Stroking his hand along my back, he pushes against me, causing me to bend at the waist. His fingers trail along my folds and gently yank on the string, pulling out the vibrating ball.

RENEE HARLESS

When I stand to face him, he moves from his kneeling position, putting the ball in his mouth moaning, "Sweet as honey."

As he places the toys into his pocket, I stare at his gorgeous face. Reaching forward with his free hand he pulls my face into a heartbreakingly sensual kiss and I aim to push all of my love and desire in return. With his other hand, he extends forward and thrusts his fingers into my core, triggering me to whimper at his perusal. His fingers stroke back and forth, crooking every few moments causing my body to shake with pleasure. All too soon, he releases me from his grasp and I stand in place panting. Behind hooded eyes, I see Alex walk over to the coffee table and grab the leather chastity belt.

Coming back to where I wait, he kneels on the floor saying, "Spread your legs."

He slides the straps around my legs, adjusting the leather and I hear the faint sound of a lock in the background.

As Alex stands up to face me he asks, "Is this ok? Is it uncomfortable?"
I tug my skirt down and complete a few paces in my office.

"No, it feels fine. I need to leave for my meeting," I state.

"I know," he says as he pulls me into a simmering kiss. "I will see you at home, love."

Rooted to my spot I stand in awe as he exits completely unaffected. Annie walks in a split second later to join me in the conference room.

As I present the final round of advertising campaigns to the vodka clients, I can't help but notice the stares from the men in the room.

Questioning myself I ask, *Do they know that I am wearing a leather chastity belt? Do they know what I was doing in my office only minutes ago? Do they know that this necklace symbolizes a collar in my arrangement?*

I am so uneasy in this moment from my lack of release at Alex's exit, that I am confusing my thoughts. They are most likely staring at the storyboard to my right.

"Gentlemen, can I answer any questions for you regarding the campaign?" I inquire.

The leader of the client group speaks up, "Ms. Winston, this is superb work. We are all very pleased with your concepts and look forward to releasing the final aspects of the campaign. We have already seen an increase in sales since we began working with you."

While he speaks, I gently rock back and forth on my heels, creating any sort of friction against the belt.

Taking a deep breath, I concentrate on my words and reply, "That is excellent news, Mr. Jones. I hope that you continue to see success with these campaigns and hire us for any future endeavors. Before we part, I need you to sign these finalized papers, then we can get started towards the end."

After signing, we all exit the conference room and Annie walks with me back to the office.

"Mallory, are you ok?" she asks. "Your face was beet red through the entire presentation."
I feel embarrassed that I was so easy to read. I hope no one else could tell what I was craving.

Trying to contain my mortification I lie, "Annie, I'm fine. I think I just ate something funny for lunch. Why don't you head home? We can work on these small changes tomorrow."

"That sounds great. I have to get ready for dinner with the future in-laws," she says as she makes a horrified face. I chuckle at her reaction because she adores her soon to be mother-in-law; she may even like her better than her actual mother.

Exiting my office building an hour later, I step up to my car and observe that placed in my seat is a large envelope with handwriting I don't recognize. Swiftly messaging Alex, I ask if he has left me a note in my car. Alarmed when he says he hasn't he tells me that I shouldn't open the envelope until we have Gregory close by.

I rush home through traffic, terrified of the stalker targeting me at work and I forget about the chastity belt that I am wearing. As I exit the main elevator on the floor where Gregory lives, an ashen faced Alex and an angry Gregory instantly greet me.

With malice in his voice Gregory announces, "I am so sorry, Ms. Winston. I had thought we had a hold of this already."

Turning to Alex, I try to calm him down.

"Alex, it will be ok. I have you to protect me."

My words seem to snap him out of his trance and he pulls me into his arms, not saying anything, just resting his head on top of my own. I toss the envelope towards Gregory so that he can open the letter and I wrap my arms around Alex.

"Ms. Winston, I will take this straight to the police. Did you want to see it?"

"No, I don't. Is it bad? Worse than the others?"

Peeking at the letter again Gregory stutters, "It's, um, descriptive, miss."

"Oh."

"And this one seems to focus on Mr. Stone as well. The police don't seem to believe me, but I don't think this crime and the terrorizing of your home are related."

"Why would you think that? Are two people after me now?"

"I'm not sure, ma'am, but because I am not a part of the government security here in the United States, I don't have the right to join into an investigation. I'm sorry, Ms. Winston, but I have to leave this all up to the police." I stare at Gregory confused. Noticing my bewilderment, he carries on, "Mallory, if it were up to me, I would take you back to England so that we can protect you there and I can participate in the investigation."

A spurt of optimism flashes across my visage and my thoughts travel. *Maybe Alex will ask me to go home with him in a few weeks. Could I leave my job and family? Do I trust and love him enough to do that?*

I plant a cheeky smile on my face remembering what I have on under my clothes and speak to Alex, "Well, that is a shame now isn't it." I grab Alex's tie and begin to tug him from Gregory's entryway persisting, "If you don't mind, Mr. Stone, we need to finish our discussion from earlier today."

Alex is quietly trailing behind me with his hands on my hips while I have his tie in my hand, over my shoulder.

"And what discussion do we need to complete, Ms. Winston?" he murmurs into my ear as I press the button to the elevator and linger for the car that leads us to Alex's penthouse. Patiently waiting, Alex stands up against me, methodically rubbing circles along my hips bones, brushing just above the leather straps of the belt. Once the elevator arrives, I step into the cart, turn, and jerk Alex's tie so that he must fall against me.

Answering his previous question, I respond, "The one discussing my virtue, Mr. Stone." As he tumbles into me, he pursues my lips in a demanding kiss. We are lucky that not one else will be using this elevator as Alex has my hands held into his, pressed into the wall above my head. He grinds his erection into me, but I can only feel the force through his belt. Once the car stops on our floor, Alex beckons me to exit first.

"Ms. Winston, please go wait for me," Alex instructs as he begins un-doing his tie.

Taking that as my cue, I head off towards the bedroom and do as he commands. He struts into the room ten minutes later, twirling a thin chain. As I remain in position, he stands in front of me and clips the chain to my necklace. It's a leash. I should feel humiliated, but instead I feel proud, magical, as if he is claiming me for his own. Alex yanks lightly on the leash, causing a metallic sound to echo in the large room.

Lifting my head up from my position, he smiles and declares, "Lovely. Come. You may walk." Following his footsteps, we enter kitchen and he goes on, "You have done wonderfully with the belt, Ms. Winston. I plan to take it off soon, but not yet."

Pausing for a few minutes, looking in the fridge, he pulls out an array of sushi that must have been delivered from the restaurant up the street.

Turning to me expectantly he asks, "How does sushi sound for dinner?"

"Scrumptious."

"Good. Go lie on the dining room table." At my hesitation he tugs the leash so I stand face to face with him. "Ms. Winston?" he questions in his dominating demeanor.

"Are, uh, you expecting guests? I'm not sure how I feel…" My sentence ends abruptly when he reaches up to gently stroke my face.

"Ms. Winston," he says, "though it would be incredibly erotic to share you as the tray for a meal with others, I will always ask your permission. I had already assumed you would be uncomfortable submitting to be in public. Perhaps one day."

"Thank you, sir, but I don't think I will do it publically, ever."
"Very well, go now."

Holding the chain in my left hand, I walk into the dining room to display myself. As I present my body on the table, I take the time to look at the leash Alex has provided. The handle piece is a series of beads that attach to a loop with a hook a quarter of the way up the chain. During my scrutiny, Alex strides in carrying the box of sushi, a bottle of plum wine, and two glasses.

"You must stay still, Mallory, but first, I need to remove your clothes and belt," he says as he reaches into his pocket and pulls out a small key that matches the tiny lock on the side of my belt. At the leathers removal Alex asks, "Do you need to use the rest room, Ms. Winston?"

Humiliated by his question I utter, "Uh, yes I do."

"Very well, go, remove your gown, and then return here."

I rush to the powder room, relieve myself, and then come back to the dining room, holding my leash in my left hand. In front of a patient Alex, I stand still and hold out my hand carrying the chain. Taking the leash from me, he asks me to turn around and to grab my ankles. Not sure what he has in store for me, I bend down reluctantly. Not soon enough, his fingers slide over my wet core and I whimper in my throat, hoping he doesn't hear. Continuing to rub the lubricant back and forth over my core, he moves his strokes to my behind, over the entrance. Once he feels it is sufficiently greased, he positions the leash in front of me and places it between my legs. Unfastening the latch creating the loop on the end, he inserts each bead slowly into my anal cavity. As each bead pushes the first deeper and deeper inside, I moan in delight. The feeling is indescribable.

When Alex is satisfied with the leashes placement, he tenderly rubs a hand over my spine and speaks, "You may stand, Ms. Winston. Please position yourself on the table. You will have to lie still once I begin."
"Yes, sir."

I use a chair as a stool and arrange myself flat onto the table. All of my movements cause the beads to slide back and forth, sending sparks to my lower belly, igniting the blaze. Pleased with my position on top of the table, Alex begins to strategically place pieces of sashimi rolls along my body. Two rows of six lay across my chest and stomach, four on each leg, one on each shoulder, one in the hollow of my neck, and one placed at the lowest part of my mound.

"Ms. Winston, as much as I am going to enjoy dinner, I am very much looking forward to dessert."
So am I, I say to myself.

Alex doesn't use any utensils to eat his meal; he leans over my body and picks up each piece with his mouth. My body flinches each time his mouth touches me, causing the beads inside me to move. For every two pieces he eats, he offers me one as well. Declining, I have lost my appetite for food; I only hunger for him. The inferno inside me is so turbulent; I fear I will detonate at any moment. Once Alex has finished all of the sushi on my body, paying close attention to the final two pieces on the hollow of my neck and on my mound, he pours a small glass of wine.

Taking a quick sip, he hums in his mouth.

"This is delightful, Ms. Winston. Would you like some?"

"Yes, please, sir."

He takes a small sip and leans over my mouth to deliver the cold liquid through a kiss.

Swallowing the chilled liquid, I moan aloud, causing Alex to respond, "That good, Ms. Winston?"

"Yes, sir. It's the best I've had."

"Indeed, perhaps you would like to meet the winemakers. I am friends with the couple that made this, but we can discuss that later." Before I have a chance to react Alex takes the bottle and pours a small amount of the wine into my navel. It is cold and I jerk to the side spilling the liquid onto the table.

"Shame, Shame, Ms. Winston. You need to stay still. You are causing a mess."

"I was startled by the temperature, sir."

"Ah I see. Too cold? Perhaps I can fix that." Alex pours another small amount into my navel and presses his tongue into the tiny pool of wine, lapping it up. My reflexes take over and my body twitches uncontrollably. Placing both of his hands on my hips, he attempts to hold me still. My leg, nevertheless, bends up to create some sort of movement for the beads.

"Darling, is it too much?" Alex groans.

Quickly becoming delirious with the need for release I whimper, "Soon, sir. Please, soon."

Alex helps me to sit up on the table, which only causes the beads to create more sparks for the flame. Standing across from me, Alex stares into my eyes and I see the desire that swiftly builds in his eyes, match my own. Our irises have both turned a startling shade of dark brown and hunter green, both almost black.

Reaching forward, Alex gently strokes his thumbs across my face, searching for an answer in my eyes. Assuming he saw what he hoped, something crosses Alex's eyes, and in this moment, I see Alex release me from his submission. He sees me as a partner. He wants me longer then the time we have remaining. I can see when the realization crosses his face. His expression hardens, but only in yearning for me. He grips the leash and jerks the portion connected to the collar, causing my head to pull towards his face. Meeting me halfway in a passion-filled kiss, his hand immediately reaches farther forward, tangling his fingers into my hair. Alex tilts my head to the side and uses this leverage to explore my mouth with his tongue.

Stepping back from the table, Alex hurriedly removes his clothes in haste. Swiftly catching my lips in another passionate kiss, he leans me back against the table. Alex follows his own movements and soon we are both lying on the dining room table.
Alex sits up momentarily while continuing to grind his hips along mine.

"You give yourself so freely to me. You are more than I could have asked for in a submissive and a lover. What do you want, Mallory?"

I reply in staggered words as I kiss along his neck and shoulders, "I. Want. You. Alex. Always. Forever."

A moan breaks free from his lips at my words and he seals our lips again in a fervent kiss. His erection slides into me slowly, penetrating my womb ever so smoothly. With each inch he glides in, I feel the beads move around in my other entrance. The pleasure is becoming too much, too quickly. The combination of his earlier retreat in my office, forcing me to wear the belt, and his invitation to act as his dinner serving dish have rapidly engulfed my core in a wildfire.

"Alex, please, sir, faster," I scream as I am becoming delirious from my need.

RENEE HARLESS

Leaning up on his hands, he cocks his eyebrow at me and bites his lip.

Smirking at me he murmurs, "I don't think so."

Bending forward to catch my lips in another kiss, he begins to massage one of my breasts. As my fire continues to burn, I instinctively wrap my legs around Alex's waist. This position helps to rocket me forward as his hips brush against my mound, grazing my clit. My body is standing on the cliff, ready to jump when Alex abruptly stops. He sits up onto his heels and pulls out of me.

Gently grabbing my knees, he lifts my legs back and delicately pulls out each of the beads. I bite my lip to hold back my orgasm and moan at every bead exits. The sensation is exquisite. After completely relieving my rosette of the metallic beads, Alex unhooks the leash from my collar and tosses the lead onto the hardwood floor while stepping off from the table.

A dismissal was not what I expected and my fire extinguishes immediately at his exit. I sit up and look at him from my perch on the table while he stands contemplating his next move. Something has changed, though I am not sure what. Alex turns around at a snail's pace, looks into my eyes and gingerly holds out his hand, not asking me to join him, but asking for permission. I place my hand in his and he heaves me from my spot on the table.

In a flash, he is walking us towards his bedroom. Once I have placed a foot inside the suite he slams the door shut and twirls me towards him, pressing my back against the now closed door. While Alex searches my face with his golden eyes, he is wrapping my hair around his wrist. He yanks my hair gently, forcing me to tilt my head up, crashing his lips against my own. Of their own free will, my arms reach up and around Alex's neck. My body has taken over and my mind lies dormant in an oversexed state. Letting my fingers tangle in Alex's hair, I massage small circles onto his scalp with my nails. Alex's hands begin sliding down my back and over my behind, resting on the back of my thighs. Sensing my need to be closer, Alex lifts me up and wraps my legs around his waist. His hands move back up to my waist and he instinctively probes my entrance with his erection. My hands tighten in his hair as he pulls me down to thrust inside. The feeling of his deep intrusion illicit an incredible sensation and a moan escapes from my lips onto his.

"Fuck, baby," Alex groans as he rests his forehead against my own.

We haven't begun moving, but we are both breathing heavily. Staring at each other, desire and want flash across both of our eyes.

Madness takes over and we both engage in a fanatical and hot-blooded kiss. I use the muscles in my legs to stay wrapped around Alex and he uses the wall as leverage to thrust back and forth, placing one arm against the door and the other wrapped around my chest and back. My hands move back and forth across his chest, back, and neck. All too soon, we both dissolve in an explosion of colors. Before I slip into a state of unconsciousness, Alex turns us around and places us on the bed.

"I am nowhere near done with you yet, Mallory," he states as he flashes a cocky grin and pulls me on top of him. Positioning me above him, he juts his hips upward as he pushes me down by my hips. My hands stretch toward Alex's chest and I rest them there with my arms extended. I begin to rock against him, using his chest as to control my movements and soon Alex removes his hands from my waist giving me the go ahead to continue the movements at my pace. His hands travel upward to massage my breasts and as he pinches each of my nipples, I tilt my head back and release a deep and husky moan. Needing to intensify the connection, Alex soon begins to thrust upward again, meeting my pace.

"I'm close," he says through gritted teeth.
I nod my head knowing that I am not far behind him.

As we both come simultaneously, my body topples ungracefully onto Alex's chest. Exhausted from our fiery lovemaking, we lay in a heap of sweaty limbs on the bed for a few moments.

Alex turns us over so we are facing each other and he lets his fingers brush through my hair as I lie on my pillow with my eyes closed.

"Would you like to take bath, love?"

With my eyes still shut, I respond to him in a whisper, "A bath sounds fantastic."

He removes himself from the bed and goes to turn on the water in the adjoining bathroom. Seconds later, I open my eyes to him lifting me from the bed in his arms. He carries me to the bathtub and sits us both in the water. I snuggle into his chest as he takes handfuls of warm water and pours them over my shoulders.

"That feels good," I moan and he turns his head to the top of my hair.

"Mallory, would you like to go to the winery this weekend; the one that made the plum wine?" Alex inquires.

Excited at the thought of another trip, I wake from my relaxed state and exclaim, "That sounds amazing. I've never been to a winery. How far away is it?"

"Well it is a few thousand miles away in California. I need to call and make sure they will be home, but we can take my plane Friday night."

"As long as they are okay with us coming on such short notice, I would love to go. I've never been to California either."
"The wine country is breath taking."

Agreeing on the trip, we relax back in comfortable silence and I soon find myself on the verge of slumber.

"Mallory?" he says glancing down at me with a shy smile crossing his face. "Come love, let's go to bed, I've worked you hard today."

As we both make to stand in the tub, I stumble bit seeming to need his help. He wraps me in a warm fluffy towel and carries me back to the bed. As soon as Alex tucks me against his side, I fall asleep.

I can barely make out Alex's faint voice whisper, "Goodnight, beautiful girl."

*   *   *

During the week, Alex and I are busy rushing from early trips to the gym and late-night client meetings that we don't get to spend much time together. I cherish the nights when I'm able to fall asleep against him; using the steady beat of his heart to help me drift off to sleep. On Friday morning, Alex takes me into work so that Gregory can usher us directly to the plane at 5:00pm. As I sit in his car, he tells me about the winery we are going to visit this weekend.

"Alex, how did you all meet?" I ask interested.

"Oh, well, they are friends of the family. I believe they hoped Samantha and I would end up together, but we are more the sibling type. Her husband Will is perfect for her."

"Oh, so they are close in age to us?"

"Yes, they are only thirty-one. She met Will when she was twenty-four traveling like Abi is doing now. They eloped quickly and have been together in California since. Her parents disowned her when she married him, so I'm the closest thing to family she has now."

"That's terrible. Why would her parents disown her?"

"Her family and mine have some strict rules for their first born, especially concerning marriage."

"Well, that's ridiculous. No one should be rejected from their family because of who they decide to love and marry."

This conversation is starting to get me worked up. I can feel the bits of anger welling up inside of me.

"I agree with you, Mallory. Calm down. She is happy with how things are, but sometimes cultures have different views on marriage and love. Sometimes, we don't get a choice on who we marry or we can't marry the person we are in love with."

I sit and ponder what Alex has said during the remainder of our journey to my office. Is this why he is nixing the option of a long-distance relationship? I know he only mentioned first-born children, but has Alex's family already chosen his wife? His mother has been hounding on him to get married, or so Abi says. Perhaps she made the choice for him. That notion leaves me crestfallen. We only have two more weeks together before he leaves me for someone else, possibly a wife. I notice we are at the entrance to my office building and I hurriedly exit the car before Alex has a chance to get out and open the car door for me.

Lowering his window, he calls out to me, "Mallory, are you ok?"

"Yes, I'm fine, sir," I reply in a sharp curt tone.

In actuality, I feel devastated by our conversation in the car. His words break my heart. To him, I am only a temporary escape until August arrives. Racing away from the car, I am barely able to keep steady in my heels and I step into the elevator to catch my breath. I can vaguely make out my expression through the reflection on the stainless-steel walls and I detect a small tear that has escaped from my eye. I swipe at it furiously wanting to erase the emotional conversation from the morning.

Deciding not to make small talk this morning with the other staff, I walk straight to my office and shut the door. I take off my suit jacket and lay it across the couch and then I get started on some of my new campaigns.

Steven and Annie join me for lunch and I listen to their conversation, participating only when I am prompted with a question. Steven pulls me aside once we arrive on our floor after lunch.

"Are you ok, Mallory?"

I sigh at his question, "Yea, I'm fine. I just had a rough morning."

"I understand. Try to get some rest this weekend. You have any plans?"

"Alex is taking me to a winery his friend owns."

"Well, that sounds like a boat load of fun. I love wine tastings. Where is it at?"

I hesitate and then crack a small smile, "California."

"California? Damn, that boy sure knows how to show a lady a good time."

"Yes, sir. He is quite the charmer."

"Well, next time he decides to take you to some Caribbean island, make it a work trip and bring me."

"I'll be sure to mention that. Have a good weekend, Steven."

"Thanks, Mallory. Enjoy yours."

At my desk, I rummage through my files in a distracted manner and decide to take a gander at my phone. I had expected a few missed calls, but I only find one message from Alex. He sent the message three hours ago.

> **Alex: I'm sorry, sweetheart. I didn't mean for my words to upset you.**
> **Mallory: I'm sorry too, Alex. I shouldn't have taken what you said to heart.**

**Alex: It's ok, love. Everyone deserves their
   happily ever after right?**
Mallory: Yes, even you, Alex.
**Alex: If only. Unfortunately, it may be too late
   for mine.**

I'm not sure how to respond to his last message. Is
he referring to me, Vanessa, or someone else all together?
I find myself considering any and all possibilities of
Alex's potential love life for the remainder of the
afternoon. By the time I realize that it is 5:00pm, I am
exhausted. Alex had asked me to be ready to go at 5:00
pm when Gregory picks me up, so I rush down the
stairwell of the building, opting not to wait on the
elevator, and find that Gregory hasn't arrived yet.

I sit on the bench outside of the building and ten
minutes later Gregory pulls the car up to the entrance.

Apologizing he says, "I'm sorry that I am late, Ms.
Winston. I had some business to settle before I could
escort you to the airport."

"Is everything ok? Where is Alex?"

"Everything is fine now, Ms. Winston. I dropped
Alex off at the airport earlier this afternoon so that he
could do the check off on his plane."

"His plane?"

"Yes, miss. Mr. Stone arrived in his personal jet. I
believe he has someone piloting it for you this weekend,
if I am not mistaken. Are you ready to leave, miss?"

"Oh, yes, sorry. I've had a rough day."

"I'm sorry. I am sure you will have a marvelous
weekend. Mr. and Mrs. James are delightful."

Gregory assists me into the back seat of the limousine and walks around to climb into the driver seat. Once the car begins, my eyelids start to droop. Before we have made it to the interstate, I have fallen asleep, lying across the bench seat.

Chapter Eighteen

STARTLED AWAKE BY A hand on my shoulder, I look up to find Gregory and Alex standing beside the open car door.

"Good evening, love," Alex says behind a small grin.

"Oh, my goodness, I must have been worn out."

"Indeed. Are you ready to go, Mallory?"

"I am. Thank you."

Alex extends his hand and I place mine in its grasp. The moment I step out of the car, I can see a flash of light off in the distance. Immediately, Gregory drops our bags and runs towards the area where the flash occurred. Alex tightens his grasp on my hand and tows me behind him speedily towards the jets stairs.

"Alex, what was that?" I ask as he continues to tighten his hand and pull me behind him.

"It's nothing," he answers. "Gregory will take care of it."

With his tone, I know that this topic isn't up for discussion. Once we reach the top of the plane's stairwell, Alex guides me to a soft, cream, leather couch.

"Hey, Alex? In case I forget," I express shyly, "I wanted to thank you for this weekend. I am really excited."

His expression softens and a shy smile spreads across his mouth before replying, "I am delighted to be taking you, angel. I think you'll enjoy their property."

"I'm sure it is beautiful. I've always heard stories about the rolling hills in Napa Valley."

Gregory joins us on the plane, but only to drop off our bags and out of the corner of my eye I notice him shake his head.

Alex responds by saying, "You know who it was; take care of it while I'm gone."

"Yes, sir."

Swiftly exiting, Alex's head of security departs from the plane and a steward comes out of the cabin to greet us. He walks to the stairwell and presses a button to secure the door hatch.

"Mr. Stone, Ms. Winston, my name is Chris. We will be taking off shortly. If you wouldn't mind, please move to the passenger seats and secure your seat belts. Once we hit proper altitude, I will serve you your meal. Is there anything I can get you before we take off?"

"No, thank you, Chris. Please, ask the pilot to proceed."

Moving to the passenger seats, Alex reaches over to hook my seat belt, intertwining our hands once he is finished. The plane begins to taxi and before I know it, we are up in the air headed for California.

"Alex, your plane is beautiful," I declare glancing around the cabin.

"Thank you. There are actually two bedrooms on this plane. One room has two queen sized beds in it, but the other is the master with a large king-sized bed and an attached bathroom. I like to use this jet when my drivers need to travel. It is sort of a benefit for being on my formula one team."

"Wow, you're an amazing boss. This airplane is incredible."

"I'll show you around once we finish dinner. I have plans for dessert," he says with a wink.

Before I have a chance to speak up, the steward exits from the front of the plane carrying two trays. He presses a button on the wall and a table maneuvers down from the wall in front of our seats. Glaring at Alex in awe, he closes my mouth with the tap of his finger on my chin.

Collecting our attention, the steward speaks up, "Mr. Stone, tonight we have filet mignon cooked medium along with twice baked potatoes and sautéed vegetables. Can I bring you anything to drink?"

I stare down at my tray; the meal looks better than any I have had in restaurants.

"Holy cow, this is our dinner? It looks fantastic," I say to no one in particular.

Answering through a chuckle Alex says, "Yes, it is. Chris, we will both have a glass of Malbec."

"Yes, sir."

Chris returns moments later with our glasses of wine and we dig into our meal. The steak melts in my mouth and the potato is divine. Sooner than I expected, I have cleared my plate and Chris clears our trays.

"May I offer you any dessert?" Chris asks.
I know Alex wanted the bedroom for dessert, but my sweet tooth is beckoning. Looking in his direction, I pout hoping he will indulge me.

Alex peeks at me and chuckles speaking to Chris, "Ms. Winston will have a crème brulé with a side of chocolate mousse and I will have a slice of key lime pie, please."

Reaching over I place both hands on Alex's face pull him into a hard peck.

"Thank you," I say with a childlike smile.

Chris brings us our requested desserts and heads back towards his personal cabin. After I take a bite of combined custard and mousse I disintegrate into the chair.

"Holy crap, this is delicious. Would you like some?" I ask offering him a forkful of custard and mousse.

Wrapping his luscious lips around the fork he releases a low moan before uttering, "Divine."
We both finish our desserts and lounge back in our seats.

Breaking our silence Alex asks, "So, Ms. Winston, are we better now?"

Knowing he is referring to our conversation this morning I respond, "Yes, Alex. I know you're right. I just can't imagine having to choose between doing something

for your parents because it's the right thing to do for your
family or following your heart for the one you love."

Alex stands from his seat and helps me out of
mine. Draping his arm over my shoulders, he places a
kiss on my head and leads me towards the back of the
cabin.

As we walk, I hear Alex mumble, "Not all of us
get a happy ever after, princess."

Pointing out the common bathroom and the guest
suite on the plane, he guides me to the master suite.

"We should be arriving around 11:00pm so we
don't need to use it this time," he proclaims, "but we can
stay and relax if you'd like."

"That would be lovely."

Turning towards me, he gently brushes the hair
off my face and then removes my blouse and tosses it
onto the chair in the corner. His fingers trail back and
forth along the skin of my neck and collarbone.

"Your skin is so soft, so delicate," he whispers as
he bends to place faint kisses along the path his fingers
made.

He moves to the other side of my neck to place
little bites along the identical path. My arms reach out to
rest my hands along his hips and I whimper as I feel his
tongue begin to lick after each nip of my neck.

"Alex, I need you," I moan noticing my voice has
a husky undertone.

He reaches down and unzips my pants, pushing
them down off my hips so that they pool on the floor. He
quickly follows this by removing my shirt next. As I
stand in the bra and panties, Alex steps back to remove

his shirt and jeans. My breath quickens as he stands in all his glory and my skin prickles as I feel his glaring eyes taking in my naked body.

I reach my fingertips out and trace the definitions of his body, my fingers brushing against every crevice and muscle. As my hand makes contact with the waistband of Alex's boxer briefs, he grabs a hold of my wrist, stopping my movement, and pulls my hand up to his mouth to kiss my palm. Gently, he places my hand over his heart and pulls my head in for a kiss. The kiss starts slow, with little nips along my bottom lip, and then he massages his tongue against my own. Our bodies begin to heat and the kiss starts to intensify.

Before I have time to comprehend that I am moving, Alex has walked me towards the foot of the bed. He lifts me onto the soft duvet and then crawls on top of me, kissing randomly over my body. Reaching my mouth, he continues the kiss with the same intensity where we left off. As he grinds his large erection into my pelvis, I groan into his mouth. Alex quickly removes his boxer briefs and makes work on the front clasp of my bra as I swiftly work my panties down my legs. He grunts between kisses and then inserts his erection into my core, pounding into my body. As I rock back against his movements, I can feel my climax coming close. When Alex rolls his hips, coming in contact with my swollen nub, I scream out and I can feel my body begin to shake.

Knowing I am close Alex groans, "Come baby," and I release my energy.

Alex continues to thrust hard before he meets his own release, working to drain the entire climax from our systems. Wrapped up in each other, Alex and I lay together across the bed as he mindlessly trails his fingers over my hipbone. While I tangle my fingers in his hair, I consider that I want to tell him that I love him, but instead I bite my tongue and hold back.

Around 11:00 pm that evening, I can feel the plane begin to slowly drop altitude. Alex and I pull on our clothes and make our way back out to the main cabin. Chris, the steward, comes to meet us in the main cabin stating.

"Mr. Stone, we will begin our descent shortly. Please secure yourselves in the passenger seats."

"Thank you, Chris."

Once the plane has stopped, Alex helps me to exit the aircraft. Waiting for us at the bottom of the stairs is an older man with a town car.

"Sir, I am here to escort you and Ms. Winston to the James' property. If you would like to get settled into the vehicle, I will gather your belongings from the plane." Alex nods at the driver and then helps me get into the car.

Unfortunately, it is dark so I am unable to see many of my surroundings, but as we make our way up a few steep hills I can see row after row of grape vines; miles of them. Our driver stops and types in a code on a box, opening the gates; we are escorted into the property. We stop at the entrance of the main building and a young man and woman greet us. I assume they are Will and Samantha James.

As soon as Alex exits the car, Samantha engulfs him in a hug. I make my way out of the vehicle on my own and in enough time to see Samantha place a very passionate kiss on Alex's mouth. He said they weren't involved, but I am finding that a bit difficult to believe as I witness her fervor. Glancing over to where Will stands, I can see his hands are in tight fists. Apparently, he was unaware of their relationship as well. While Alex and Samantha are busy catching up, mainly her continuing to pull Alex into hugs and kisses, I walk over to Will to introduce myself.

"Hi, I'm Mallory. You must be Will," I say.

"That would be me it's nice to meet you, Mallory." As he shakes my hand, we both turn to look at Samantha and Alex where they both seem to be lost in each other at the moment.

I can feel the spurts of jealousy taking over my body and I am relieved when Will asks, "Would you like to come inside? I can show you to your room. Which by the looks of it, you may want to keep to yourself?"

"You're probably right. He said they were more like siblings, but I don't act like that with my brothers. Maybe it's a European thing."

We walk into his lovely home making small talk as he points out the living room and powder room. He grabs the small overnight bag from my hands and escorts me to a quaint room at the end of a long hallway.

"I had planned to have you and Alex stay in a room on the other end of the hall," he announces, "but I figured you may like this room for the night." In the room is a small double bed, just big enough for one person. "There is a bathroom attached so you won't need to leave during the night unless you want to. I, myself, am a bit furious at my wife. Of course, I should have guessed this would happen. She's been in love with him since they were little, but she swore he didn't feel the same."

I tuck my hands into my pockets and look around the room speaking softly, "I'm sure they are catching up, it has been a while. But thank you for letting me stay here tonight, it would be a bit awkward to sleep with Alex after witnessing that."

"I'm sorry, Mallory. You seem like a sweet girl, but be careful." I cock my head at his words and he continues, "Holler if you need anything. My bedroom is two doors down on the left. See you in the morning."

"Good night, Will."

Stepping into the bathroom, I wash my face and stare at my green eyes in the mirror. My emotions are all over the place, but I am mostly furious and hurt. Without even considering the make out session, I am miffed that Alex didn't even introduce me. We haven't been here for thirty minutes and I am already cast aside. Turning off the light to the bathroom, I lock the bedroom door and crawl into the beckoning bed. It is soft and clean, reminding me of home and I curl up into a ball letting the few tears of rejection skim along my cheeks. If it was possible for me to leave, I would, but then I think of Will. How heart breaking to see your wife run to the arms of another man. Another man that you were told had no history with your wife. I'll suck up my jealousy and pride for Will, because he doesn't deserve to witness this alone.

As tired as I am, sleep escapes me and I find myself tossing and turning between the sheets the remainder of the night. At some point during my restless slumber, I hear Alex and Will talking in the hall. I glance at my phone and see that it is 3:00am.

I hear Alex shout, "Why isn't Mallory in my room?"

"Because I put her in a different room. She doesn't need to have you around her right now."

"What the bloody hell does that mean? I brought her here. She is my girlfriend."

"Yea, what an amazing boyfriend you are; making out with another man's wife while your girlfriend and the husband look on. You didn't even take a breath to introduce her. That makes you a shitty friend and a shitty boyfriend."

"We weren't making out, that's just how we are."

"Really, what do you call it? Mallory said that you told her that you and Samantha were like siblings. I've only met you a handful of times and I knew that wasn't the case. You should have told her that you both were in love with each other. I wish someone would have told me, I wouldn't have married her."

"What the fuck, I don't love her like that."

"You could have fooled me, my friend. If you're smart you will let Mallory cool off. She's too nice to be with a dirt bag like you anyway. About time she saw your true colors."

"Will, what the hell? I don't love Samantha and I wasn't making out with her. If you saw anything, I was only standing there. I have no control over what your wife does. What do you have against me?"

"How about I tell you when the divorce is finalized? I think you'll get a real kick out of it."

"Divorce?"

"Oh yea, didn't she tell you during one of your weekly phone chats? We've been legally separated for three months. I am making her stay in the guest house since the winery was mine before the marriage."

"Shit. I should go talk to Sam. She should have told me."

"Alex, if I were you I would stay here tonight with a locked door. One, because I don't trust her to stay out of your room and two, because Mallory is a good girl that you don't deserve. I'm willing to play nice for Mallory's sake, since you brought her into this mess, but let me give you a piece of advice, figure out if you really don't love Samantha or Mallory. Neither of them needs to be lead on. I'm hoping after this mess we can remain friends, but knowing the things I do, I find it doubtful."

"Christ, what the hell happened?"

"Like I said, we'll discuss it after the divorce if finalized. I suggest you go to your room and figure things out. If you're not here in the morning, I'll let Mallory know what you decided. Who knows, maybe she'll move out here with me after this is over."

I can hear anger lace Alex's voice.

"You stay the hell away from her you understand? Regardless of what happens with you, Samantha, and me, Mallory is mine, always."

Will's voice is much fainter, like he is walking away.

"Interesting Alex, you sure you don't love Mallory either? Sleep well and lock that door."

RENEE HARLESS

I lie on my back and replay Will and Alex's words through my head. So Will thinks that Samantha and Alex are in love, but that Alex loves me as well and Alex denies loving either of us. What interests me the most is that Will and Samantha are getting a divorce. I wonder if she will be moving back to England to marry Alex. Closing my eyes, I picture Alex standing at the altar as a white dressed woman walks down the aisle. In the past, I had pictured my face when he lifts the veil, but this time I see the image of Samantha. A cry escapes from my throat and my body begins to shake in sobs. During my tears, I can hear a soft knock at the door and Alex calling my name in question. I continue my crying fit as he turns from my door and heads to his room, I hope.

During some portion of the early morning, I catch a few hours of sleep. When I finally open my eyes, I see that it is a golden sunny morning in California. Slumping into the bathroom, I splash water onto my face hoping to mask my bloodshot eyes. Following a quick shower, I put on a bright yellow sundress hoping that it will improve my melancholy mood. As a side thought, I make sure to leave my collar on the dresser. Walking downstairs, I note the eerie silence of the home and as I find my way to the kitchen, I see Will standing over the stove cooking an omelet. In the attached dining room, I catch a glimpse of Samantha and Alex sitting at the large table. She is leaned into him, attentively listening to his every word and her face shows every glowing sign of being in love. I recognize the expression because it shadows my own.

"Good morning, Will," I say strolling further into the kitchen.

"Hey, Mallory. I thought it might be a while until we saw you. What can I get you for breakfast?"

As a horrible sounding grumble reverberates in my stomach, I chuckle.

"An omelet with cheese, spinach, and mushrooms if you have any left."

"Certainly. It'll be ready in a minute."

At that moment, Alex looks up and smiles, noticing my arrival. I see Samantha's face turn from love to anger and hurt.

Attempting to rush out of his chair Alex asks, "Mallory, can we talk?"

But before he gets the chance to unseat himself completely from his chair I answer in a harsh tone, "No."

"What?"

"No."

When I sit down at the breakfast bar in the kitchen, Will passes over my omelet.

"Thanks, Will," I say sending him a soft but sad smile and he returns a similar one as he replies,

"Anytime, beautiful."

Just as I am finishing my breakfast, Alex and Samantha stroll into the kitchen. After last night, I would have expected his arm to be draped over her shoulder or their hands laced together. Instead, Alex comes to stand beside where I am sitting and Samantha joins him.

He announces, "Mallory, may I introduce you to Samantha?"

"That's ok there is no need for an introduction."

I can see anger flash across Alex's face, but it quickly diminishes and I have no need to glance in Samantha's direction.

"Mallory, don't be rude."

Jumping from my chair, I stand in Alex's face. He will not get submissive Mallory. In this very moment, he will be seeing Senior Executive Mallory, the Mallory that is tired of being in everyone's shadow, doing what is expected, and swallowing her tongue.

"Rude? I'm sorry, rude was when you jumped into the arms of a married woman the minute our car arrived and allowed her to shove her tongue down your throat. Rude, was when you didn't even have the decency to introduce me to your so-called friend and her husband. Rude, was when Will had to escort me to a different bedroom because we were unsure of when you would be returning and whom with. So, Alex, don't for a second consider my lack of needing an introduction to Samantha as rude."

Standing there in silence, I can almost see a hint of amazement in Alex's eyes.

Will begins a small clap breaking me of my stare.

"Well said, Mallory," the appreciative husband proclaims. "Instead, how about I introduce you to my soon to be ex-wife? Samantha, this is Mallory. Without a doubt, Mallory is one of the most patient and kind-hearted people I have had the pleasure to meet. Only someone of her caliber would be able to stay the night and come down here in the morning to face you."

I can see Samantha's eyes begin to well up and my heart hurts for her a bit. I know what it's like to love someone and not have them love you in return. Tucking away my pride and jealousy in my pocket, I extend my hand to shake hers.

"Samantha, it's nice to meet you," I say in the most genuine voice I can manage.

In a naturally sexy and husky voice Samantha replies, "Likewise, Mallory, I've heard a great deal about you. Even from the first night at the bar."

Astonished, I glance in Alex's direction as a sheepish grin crosses his face and he shrugs his shoulders. Looking back, I examine Samantha. She is a tall woman, about five-foot-eleven and willowy with long, straight, blonde hair and dark brown eyes. She isn't your typical beauty, but I can see why men would be attracted to her, if not only for her voice.

Breaking me of my interest in her appearance she continues, "Mallory, I'd like to apologize for my actions yesterday."

My body tenses up again remembering their kissing at our arrival.

A bit harsher than I intended I respond, "I don't care to hear an apology, nor do I condone you giving one. You were well aware of your actions and, if I'm not mistaken, they were premeditated. What I cannot understand is why a woman married for five or so years would need to cheat in front of her husband with a lifelong long friend that is accompanied by his girlfriend? Cheating is wrong and disgusting, period. I do, instead, accept your need to feel regretful of your actions."

Turning in Alex's direction I add, "As for you, Alex, I am not willing to accept an apology or remorsefulness of your actions. You may not have been the one to initiate anything, but you didn't stop them from continuing either. That makes you equally at fault." As Alex makes to grab my hand, I snatch it away quickly snarling, "Don't. We don't share, remember?"

Sorrow and pain rack my body at my dismissal of Alex and I turn around to face Will so that Alex cannot see me cry.

Above a whisper I say, "Will, I am going to walk around outside. I called a cab earlier; will you please let me know when it arrives?"

"Sure thing, beautiful," he says mournfully as I write down my cell number.

With grace, I walk towards the back of the house en route for the French doors, planning to explore the flower garden I saw from my bedroom window. Above the whoosh of my sandals on the floor, I can hear Will speaking to Alex, "You sure screwed this up buddy."

Through each row of flowers that are cascading like a canopy around me, I totter in the garden. The flowers are designed in a maze and I slowly find my way to the center. The dew on the flowers call my attention and I rest on a cold bench, glancing through the canopy towards the sky. I hear the crackle of footsteps behind me on the pebbled path and, thinking that it is Will, I turn my body around. Instead of joy, I am stunned to find Samantha walking towards me.

"Mallory, can I speak with you for a moment?" the tall blonde asks.

Ruthlessly I answer, "I prefer you didn't, but seeing that this is still your home, I can't stop you."

She continues to walk along the pebbles and sits on the damp bench across from me.

"You were right, earlier," she begins. "I'm not truly sorry for what I did yesterday, but yes, I do regret it. I have been in love with Alex since we were children and our parents had always planned on us getting married, but it seemed like once our parents decided that was what should happen, Alex decided against it. I know that we have an odd relationship and I think at some point he may have loved me, but he doesn't feel that way any longer."

Unfazed by her story I ask, "Why are you telling me this?"

"Because I took advantage of his friendship yesterday; a friendship that means the world to me. This closeness has ruined my marriage and I won't let it ruin your relationship with Alex. He told me about your affair; that you two agreed to be together for a couple more weeks, but you're special to him and after yesterday I realized that. He was truly disconsolate after having a conversation with Will last night. Will came to me not long after and said that Alex looked like a lost boy when he realized you had locked him out of your room. Alex told me this morning that he heard you crying. I am sorry for causing you pain, Mallory," she emphasizes. "Will was right when he said you are a sweet girl; you don't deserve this. Please talk to Alex. If I only had two weeks with him, I'd take it."

"I'm sure you would, except he doesn't want me either. So what difference would it make?"

Considering what I've said she counters, "I think Alex may surprise you if you give him a chance."

With that final comment, she removes herself from the bench and walks out of the labyrinth of flowers. I try to sift through her words searching for something to help my situation with Alex, but I find nothing. I ask myself, *If I was special to him, he would have pushed her away or come to me right after it happened, right?*

Attempting to fill my mind with something beautiful, I pull out my phone and begin to take close up pictures of the various flowers in the garden. This miniscule task helps to keep my mind off Alex as I continue to snap photos of the garden full of lilacs, roses, carnations, and hydrangeas, all in full bloom.

As I begin to admire the pictures I have taken, I hear Alex's tormented voice, "May I join you?"

I don't respond, but shrug my shoulders showing my indifference. Instead of sitting down on the cool bench across the way, Alex joins me on the bench I am currently occupying. He runs his hands through his hair various times, as a nervous gesture, and leans his forearms against his knees, turning his head in my direction.

"Mallory, please talk to me," he pronounces in anguish.

Gazing at him I ask one word filled with a thousand questions, "Why?"

He looks at me with a confused expression reacting, "Why, what?"

Huffing out a breath I turn my body to face him directly as anger begins to boil in my veins again.

"Why?" I question. "Why didn't you push her away? Why did you rush to her side when we arrived? Why did you only realize your mistake when you spoke with Will last night? Why didn't you tell me the real reason you wanted to come here? And why won't tell me what you're hiding from me?"

With a sigh he sits up to face me.

"That's a lot of whys," he says with an attempt at humor, but doing nothing to break my shell of anger. Continuing to glare in his direction, I wait for my answers. Sensing my annoyance Alex begins, "Mallory, I am beyond sorry for my actions. You are right that I am just as a fault, though I didn't initiate the transgression. I think I was too caught up in seeing Samantha after all these years that I was unaware of how you or Will would perceive things." As red continues to burn in my eyes Alex adds, "I didn't know that she had planned to kiss me like that, Mallory; you have to know that. If I had known she was still in love with me, I wouldn't have brought you here. You must know that I would never have purposely treated you like that." Noticing the tears that begin to fall down from my eyes, torment takes hold of Alex's voice as he says, "I want so badly to make this right, Mallory. We only have two short weeks left before I return to England and I want to spend those with you." Squaring my shoulders, I take a chance and decide I want all of my questions answered.

"Will she go back to England once her divorce is finalized? I'm sure your families will be pleased with that. You get the love of your life and she gets hers, you both get to please your families, and you get to keep whatever secret it is you are keeping from me. Happy day for everyone."

Pathetically trying to lighten my mood Alex replies, "Mallory, no. I have no intention of returning to England with Samantha. If I brought anyone home with me, it would be you, sweetheart. Besides, you are currently my mother's first choice."

His second attempt at humor causes me to crack a tiny smile as I say, "That is not something to joke about, Alex. I won't hesitate to call your mother and tell her what you said."

"Who said I was joking? My mother loves you."

"She has only spoken to me once."

"That's all it took, darling." Reaching across, Alex tentatively places his hand over mine and whispers, "I am truly sorry for everything that I have done to cause you to hurt, Mallory. It killed me to hear you sobbing last night and to see you so disappointed this morning, knowing that I was the cause."

He gently rubs small circles onto the back of my hand and I am torn at the decision I need to make. Either I stay and trust Alex for the next two weeks or I turn my back on what we have built in the past month and half.

Our silence is broken by my cell phone ringing and I peer down to see Will's number flashing across my screen.

Answering the call, I ask, "Hi, Will. Is the taxi here?"

"Yep."

"Ok I will be up front shortly."

Ending the call, I turn in Alex's direction and softly murmur, "My taxi is here, Alex."

Tugging me towards him he speaks to me with urgency, "Mallory, please. Stay with me. We don't have to stay here, we can go get a room in town. Please, just don't go. Not yet."

With a glimpse into his eyes, I find love and sincerity and as I stand from the bench, I make my decision. I tug my hand from Alex's and he places his in his lap.

Asking him to follow me I command, "Alex, come with me."

He doesn't respond and his body looks as if it has shut down. He sits robotically, blending into the frigid and dew stained bench. This moment reminds me of the time in his home he turned off all emotion.

"Alex?" I ask then I repeat his name again. When he doesn't respond again I tentatively walk out of the garden towards the front of the house.

The taxi driver is waiting with Will and when I arrive to the front of the property, they both turn in my direction.

"Will, I'm going to stay," I express as he stares at me shocked, "but I'd like to stay at another place; maybe a hotel in town. I just feel uncomfortable staying here. Do you think you could drive me into town later?"
I hand the driver some cash for his trouble and turn back to Will as the driver leaves.

Speaking up Will says, "That man is one lucky son-of-a-bitch I tell you."

I chuckle, "That's not very nice. I've spoken to his mom and she seems lovely."

Joining in my laughter, we walk back into the house and I head toward the kitchen with the plans to make a fruit salad and prepare a picnic. I grab a bowl of fruit from the fridge and toss a blanket from the back of a love seat over my arm.

Outside, I find Alex and Samantha in a heated discussion so I walk slowly without the intention to interrupt, but once I get close they both notice that they have a spectator.

Rushing towards me Alex wraps me in his arms exclaiming, "Mallory, you're still here? I thought you left." Though the electricity of being wrapped in Alex's arms overwhelms me, I am aware of Samantha sneaking off to the side to head back to the house.

Snapping back from my gaze, I say to Alex, "I wasn't ready to leave you yet, Alex. Come with me." Taking the directions Will gave me, we head towards the end of the property between a few small hills. I was told that there was a small beach and lake on the property with a cabana. Walking in silence towards the lake, our hands are intertwined and I can feel the sparks igniting between us, even through the turmoil of our lives, our bodies still crave each other.

We reach the top of one of the hills as the lake and cabana come into view and I find myself in a peaceful state of mind due to the scenery and exercise.

"We're here, Alex," I sigh.

"This is wonderful, Mallory. Thank you, for bringing me here."

"I figured we could use some time away from everything. Will has agreed to take us into town for a hotel when we return."

Stepping into the cabana, I lay the blanket onto the hard-wooden floor and sit down opening the bag full of grapes.

Gesturing to the blanket, I call out, "Come join me, Alex."

He finally makes his way over to where I sit and saddles up close to my body. Offering him some fruit, he declines and instead he grabs a piece of cloth used to tie back the cabana wall, holding it out to me. My eyebrows furrow in confusion as he moves slowly towards me, wrapping the cloth over my eyes as a make shift blindfold.

He takes the grapes from my hands as the deep silkiness of his voice commands, "Lay back, Mallory."

Twisting my body to lie back onto the blanket, I feel pillows behind my head create a lounge in the cabana; Alex must have placed those there. Sweetly, he begins to feed me small pieces of fruit. Each piece exploding in flavor as it reaches my tongue and soon Alex begins to feed me the fruit using his mouth. Our lips slightly brush against each other and I lose my breath each moment.

Offering me another morsel, I shake my head that I am finished and I feel Alex press his wet fingers onto my lips. I take a hold of his hand and suck each finger into my mouth licking off all the excess juice from the fruit.

Sliding his hand around to the back of my neck, he presses a demanding kiss on my lips. Throughout all of the anger I held towards him yesterday and this morning, I never lost my desire for him. Urgently meeting his kiss with an equal need from my body, I moan into his mouth and he lays us both onto the blanket, removing the pillows. Alex lets his hand travel up my thigh and underneath my dress, while our tongues dance against each other as he slides a finger underneath my panties. I whimper into his mouth when he glides along my swollen nub and then when he inserts two fingers into my wet center, my hips pulse back and forth. Quickly removing his hand, he reaches up to eliminate the blindfold before brushing the back of his knuckles against my cheek.

"You are a remarkable woman, Ms. Winston," he murmurs. "I am lucky to have you."

As I smile at his admission, he tangles his fingers in my hair then tilts my head towards him to places another series of kisses against my lips.

Between each peck Alex proclaims, "You.Mean.The.World.You.Are.Everything.To.Me." It takes me a minute to piece it all together, but once I understand his declaration I return his smoldering kiss. Unexpectedly he grabs both of my wrists and positions them above my head, wrapping my wrists together in a make shift restraint with the cloth.

"Keep your hands above you, Ms. Winston. We don't have much time," he commands.

"Yes, sir," I reply.

Alex then pushes the hem of my dress up to my waist and rips down my panties pronouncing, "You're soaking wet already, darling."

As he glides his two fingers back into my entrance, he crooks his finger to shoot sparks towards the fire burning in my belly. Wanting more, Alex pulls back and unbuttons his jeans, tugging them down to his knees along with his boxers. Both of my knees are positioned over each of his elbows and he enters me quickly. After a few hard thrusts, Alex grabs a discarded pillow and places it under my hips. When he slides his erection into me again, I groan with longing. His cock is so deep inside me this way.

I scream, "Alex, please. Oh God."
My body hurriedly pushes toward its release.

"Come, beautiful," he commands and it drives my body over the edge towards its climax. Alex reaches his shortly after.
On the hardened floor, we lie against each other catching our breath and I pull my restrained arms over Alex's neck. Once we have both collected ourselves Alex leans up and gazes deep into my eyes.

"Thank you"

Understanding his thanks, I reply truthfully, "You are worth it."

Back at the house Will takes us to one of the luxury hotels in town and pays for our room, which Alex fights against. We spend the remainder of the afternoon and evening exploring the small town, walking in and out of trinket shops and local markets holding hands and looking very much in love, or so the older shop keepers continue telling us.

*   *   *

As we set to depart this morning, Samantha gives me an awkward hug, whispering in my ear to take care of him. I'm not quite sure what she intended by that comment. Will offers to let me visit whenever I feel like getting away and I agree wholeheartedly as he was a magnificent host and I would love the opportunity to explore the vineyard.

Our flight back to Baltimore seems longer, though Alex explains that it is due to the time change. Once we exit the plane, Alex and I decide to forget about the incident with Samantha. He is right that it was out of his control, but agrees that he should have stopped it. Since leaving the vineyard, Alex has been extremely attentive to make up for his wrongdoing.

Arriving at his home, both exhausted from the long fight, we head straight to the bedroom. Peeling each other out of our clothes, we lie in bed facing each other sneaking kisses in-between our conversation. We both fall asleep quickly after Alex pulls me into his side, my head resting on his chest, my hand across his heart.

*   *   *

Alex and I return to work and spend the next two weeks enjoying each other's company. As each day passes, I can't deny that I have fallen so hard and so irrevocably in love with Alex; I know his leaving will be torture to my heart. He has taught me more about myself in the two months of us being together, than the world has in my twenty-nine, almost thirty years of life. Alex has shown me a new side of my sexuality and I thrive on being at his command. And, although I still am his submissive, he has learned to treat me as his equal; even asking if I am ok proceeding with certain scenes. Unsure of how I will be able to return to a normal vanilla relationship after our affair, I am tempted to stay alone. I could pursue another BDSM relationship, and Alex has pointed out locations I can frequent to find another master, but it would be uncomfortable submitting to anyone other than him.

He continues to treat me like a princess during our time together and on our last evening, Alex escorts me from work that Tuesday. He looks remarkable in his tailored suit, hugging his body like second skin.

"I have a special evening planned for us tonight, Mallory," he announces.

Behind a choked-up voice I say, "Alex, thank you, but we don't need to do anything special. I just want to be with you before you leave."

"I know, darling, but I want to do this for you."

He ushers me towards a waiting limo and waits for me to slide into the seat before getting in himself.

Lying across the seat in front of us is a garment bag and, after noticing my questioning look, Alex states, "I have an outfit chosen for you this evening. When we arrive at our location you may put it on."

Smiling at his command I answer, "Yes, sir."

Across the seat, he intertwines our hands as we make our way to his surprise.

We arrive thirty minutes later to a marina of luxurious boats. Gregory opens our door and helps me out after Alex has exited.

"Mallory, please go change in the marina club house across the way," he says. "Gregory will wait for you and escort you the rest of the way."

I reach up on the tips of my toes and kiss him on the cheek responding, "Thank you, sir."

Turning on his heel, he walks down the dock and Gregory ushers me to a room so that I can change, leaving me at the entrance.

Cautiously, I step into a small room and hang the garment bag on the hook attached to the door. I slide out of my work attire and fold them onto a chair before I open the garment bag. My eyes are stunned to find a simple, navy, long sleeve, dress made of jersey. I ease the dress out of the garment bag and hang it on another hook inside the room also finding in the garment bag a navy lace bra with matching panty and garter belt. In a separate bag, which Gregory placed in my hands before I entered the room, I find a pair of nude stiletto heels and silk thigh high stockings.

I remove the rest of my under garments and place them with my work clothes before I run my hands over the new soft lace and sigh. This evening is bittersweet and I am thrilled to spend it with Alex, but I am utterly heartbroken that he leaves me in the morning. As I slide each of the silky pieces of lace onto my body, I think back to my hope that Alex would decide to stay with me. I know it is an impossible thought, he is a gorgeous man with millions of dollars that can have any woman of his dreams, but I still had that bit of hope that he loves me too. After two months, I'm still at a loss as to why he has had any interest in me.

Removing the dress from its hanger, I find that the dress is not nearly as conservative as I first thought. The back is almost nonexistent and the entire dress falls extremely short. I slide the material over my body and step into the shoes pulling my hair from the French twist, bringing it over my shoulder. Slowly I turn to face the lone mirror in the room. The dress skims my curves and hits me mid thigh. Twisting to see the back of the dress, I notice that it barely covers my behind, instantly proving why Alex chose this one in particular.

Into the darkening night I step out of the building and Gregory escorts me past hundreds of gorgeous vessels, each one more elaborate than the first.

My escort stops suddenly in front of an enormous yacht and I ask, "Gregory, are we going somewhere?"

"Only out for the evening, Ms. Winston. We will return in the morning."

Not expecting to dine on a yacht I announce, "Oh, ok. I've never been on a boat like this."

"Enjoy yourself, Ms. Winston. You are a remarkable woman and it has been pleasure getting to know you. Mr. Stone is waiting for you on the deck. I hope to see you in the morning."

Surprising Gregory in a tight hug I cry, "I'll miss you, Gregory."

A small tear falls from my eye and I turn around, quickly brushing it away. Gazing up at the large vessel, I walk onto the yacht and find Alex standing against a railing in his soft, gray, linen suit. He really is a stunning man. At the entrance of the deck, I halt my steps and watch Alex turn around when he senses me near.

"Mallory," he broadcasts. "You are by far, the most beautiful woman I have ever laid eyes on." His comment makes my cheeks redden and I gaze down at the ground as he continues, "Please don't hide your lovely face, darling. Your eyes are too magnificent to keep veiled." Smiling as I look up at him, he struts over to me and takes one of my hands. "Dinner is ready for us inside the cabin and we will depart the marina in a few moments, but I want you to know that I have never in my life wanted things to be different for us. Unfortunately, I can't change them, so I hope that this evening we can just pretend things won't be different in the morning."

To hide my aching heart, I stare into Alex's eyes and utter softly, "Sure, Alex. I can do that."
We gaze off at the sea from the deck, wrapped in each other as the boat departs from the marina.

When the temperature begins to cool out on the deck Alex takes my hand and guides me to the dining room on the yacht. Along the way, he points out the master bedroom and some other smaller bedrooms inside the cabin.

Once we reach the dining room, I see that the table has been arranged and the food is waiting for us. Alex opens the trays and we are served with some Mahi Mahi with mango salsa and sautéed vegetables. The Mahi and salsa is phenomenal with the chilled Riesling Alex has poured to accompany the meal.

"Alex, is this your boat?" I ask amidst conversation.

"You would think," he chuckles, "but unfortunately no, the concierge helped me to set it up. Though, after seeing her, I may look at purchasing one of my own."

"Do you need a boat?"

He laughs, "Probably not, but I could always use more toys."

Joining into his laughter I chuckle, "Good point."

"You look stunning in that dress, Mallory. I will enjoy peeling it off of you later."

"Thank you, it is lovely. I bet you will like what's underneath more.," I say behind reddening cheeks.

At my statement, his hand skirts up my thigh and his fingers skim the straps from the garter, moving up towards the lace panties.

"Oh, I can guarantee that I will enjoy them," he says without breaking his demeanor.

Agile fingers glide inside my panties and caress along my folds, eliciting such pleasure that I find myself closing my eyes and gripping the table. As I part my lips and let out a moan, Alex pulls me across the table into a scorching kiss. I massage his tongue with my own as he mimics the movements of his fingers thrusting into my core. Suddenly, he removes his fingers from my panties and my hair while standing from his chair.

"Come with me, Mallory," Alex beckons and I take his hand following him into the master bedroom.

Unable to appreciate the light décor of the cabin, Alex rushes us into the room.

"I want tonight to be special, Mallory." Sitting me onto the bed, he kneels onto the floor, removing each of my shoes and slithering his hands up each of my legs towards the hem of my dress.

Pulling me from the moment he whispers, "Stand and take this off."

Allowing me room, he rests back onto his heels and I stand at the edge of the bed. My hand skims down my sides as I reach down towards the bottom of the dress and pull it over my head. Alex reaches up, takes the dress from my hand, and then glides his hands around my waist. Sitting forward, he places soft kisses along my navel and hipbones.

"So beautiful."

With each kiss, I can feel myself drenching my panties. Standing rapidly, Alex crushes his lips against mine and I crave all of him at one moment, I cannot get enough. Alex must have the same thought because he reaches his hands around my hips and lifts me so that I can wrap my legs around his waist. Turning around hastily, he presses my back against the wall while nipping at my lips as he reaches a hand up to pull down the cup of my bra. Releasing my breasts, he bends down and swirls his tongue around my nipple. The feel of his wet mouth sends electricity straight to my womb. I whimper when he takes a bite at my hardened peak.

"Alex, more please."

"Oh baby, I haven't even gotten started."

Setting me back onto my feet, he reaches forward me to unhook my bra.

"Lovely," Alex says, dazzled as he massages my breasts.

I extend my hands forward, peel off his jacket, and then make my way to the buttons on his shirt. After helping to shrug off his shirt, I pull his head in for another round of kisses. Feeling the dampness in my panties, I know they are ruined from the pooling of moisture that his touching has aroused in me.

"Alex. Pants," I breathe out huskily.

He steps back, unlatches the button of his slacks, and pulls them down, leaving himself in gray boxer briefs and sporting a large erection. Again, Alex kneels at my feet and he unhooks each of the garter straps, unraveling the stockings from my legs. Barely touching my skin, his fingertips leave a trail of fire along my skin. Ripping the panties off me, he promptly removes the garter belt. When he has finally removed all of my clothing, Alex presses his nose and mouth into the apex of my thigh.

"Mallory, your scent and taste are intoxicating," he exhales. "If it was possible to bottle them up and take them with me, I would."

My breathing has become shallow and I reply to Alex in a husky voice, "Take me now, Alex, please. I can't stand it any longer."

Grunting at my desire, Alex stands and tugs my hair back, placing wet kisses along my neck.

"I don't want this to end too soon, Mallory, but I can't hold back either," Alex replies with a huff as he lifts me into his arms and walks me over to the bed, positioning me on the duvet.

Moving from the bed, he reaches into a dresser drawer and pulls out a spreader bar for my ankles and two sets of leather handcuffs. He fastens each of the handcuffs to a wrist and the headboard and then attaches the spreader bar to my ankles, adjusting it to keep my legs at the max length apart. We have played with this before and I remember how the feeling of being restrained intensified my orgasm.

"I won't be blindfolding you tonight, Ms. Winston," Alex states. "This time, I want you to see and remember everything we do."

"Thank you, sir, but I always remember everything we do, even if I can't see it."

"Good, that is how it should be." Reaching down, he strokes his hand across my center and then brings his fingers to his mouth and closes his eyes in ecstasy, moaning, "Ms. Winston, you have the most divine taste. It is a delicacy."

Stepping out of his boxers, Alex comes to straddle my body and places soft wet kisses along every inch of my skin, beginning at my wrists and working down to my ankles. As I begin to fall into the abyss, he pauses and rests above me and then, without haste, he pummels his cock into me, shocking my system.

"Jesus Christ, Mallory!" he cries. "I can't get enough of you."

With my orgasm so close I feel a blindfold of my own covering my eyes as I scream out, "Alex, yes, please, harder!"

Alex begins to pick up the pace of his thrusts and behind my eyes, I can see the rainbow of colors blossom.

Within a few more thrusts, my orgasm is unleashed as Alex murmurs, "Mallory, you feel so good. I won't last much longer, baby."

Releasing his seed moments later, I groan at the sensation of his pulsating cock. Seconds later, he reaches up to unhook the handcuffs and then he unhooks the spreader bar.

After massaging my limbs, we lie together on the bed and make small talk for the next hour.

Taking a deep breath and addressing the elephant in the room Alex asks, "Mallory, do you have plans after I leave?" When I shrug my shoulders noncommittally Alex continues, "You are welcome to stay at The Braxton for a while, especially since the investigation on your apartment is still going."

"No, Alex, I don't have plans to stay at your place. I may stay at Lily and Kyle's place until the investigation is over. They will be travelling for a bit."

"Good," Alex replies considering my words, "at least I know that their building is secure. Just, be careful for a while, Mallory. I'm sure they will have the investigation solved soon, they seem to have a major suspect."

"I will, Alex."

Sighing against his chest, I rest my hand over his heart.

Drifting into a calm slumber, I hear Alex whispers, "Thank you, Mallory, for everything. These past two months have been beyond anything I could have imagined. You have brought a light and energy to my life I never knew existed."

I don't respond to his statement, as I don't think he intended for me to. His breath tickling my skin evens out and I feel his heartbeat slow down to an even speed.

When I think he is asleep, I speak softly some of my final words to him, "I love you, Alex. I will be yours, always."

Closing my eyes, I find my body rushing towards sleep, but before I reach unconsciousness, I hear Alex reply in a hushed and pained tone, "I know."

Chapter Nineteen

AT SOME POINT DURING the night, I feel a hand sweep across my face and a kiss brush against my lips. In my dream, I hear a voice that sounds like Alex's whisper in my ear, "I'm sorry, Mallory. I have to go. I will be yours always too, my love. Goodbye."

As rays of early sun dance across my face through the window in the cabin, I wake and stretch in the bed and then remember I am on the boat. Glancing around, I notice Alex is not in the bedroom with me and feeling across his sheets, I realize they are ice cold; he must have left hours ago. I sit up in bed and see a bag in the chair in the corner. Perhaps he is waiting for me on the deck and brought me a change of clothes. Opening the bag, I put on the gray trousers and dark purple blouse along with the nude shoes from the previous night.

I search for Alex on my way up to the deck, but I don't find anything to show he is close by. As I walk onto the deck into the open air, I see Gregory waiting on the dock. I glance about, but instead of finding Alex, I find a single purple rose in a vase and a folded note placed onto a small table. Realizing that Alex has left, a lone tear escapes my eye, but I fight to hold back the others. I knew this day was coming and I need to contain myself from letting the pain take over.

At the table, I lift the magnificent rose to inhale the sweet scent of the flower. These particular flowers had quickly overtaken my love for lilies and they will always remind me of my affair with Alex. With shaking hands, I tear open the envelope to read the letter left from my English lover.

Mallory, I am sorry for leaving you without a proper goodbye. It was cowardly of me and you deserve more from a lover and a friend. I wish you all the luck and happiness in the world and I hope that one day we will meet again. I did hear your profession of love and it was spineless of me not to respond. I am not worthy enough for your love and I pray that one day you will meet the man that is deserving of you. I yearn that that man could have been me. Please keep yourself safe and never underestimate your importance to the world and to me. I pray that you will grant me your forgiveness one day.

Yours ALWAYS,

Alex Stone

My heart is shattering into billions of tiny broken pieces as I re-read the words repeatedly. He left me, in a note. I remember the goodbye in my dream and my heart aches more as it must have been him. The air leaves my lungs as I lean against the table and in a spurt of rage, I take hold of the vase containing the rose and throw it across the boat. Falling onto my knees, I let the sobs take over as I feel my heart ripped from my chest.

Gregory finds me moments later and kneeling in front of me says comfortingly, "Miss, can I help you? I'm sorry we must leave this way, but I'd like to escort you to work before I need to catch my own flight."
Staring down at the wooden paneling of the deck, I let my body release its despair. Slowly I compose myself enough to let bitterness take over. After taking a deep breath, I wipe my eyes and look over to where Gregory kneels.

"I'm sorry, Gregory," I apologize "Thank you, for being so kind to wait for me this morning. I am only outraged that your boss didn't have the decency to say goodbye to me in person. Now I know he never cared at all; that all of the words on this note and every other note, have been lies."

With fury, I angrily fist the note in my hand and strut towards the exit.

Gregory stays quiet as I walk off the boat and he continues his silence as he drives me to the office. Once we arrive at my building, Gregory turns around to look at me from his seat.

"Ms. Winston, you have access to Mr. Stone's residency for the next month as they wrap-up the evidence portion of your investigation. We have asked The Braxton to arrange for all your belongings to move back to your residency at your request."

"Thank you," I answer as I stare out the window.

"You're most welcome, ma'am. May I speak up about the matter at hand, miss?" he asks nervously and at my nod continues, "Mr. Stone may be my boss, but he has also been a friend for a number of years. Within those years, I have never seen him act with a woman the way he was with you. You were and are very special to him. I am sorry things ended the way they did, but I do not foresee him being nearly as happy within anyone else as he was with you."

How is this supposed to make me feel better? I do not want to imagine him with other women.

Biting back my tongue I respond to Gregory, "Thank you. It was nice meeting you Gregory and I wish you well. Unfortunately, I didn't mean enough to Alex because he still left."

As I exit the car and walk past his window towards the building, Gregory speaks up from his seat. "Before we depart, Ms. Winston, you should know that Mr. Stone was equally as upset to leave you this morning.

He was reluctant to board that plane." With a sigh Gregory adds, "His formula one team is his passion, but I don't even believe they hold his heart any longer."

With those final words, he closes his window and drives away from me. My last slice of Alex has left and my brain and heart lock themselves away. Within a few seconds, I officially become a shell of the person I used to be. The life has drained from my soul and I process life on autopilot.

*   *   *

Walking into my office, I begin my day by focusing on completing project after project at lightning speed. I answer any questions from my staff, but I make no attempt to socialize as I would normally. I'm not sure I can ever return to my row home, so I decide to make plans for housing. My reasoning to not return is not because of the crime, but because Madison and Mika are no longer the friends they used to be. For some reason in the two months I have been with Alex, we have drifted apart. Madison still believes I am the reason David left her and Mika has dropped all form of contact.

I contact The Braxton concierge and she helps me to locate a small apartment to rent immediately and promises to have my things removed from Alex's home and brought there by the end of the day. She faxes me the monthly lease and photographs of the apartment, gushing that the property owner is a nice old man.

Before I end the call, the concierge adds, "Ma'am, I am sorry to hear you will no longer be staying with us, it was a pleasure getting to know you through Mr. Stone."

"Thank you. Could you also have my car brought to my place of work?"

"Yes, miss. I will get the address from security."

The rest of my day, I spend purchasing some furniture from a local store and paying for it to be delivered this afternoon. My final task of the day is to check my savings account.

With resolution formed in my mind, I walk out of the bank and drive back over to my old home. For a few moments, I stare at my beautiful row house and peek back down at the paperwork in hand. Knowing I won't be happy living here any longer I have gone to my lender and had my name removed as the primary holder of the mortgage along with my portion of the monies that needed to be paid for the remainder of the year. This will allow the girls to rent out the lower property or sell.

Placing everything in a large manila envelope along with my keys, I step up to the front of the house and ring the doorbell, waiting for someone to answer, hoping it is Madison. Unfortunately, neither girl is home, so I dig the front door key from the envelope and open the main door.

The walls that encase my old home are now crisp white, no longer showing the profanities that were painted there. I pass by my old door and make my way up the steps towards Madison's apartment. Noticing her mailbox is empty; I realize she must have just left. I place the envelope under her door and walk back down the steps, saying goodbye one last time to my home of seven years. As I begin to drive away, I can see Madison enter the main door and sigh contentedly that I won't have to say goodbye to her in person.

Driving across town, I follow the directions the concierge gave me and I pull up in front of a new development of reconstructed row homes. My apartment is on the third floor and as I climb the stairs, I am glad I won't have to carry any furniture or boxes up these steps. When I get to the landing, an older gentleman is sitting in a corner chair waiting for me.

"Good evening, you must be Mallory Winston," the kind, elderly man says with a gentle smile.

"Yes, sir, I am. Thank you so much for renting to me on such short notice."

"I am delighted to have such a sweet young lady living in my building. I had planned to rent to my granddaughter, but she has decided to study abroad for another year. I live on the first floor and my niece's family lives on the second floor. She is a single mom with two little ones, but they are pretty quiet."

In love with my new landlord already I reply, "Thank you, sir. I love children and I look forward to meeting some of your family. I've had a rough couple of days and I am excited to get settled in."

"Splendid. Here is your key, Mallory. You can call me anytime if you need anything. The concierge at The Braxton spoke to me about the defacement of your previous property. I am an old Southern man from Georgia and I take care of my own."

"That is sweet of you, sir."

"Please call me Fred. It seems that all of your things have been moved in so I will leave you to your new place. Enjoy your night."

Taking a tentative step into my new apartment, I look around at the space. It is only slightly smaller than my previous home, still boasting two bedrooms and two bathrooms with a separate living room and kitchen. The entire apartment was redone recently and everything is very modern. I walk into the bedroom and look at my new set of furniture pleased with my choices. Opening the closet door, I find that all of my clothes and shoes have been organized. It was kind of Alex to let me keep the clothing since all of mine were ruined. I walk back out to the living room and notice the bouquet of white peonies on the coffee table with a small note resting beside it.

I hope that you will find this new place to suit your needs. Though you are no longer staying with us, please don't hesitate to call me if you need anything. I am sure you are exhausted from all of the moving so I have placed a finished lasagna in your oven to keep warm, it is one of my specialties. Happy Housewarming.

Nancy Wells

Marching into the kitchen, I smell the wonderful lasagna and pull out a plate from the cupboard to place a small square of the pasta dish on it. I take a few bites of food, but I don't notice any flavor. With a sigh, I toss the rest of the lasagna into the trash and wash the plate. Deciding to end my day early I enter my bathroom, strip from my clothes, and turn on the water as hot as I can stand it. When I step into the scalding water, I yearn to feel my skin burn the way Alex's touch used to, yet I feel no warmth. Sinking deep into the tub, I can see my skin redden from the heat and still, I feel nothing. When my skin begins to shrivel in the water I step out of the bath, noticing my skin resembles the same color of pink from the nights Alex used to dominate me. I sigh as I stare at myself in the mirror wondering if the pain of losing him will ever go away. I'm not sure who the woman is I am staring at in the mirror; her emerald eyes hold no life, no energy. The once brilliant color has drained and is now a dull resemblance of what they used to be. Exhausted from the brutal beating my heart took today I crawl into bed hoping to fall asleep quickly and dream of the man that holds my heart.

I pass the next two days at work on autopilot. Annie is preparing for her wedding, but even in her excitement, I am withdrawn. Stephanie is bringing Seth to the reception, so I offer to give my extra seat to her, as I don't have a date to bring to the wedding. I had invited Kyle when I found out Alex wouldn't be here any longer, but in the last week Kyle has joined Abi in her venture across the country. A sob escapes when thinking of Abi.

She had become a good friend and I hope that I am able to stay connected with her.

On the day of Annie's wedding I go to the closest boutique to find a dress to wear, not pleased with anything I own. After shopping endlessly for a few hours, I settle on a dusty pink chiffon number and pair it with some matching shoes and a cream shawl. I curl my hair, pin half of it up, and then head out to the coast for the wedding.

The affair was beautiful and I was delighted for Annie; she made a gorgeous bride. Finding my seat at the reception, I make small talk with some of the other guests and I bump into Seth towards the end of the night.

"Mallory, where's your boyfriend?" he curiously asks.

Smelling the alcohol reeking from his body I reply, "Oh, um, he is busy and couldn't make it."

"Well, that's a shame. You look mouthwatering this evening," he says as he tugs me into his arms and tries to kiss my neck.

"Seth have you been drinking? Where's Stephanie?" I question as I try to push him away.

"She went off somewhere. Come on, Mallory. We could have some fun later; now that the girls aren't around."

Finally escaping from his grasp, I step back closer to the crowd.

"I'm sorry, Seth," I announce, "but that isn't going happen. I'm sorry I missed Stephanie. Please tell her hello from me."

I move out of the hall and walk towards my car hoping that he isn't following me.

*   *   *

I spend the following month working with clients and finishing campaigns. I haven't answered any phone calls since the day that shattered my soul and have only spoken to my family once, through an email, telling them that I was focusing on work and was too busy to talk for a few weeks.

Trying to piece myself together and start from scratch, I realize nothing from my previous life exists in my new one. I have a new home, new friends, and a new job. And I hope to create a new me. But the hardened exterior brings me back to the wax from the candles Alex once used on me. I feel like the wax now, hard with nothing on the inside except the wick that constantly burns, as I burn for Alex. I removed everything from my existence that reminds me of my time with Alex. Color is no longer found in my life; everything is now shades of black, white. The color purple isn't my first choice in the floral shop anymore, I find myself gravitating towards the simple white daisies. My only emergence into the social world has been my daily lunches spent with Nancy. After I received her note, I made it a point to thank her in person. She is a sweet older woman and looks after me like a grandmother would. We meet every day of the week at a small café she likes to frequent and we talk about her life, my life, our families, and any strange celebrity gossip. She has become the highlight of my days.

Summer has officially ended as the chill of fall bears down on Baltimore. The leaves have begun to change into magnificent autumnal colors while the air brings a bite to your skin with its crisp coolness.

I find myself walking to work this breezy Friday and I don't feel the chilled wind on my skin, but I walk at a quickened pace with the rest of the walkers I pass. Today is my birthday, September 26, yet I feel as if I have aged beyond my years in the past two months. Nancy and Fred have been my sole companions as the phone calls have stopped and no one knows where I have moved. I am now living a lonesome solitary life, but I can't bring myself to enjoy the things the world has to offer. It is all meaningless to me without him, without Alex.

As I exit the elevator on the floor of my office, an empty reception desk greets me. Usually Stephanie is here by now with the apprehensive smile on her face to greet me, but perhaps she is running an errand. Our new assistant continues to follow me around the office. At first, I found it interesting that he wanted to learn so much, but now it's just annoying. Steven was supposed to retire two weeks ago and the company threw him a retirement party, but he continues to find reasons to work on a project.

I walk past Annie's office, but she isn't sitting at her desk either. Checking my phone to verify that today is a workday and not a weekend I place my phone back in my bag and walk into my office. Everything looks the same as it has for the last few months since I took over. I replaced the vase of flowers on the coffee table with business magazines, but that has been the only change.

I sit at my desk and as I wait for my computer to boot up I hear my office phone ring. Checking the caller ID I see that it is my mother.

"Hi, mom," I answer.

"Good morning, darling. Happy birthday."

"Thanks."

"It's a big one today. Turning thirty is a blast. Are you doing anything fun tonight?"

"No, I don't have plans to go out, but we'll see."

"Mallory, I'm starting to worry about you. You used to always have such life in you, but it seems drained now."

"Sorry, mom, I've just had a lot going on."

"I know, darling. I also know you don't want to tell me that Alex is the cause for all this, but I'm not blind or dumb. You have been different since he left. I know a broken heart takes time to heal, but you weren't together that long, sweetheart."

"Mom, please, can we not talk about this? I am doing the best I can. Madison and Mika don't even talk to me anymore, so I have no friends to go out with even if I wanted to."

"They didn't even wish you a happy birthday?"

"No, mom, and I didn't expect them to. Look, I need to go I have a Directors meeting in a few minutes."

"Alright, sweetie. Your father and I love you. Enjoy your birthday."

"I'll try. I love you too, mom."

My meeting lasted longer than expected so I dial Nancy to let her know that I will be late for lunch. Bumping into Annie on my way out, I let her know that I will be back in an hour.

At our typical spot, I meet Nancy and she greets me with a large hug and then hands me a gift.

"Happy birthday, Mallory," she cries joyously.

"Thank you, Nancy. You didn't need to get me anything."

"Stop that crazy talk, of course I did. I hope you like it."

I open the box and greeting me is an 11x14 photo of the Orioles team with each player's signature. With the photograph, she has paper clipped two box seat tickets for any game I would like to attend.

Knowing these are special tickets set aside for player's family I exclaim, "Nancy, this is incredible. How did you get these?"

"Well, I may or may not be a grandmother to one of the players."

"Really? Which player?"

She chuckles, "That's my secret. I'm glad to see a smile on your face."

"Are you kidding? This is one of the best birthday presents I have ever received." Standing up, I hug her from across the table as she continues, "You are quite easy to please, my dear. Now let's eat, I am starving."

Enjoying the fall day, I walk back into my office with my present from Nancy under my arm.

Situated in my chair, Annie comes rushing in carrying a small box and shouting, "Mallory, I could kill you. Why didn't you say today was your birthday?"

"Because I didn't want you to make a big deal out of it."

"Well gee; you are such a spoil sport. It took me forever to get this for you while you were away at lunch so you better fucking enjoy it." I laugh at her anger as she opens the small box and shoves a cupcake in my face proclaiming, "Happy birthday, best boss ever."

"Thank you, Annie."

"You're welcome. You know we have finalized the vodka campaign. You could take the afternoon off. Do you have any plans tonight?"

"I was already thinking about doing that and no, I don't have any plans. My parents are traveling to Blacksburg to visit my brothers and to watch Virginia Tech play, so they won't be visiting and well, you know about Madison and Mika."

"What? They didn't even suck it up enough to wish you a happy birthday?"

"Nope, but that's ok. I just got a wonderful present from Nancy and a lovely cupcake from you. It is almost too pretty to eat. Almost."

"We should go out tonight."

"What about your husband. Won't he mind; you being newlyweds and all?"

"Nah, he is playing poker tonight. We can do something small and just head out for drinks at the harbor."

I stare down at the cupcake and think about what my mom said. I need to let this go, I need to enjoy my life again. I used to be happy.

"You know what, Annie," I announce, "that sounds great. Where should I meet you?"

"I can pick you up if you'd like that way you don't need to drive."

I release a sigh. I hadn't told anyone where I was living.

Avoiding the driving situation, I say, "It's fine. Why don't we meet at Shotti's Point at 8:00 pm?"

"Great, see you then. Now go home, so I can go home."

"Alright. I'll see you later."

Grabbing my box from Nancy and the cupcake from Annie off my desk, I step out of my office.

Exiting the elevator, I stride into the lobby of our building. Glancing around I locate a security guard and ask him if he would like my cupcake since I'm not really in the mood to enjoy it. He gladly takes it and devours it in two bites; thanking me as he shoves it in his mouth.

Leaving the building, I turn down the sidewalk leading me to my new home. Suddenly, I feel a hand wrap around my arm and I scream out in surprise.

"Mal, are you leaving?" a voice asks. "I didn't get to wish you a happy birthday."

Turning I find Seth smiling down at me.

"Seth, you scared the shit out of me."

"I'm sorry. Hey, are you headed home?"

"I am. I walked today."

"Well I had a half day today. Can I take you out for some coffee or drinks?"

Peeking down at my watch, I sigh; I haven't been a great friend to Seth recently so I relent and I agree to join him for coffee. He wraps a hand tightly around my arm and begins to squeeze.

"Seth, can you let up? You're hurting me," I pronounce trying to jerk my arm free.

He doesn't respond but continues to walk towards the back corner of the parking lot where very few cars are parked; heading towards a large black SUV, not the car I am used to him driving. Opening the passenger door to usher me into the car, he leans in and straps me into the seat tugging the straps hard to secure them in place. My bag, which also contains Nancy's box, is tossed into the back seat.

As Seth comes around and gets into the driver's seat, I try to calm my nerves and ask, "Seth when did you get this car? Is it new? Can we go to the Mocha Lounge for coffee? I love their chocolate lattes."

"Mallory, shut it," he says harshly.

I quickly close my mouth as he faces me and I rub the arm that he had gripped in his strong hand. Anger and excitement stretch across his face, distorting his all-American boy features. This is not the Seth I know; this Seth seems violent, sinister. As he begins to pull out of the parking lot, he hands me a small drink from the cup holder.

"Drink this, now," he commands.

Taking a deep breath, I stutter, "What…What is this?"

"It's a birthday present."

RENEE HARLESS

I take the small cup from him and look down at the clear liquid. Peering over to him once more, I see the outline of a gun on his hip. Sniffing the contents, I smell something berry flavored that reminds me of an energy drink and I glance back at Seth who is watching me carefully as we are stop at a red light.

"Drink," he yells at me in rage.

Pinching my nostrils, hoping not to taste the liquid, I quickly swallow the contents of the cup and hand it back to him. He crumbles the cup in his hand and sends it into the back seat. Confused at the situation, I turn to look out the window as I wait to arrive at the coffee shop.

Chapter Twenty

OPENING MY EYES, I find myself in a dark, almost blackened room that I don't recognize. *Where am I?* I ponder as my memory begins to drift back to me and I remember riding in the car with Seth and drinking something from a cup on our way to the coffee shop.

I glance around again, but I can't distinguish any of my surroundings. The walls are all brick and the windows are covered in darkened cloths. Suddenly, I realize that I am numb all over and I can't feel anything. Panic grips me and I begin to breath heavily. Unexpectedly, a small light bulb is flicked on and I can see that my body is restrained to a chair with zip ties at my ankles and my wrists.

Barely above a whisper, I hear someone say, "If you make any movements they will only cut into your skin."

I look around for the faint voice and I find Stephanie also tied to a chair about ten feet away from me.

"Where are we?" I ask.

"I don't know. An abandoned warehouse along the harbor I think. I can hear some boats every now and then."

"Why are we here?"

As a fog horn sounds in the distance she shrugs her shoulders and replies, "He brought me here early this morning when I was leaving my place. I'm so sorry, Mallory, but he is crazy. I think he plans to kill us."

She starts to sob and trying to calm her I murmur, "Stephanie, we'll get out of this."

Her sobbing continues and all too soon, Seth enters the room and smacks her.

"Keep quiet, Stephanie, or I will repeat what I do to Mallory to you. Get it?" he snarls.

She quickly nods her head in reply and looks in my direction following Seth with her eyes.

"Well, Mallory," Seth begins. "I am so glad to see you are awake. This is going to be fun. Are you scared?" I shake my head.

"Well, we will have to fix that," he acknowledges before walking away for a few moments and then returning with another chair and a wheeled cart.
The tray on the cart contains various surgical equipment and about twenty-five different carving knives.

Alarmed I ask, "Seth, what are you doing?"

"Granting you a birthday present, doll. See, I've been in love with you for years, but you never wanted me like that. I was sure it would just take time, but you didn't want anyone else either. Maybe you couldn't love anyone. Then one day you are dating Mr. Stone, giving yourself to him; whoring your body out to his every whim. So I knew your heart was there, but how could you love this man and not love me? Then I realized, it's because you are trash, a gold digging slut. So I plan on treating you like one."

Shocked by his admission I shout, "It was you. You broke into my home, destroying it and you sent the letters."

"I did enjoy breaking into your home, though I did have a bit of help."

Stephanie chirps in, "Mallory, I'm so sorry. I didn't mean it. He made me…"

Seth cuts her off, "Shut it, Stephanie, I am warning you."

With a bit of resolve I say, "Its fine, Stephanie. The police will figure it out."

"So gullible, Ms. Winston. No one will find anything. There is no way to link us to the crime. I even hacked into your stupid security system and cleared the evidence from that night before the police could use it."

"Why now, Seth? What do you want?"

"Well, I have been watching your every move, Mallory. You escaped me for a bit when you moved using a police issued name, but I soon found your whereabouts in their records. They were very easy to track. In no time, I realized that you and Mr. Stone had parted ways as he had left the country, ridding you of his extra security. So now that you have been left vulnerable, I seized my opportunity, planning it when least expected. Today is your birthday and since you don't venture out of your home any longer, I thought that this would be a perfect opportunity. Do you know what tomorrow is, Mallory?"

I stare at him stunned, but I can't fathom what he plans to do.

Without waiting for my reply, he continues, "Tomorrow is my birthday and you will be forced in gifting me your heart. I plan to take it from you." I gasp at his words, fear evident on my face and he laughs, "Oh, we will have some fun first. I plan on getting my fill of you for the next twelve hours before I pry your puny heart out with my hands."

Exiting the room, but leaving the light on, my tears begin to cascade from my eyes. The moisture falls for those that will miss me, for those that won't know how much they meant to me, and for those that will never know I am gone. As the sobs rack my body, I close my eyes and think of Alex. What will he do if he realized Seth had done this to me; if he finds out I'm dead? I think of all the wonderful nights we spent together curled up in each other's limbs, making love, and learning about each other. I will treasure those moments in the few hours of life I have left.

Walking menacingly back into the room, Seth has changed his clothing into an all black attire of jeans and a long sleeve shirt and he stands in front of me after grabbing a knife from his table. As he trails the back edge of the knife along my collarbone, I shiver in fear realizing the numbness is wearing off and I can feel the chill of the cold steel.

"You're too covered up, Mallory," he says licking his lips. "I want to look at you."

I peer down as he trails the knife slowly down my breastbone, only then noticing that I am wearing my dark purple wrap dress. My favorite dress, that holds a few memories, is being cut in half by a mad man. Once he shreds it to his liking, he tugs it down my shoulders so it rests on the chair. He steps back and stares at me in an appreciative gaze and I can feel the bile rising in my throat as he rubs his hand across a growing erection.

"You look mouth wateringly delectable in that getup, Mallory. Tell me, did he buy those for you?" Seth groans.

I reply, "No."

"Well, it's a shame he won't get to see them on you."

Reaching forward he unclasps the front of my bra and I scream out begging, "Seth, stop, please! I won't tell the police if you let me go. Please."

"I don't think so, Mallory. Groveling doesn't suit you." Pushing the bra away from my skin, he reveals my breasts and murmurs, "My god, they are better than I imagined."

Taking his fill of my flesh, his hands make their way to my chest and he kneads them demandingly. The roughness of his touch causes me to cry out in pain.

"Did he touch you like that, Mallory? Hmm?" Seth asks as stands back from me and sets an angry gaze in my direction.

"What do you think, Stephanie, beautiful aren't they?"

RENEE HARLESS

She has averted her attention to another wall, but he stalks over and tugs her face in my direction.

Angry, Seth states, "Stephanie, perhaps I should give her a heart for the one she will be missing. What do you think?"

She whispers in reply, "I don't know, sir."

Punching her across the face he yells, "Of course, you don't know. You aren't good for anything."

I cringe at his treatment of Stephanie. This isn't the Seth I had gotten to know over the last seven years and I wonder what has changed in him. Was he hiding this character all along?

Walking back over to me, Seth exchanges his knife for a small paring blade. He bends in front of me and presses the tip of the blade over my left breast. As the blood trickles down my chest, I can see that he is carving a small heart onto my skin. Finishing his carving, he takes the chair and table and moves them back to the well-lit area of the room.

Strutting over to Stephanie, he places a wet kiss on her mouth, but she seems to be unconscious from his earlier punch.

Moving back over to me, he pushes my hair aside and, as I recoil from his hand, he bends forward and licks from my collarbone, moving up my neck.

Sensing an opportunity, I take a chance; I refuse to wait in distress, I will fight for my life. As his face inches closer, I slowly turn my head towards his movement, as if embracing his touch. When his neck is in reach, I react quickly, removing my neck from his lips and biting into his. I bite as hard as I can, tasting blood and skin.

"You fucking bitch!" he cries out grasping his neck.

He swings at me, backhanding my face, and knocking me to the ground. The movement causes me to cough up the skin and muscle that I took from my bite and though I keep my head tilted, it still hits the concrete.

I am knocked unconscious for a few minutes, but when I come to, I see Seth lying on the floor. My bite wasn't deep enough to cause him to bleed out, but it was enough to cause him immense pain and to possibly black out. Feeling searing pain in my shoulder and hips, I must have bruised them from the fall. But even in my pain I move my body enough so that I can slither across the rough concrete floor. I have to mask my cries as I can feel bits of rock imbedding themselves into my skin, but I am only a few feet away from the table holding the knives. With hope restored, I continue to squirm across the floor, optimistic that I can reach them and cut the zip ties. My through the back of the chair.

"You fucking whore," Seth yells out as he kicks me again.

Stumbling into an adjoining room, he drags the tray of knives with him. My hope vanishes and I lay on the rubble letting the darkness take over my body.

*   *   *

Startled, I wake to screaming in the background and look around. I am no longer attached to the chair on the floor, but to an older hospital bed and my arms and legs have bed handcuffed to the railings. The screaming continues and I know that Stephanie is in incredible pain. The blinds encasing the windows of the room I am trapped in open to Seth's demented face. In the backdrop, I can see Stephanie hanging from some chains by her wrists with her toes barely touching the floor. Carved across the side of her body is the name SETH. I cringe at the sight and look back at him with horror etched across my face. Rapidly the blinds close and I am shrouded again in darkness. I wiggle my hands and feet against the handcuffs, but they are too tight and they begin to cut into my skin. I glance around the room looking for anything that could help me, but it has been stripped bare. Only the bed and I remain in the room.

Another few hours pass, though I have no recollection of time. I am assuming it is midmorning as I can hear a few faint foghorns in the distant. Seth staggers into the room with his tray of knives and I see that he has a tight bandage wrapped around his neck.

"I'm going to make you pay for what you did to me," he growls as he comes forward and presses a hand against my throat with the intentions to strangle me. As my vision begins to blacken, he removes his hand and I gasp for breath as the air burns my lungs.

"Too soon," he says, "I want to hear you scream when I cut you open. I plan to slice you from neck to core. How does that sound, Mallory?"

I don't respond when the panic takes over my body. He jumps onto the table, causing my ankles and wrists to dig their open wounds into the handcuffs as he takes a sharp blade and trails the back of it from the

hollow of my neck to the waist of my panties. Quickly, he
turns the blade and severs the panties into half.

Again, he takes the back of the blade and glides it
across my center speaking, "It would have pleased me to
find you aroused during this. I know you like it rough,
Mallory. You like to be beaten and demeaned."

I scream out at him, "He never beat me or hurt
me, Seth. He isn't crazy, like you."

"Crazy, am I? Well, let's see about that you little
gold-digger."
I close my eyes at his words; I don't want to watch him
torture me

In his madness Seth shouts, "Look at me you
fucking whore. I didn't give you permission to close your
eyes." While landing a punch across my face.

The warmth of blood drips from my nose onto my
breasts as Seth inches higher along my body and begins
to press his calloused and bloodied hands on my chest.

"You sure this doesn't feel good, Mallory?" he
asks. "I bet you're enjoying this."
Disgusted, vomit furiously releases from my body,
splatters across the bed, and covers Seth.

"God dammit," he screams, jumping off me and
running out of the room.

I take in a few shallow breaths at his escape, but
my hopes at stalling him are crushed quickly when he
returns with his shirt removed and a ball gag in his hand.
I bite his hand as he shoves the gag in my mouth and he
smacks me across the face again.

Through gritted teeth Seth says, "I had intended
on being more pleasant about this, Mallory, but now you

have left me no choice. I will see to it that this is extremely painful. You will watch as I rip your heart from your chest. It will be mine, forever."

Rearranging the knife set on the table, Seth jumps back onto the bed straddling me. Too heavy for me to buck off, I cry out behind the gag as he lands on my bruised hip. Taking a knife from his set, he leans over my body right above my rib cage.

"I think I'll start in the middle and work my way down and then back up. That seems like much more fun."

Holding the blade precariously above my skin, I see a glint of sun from behind the blinds glisten off the knife blade. With my eyes open, I close off my mind, turning into my shell and behind the gag I say I love you to my family, to Nancy and Fred, and to Alex. With a final prayer, I beg that Stephanie is unharmed, that Alex knows how much I love him, and that I reach a quick death.

Off in the distance I can hear some movement over the sickening laughter from Seth as he toys with the blade in his hand. He has yet to slice my skin, but instead taunts me by pressing the tip in various locations creating his own form of connect the dots. The thought that Stephanie has broken free warms me and I am pleased that she will get to live her life.

At the sound of breaking glass, I shake out of the catatonic state I placed upon myself. In slow motion I see the glass from the windows in this small room continue to be broken by a small battering ram. Men and women in uniforms crowd the outside of the room and yell at Seth to drop his weapon. I am in shock to see that I have been rescued. In fear, Seth falls from the bed slicing me across the side with the cold steel. In his attempts to free himself from the room using a small door in the back, he knocks my bed over to thwart the police. I collapse onto the floor hearing various bones break from the weight of the bed and the restraint of the handcuffs. Before my world turns from gray to black, I can hear the faint sounds of gunshots.

*   *   *

In an unconscious state, I can vaguely hear doctors and nurses speaking to my mother. At some point during the comatose of my body, I feel a soft kiss pressed to my forehead along with some fallen tears.

"I'm so, so very sorry, Mallory. You are my world. Please, come back to me," an agonized deep voice says. These are the last words I hear before, I again, am led from the light towards the darkness. Words from a voice that remind me of the man that will forever hold my heart.

"Mallory, sweetheart can you hear me? The doctors are worried you haven't woken yet."

I can hear my mom's light voice laced with agony. I try very hard to open my eyes, but they feel incredibly heavy.

In the background another voice speaks, "Ma'am, just give her time. Her body needs a lot of rest and she will wake when she is ready. Her brain scan today said that everything is working normally. There isn't any reason to worry."

RENEE HARLESS

Quickly, I fall back into another deep sleep.

Prying my eyes open, I look around at my surroundings. I recognize a faint beeping and I peek down to see that I have tubes attached to my hand, a hand covered in bruises. I look over to find my other arm wrapped in a cast and placed in a sling. *Why am I here?* I ask myself as I look around a few more times. Suddenly, I remember everything that happened with Seth and I begin to cry. Sobs escape my chest and I can hear the beeping of the machine pick up in pace.

A nurse rushes in moments later, "Miss, are you ok? Are you in pain?"

I continue to sob and the nurse looks around a bit confused at my emotional state. Another older nurse enters the room and comes to sit on the edge of the bed. She pulls me into her arms, as a mother would, and strokes my head as I cry onto her chest.

"It's ok, dear. You've had a tough couple of days. We are so glad you pulled through," her gentle voice murmurs.
My crying begins to lessen and she eases me back on the bed.

Between sniffles, I ask them through my dry voice, "How long have I been here?"

"You've been in this facility for about two weeks."

"Two weeks?" I exclaim and then wince in pain.

"Be careful, dear. You have taken quite a number of hits to your head."

"What happened to me?"

"Do you remember anything?"
I nod my head.

"Ok, well first let me go get your doctor. The police have been asking for a statement from you as soon as you wake up. The doctor will come in with them to discuss your condition and then you can see your family."

"My family is here?"

"Of course, dear. You have had a number of visitors in the past few weeks. Just sit tight."

A doctor comes into my room a few minutes later followed by the nurse and two police officers. I tell them what I remembered happening and ask about Stephanie.

"She is doing well. The hospital released her yesterday and she is staying with her family. Do you want to press charges against her for assisting in the crime against you at your apartment?" the young officer asks.

"No!" I yell out. "She was manipulated by Seth. I place all the blame on him."

"Alright then I will be sure to let her know. She is a nice girl."

"Yes, she is. Can you tell me what happened? Where is Seth?"

Beginning the story, the officer states, "Well, your friend Annie called the station filing a missing persons report on Saturday morning and then we received a second missing persons report from another woman named Nancy in the early afternoon. We typically wait a few days to begin investigating, but since you already had an ongoing investigation, we acted fast. Your friend Nancy requested some security details from your old residence and learned that a GPS tracker had been placed on your phone. At first, we hit a dead end when we found your purse and phone shoved in a trash can along the harbor, but while digging for evidence using your work security tapes, we were able to locate the vehicle you were taken in. We scanned the stoplight cameras and tracked the vehicle to the abandoned warehouse. Seth was shot and killed during his escape. I am sorry to say that he will not suffer and rot in a prison cell."

I nod in understanding.

"You did well, Ms. Winston. He had lost a lot of blood already and wouldn't have lasted much longer. I am assuming that you were the one to bite his neck as the doctors found bits of his blood along your mouth."

In a whispered tone I respond, "I didn't want to die. I needed to live."

"We will let you rest, Ms. Winston. You are safe now."

The police officers exit the room and I peek at my doctor. He is a younger man, probably in his mid thirties, with light brown hair and blue eyes. I can tell that both of my nurses are smitten with him as they stare in his direction with large grins on their faces.

Startling me, the doctor asks, "Ms. Winston, I'm Dr. Young. How are you feeling?"

"Sore, everywhere."

"I bet," he chuckles. "Well, would you like me to go over the extensive list of your injuries?"

"Please call me, Mallory. And yes, if you don't mind."

"Well, Mallory, let's begin from the top and work our way down. You have several small fractures along your skull, which is why your head is in a wrap. You also suffered a concussion during one of your falls. Your left shoulder wasn't broken, just dislocated, but your arm was fractured in three places. Both of your wrists are bruised heavily, along with your hands. He left you with a small scar on your chest that we can have removed by a plastic surgeon, if you wish. Your body naturally healed each of the knife piercings along your ribcage, so you won't have any scarring there. Unfortunately, you sustained a very deep knife wound to your left hip, which is also broken. The stabbing nearly missed your vital organs and we performed a surgery to patch up what we could. Your broken hip has a few screws in it for now while it heals. Your legs are fine, as are both of your ankles and feet, minus some bruising. Wow, that's a mouthful. Do you have any questions?"

"When can I go home?"

He laughs and looks up from his chart and the nurses join in. I blush at their amusement.

"It will be quite a few days before you can go home and then we need to schedule some therapy for your hip, arm and shoulder."

"Oh, so it will be a while?"

"Yes, Ms. Winston, I mean Mallory. I'll send your family in if that is ok."

"Yes, please. Thank you."

"You're most welcome. Let me know if you need anything." He shoots a wink in my direction and leaves the room. The older nurse steps over to me and moves the bed to a sitting position.

"Dr. Young must like you," she says.

"What makes you think that?"

"He never stays in a patient's room. He always has the nurse relay the condition information."

"Really?"

She nods her head proclaiming, "You lucky girl. If I was twenty years younger I would have been all over him."

I laugh at her words and she exits the room as my family enters.

My mom immediately rushes over to hug me and my dad stands at the foot of the bed with tears in his eyes.

"Baby girl, I am so glad you're awake. We have been so worried about you. How are you feeling?"

"Sore, but better than I expected. I think they have me doped up on pain meds. You guys didn't have to stay here."

"You silly girl, of course we did. Your nice friend Nancy let us stay in a guest suite at The Braxton, so we haven't been sleeping here. I am so glad you're ok. I can't believe Seth was the one to do this. He seemed like such a nice boy."

"Yep, he had us all fooled." My mom moves over to wear my dad stands and I say through watery eyes, "Hi, daddy."

"Hi, sweetheart. I'm happy that you're ok. We love you very much."

"Thanks, daddy. I'm getting a bit tired from the medicine. I think I'll go back to sleep for a little while."

"That sounds good, darling. We'll be back to see you in the morning."

"I love you."

"We love you too, baby."

Closing my eyes, I drift into a drug induced slumber.

Later I wake to a high-pitched squeal coming down the hall and barging into my room.

"Mallory Jane Winston, how could you do this to me?" Madison pronounces as she smacks my arm and I yelp in pain. "Oh my god! I am so sorry," she apologizes.

Soon the older nurse rushes into my room, quickly followed by Dr. Young asking, "Mallory, are you ok?"

I take heavy breaths and nod sighing, "Sorry, I'm ok. She smacked my arm accidently."

They both send glaring stares at Madison and for the first time in my life, I see her cower.

Embarrassed she whispers, "Sorry, I'll be more careful."

After the nurse exits my room, Dr. Young stays by for a few moments to speak to me.

Catching my attention, he says, "Visiting hours are almost over so I'll leave you two, but I'll be back once those hours have ended. Holler if you need anything."

"I will. Thank you."

Madison gawks at Dr. Young as he exits.

She utters, "Damn, who is that fine piece of man?"

"That would be my doctor. Madison, what do you want? I haven't heard from you in three months."

She sighs and then brings the chair close to my bed.

"I know and I'm sorry," she reveals. "I finally got the nerve to confront David about the relationship and he also told me you weren't the reason behind the breakup. Mika lied. He had been sleeping with her, not you."

"Why would she do that?"

"I don't know. She seems different recently. I don't even hear her come home anymore. Mallory, why did you move out?"

"I didn't want to live with people that don't want me in my own home, so I paid you my amount and found a temporary place. I needed to figure things out. I've had a difficult month."

"Why what happened? Well, besides the obvious."

"Alex left me. He went back home."

"Oh, but he's in love with you," she says with such conviction.

"No, he isn't."

Madison and I sigh and she looks heartbroken as she looks over my injuries.

"How did we not suspect him?" she asks. "He was always so nice."

"I don't know. The police had questioned him and everything. He wasn't even a lead suspect."

"I'm so sorry, Mallory. I hope we can go back to being friends. I miss you."

"We were always friends, Madison. We just hit a bump in the road."

Gripping me in the best hug she can muster she declares tearfully, "I love you. Hey, we never got to celebrate your birthday. Maybe when you get out of here we can go out! You can even invite Dr. Sexy."

"Who is Dr. Sexy?" A deep voice calls from the door.

We both turn to see Dr. Young standing at the edge of the room, leaning against the doorjamb. Both Madison and my cheeks blush from embarrassment.

"Mal, I'm going to go. I will come by and see you tomorrow," she whispers as she exits quickly, only glancing back at me once she passes Dr. Young and fans her face. I chuckle as she leaves.

Dr. Young beckons my attention and exclaims, "She is a funny one. You can call me Bradley, by the way. Though, Dr. Sexy does have a nice ring to it."

We both laugh at the nickname as he sits on the edge of my bed.

"So, Mallory," he continues, "I am about to run through my nightly rounds before I head out. Tell me, how you are doing?"

"I'm ok. My body is a bit sore, but I'd like to stop taking the meds as soon as possible."

"Smart girl. I am hoping we can discharge you by the end of this week. You seem to be progressing well, but we will take it day by day."

"That would be great. How long will I be out of work?"

"Not for long, though it would be ideal if you could work from home while you complete therapy. Do you have someone that you can stay with or that can stay with you when you are discharged? You may need some help getting around and bathing."

Looking down I sigh, "No, I don't have anyone."

"Really? No boyfriend or close friend that could take care of you?"

I shutter my shoulders noncommittally. "No."

"Well you just let me know if we need to hire a day nurse for you. Or, you know, Dr. Sexy can do some house calls," he says with a laugh and I join in. "Get some rest, Mallory. I'll see you in the morning. Dr. Chang will be your attending doctor for the evening."

"I will. Thank you."

"You are most welcome."

As he exits my room, I take a few moments to look around. I hadn't noticed earlier, but my room is engulfed in flowers, balloons, and cards all wishing me to get well soon.

The older nurse strides into my room carrying a vase full of flowers. My breath leaves my lungs when I see the bouquet of dark purple roses with lavender calla lilies sprouting above. The arrangement is stunning.

"These are quite beautiful, Ms. Winston," the nurse states. "The young man that brought these in the day before last asked me to set them aside until you woke up. He was certain you would be awake before they wilted. I think they are even lovelier now, then when he brought them here."

"Who brought them, ma'am?"

"A charming fellow with an accent. I believe his name was Rock or Stone or Pebble. Something like that. He seemed heartbroken after he saw you and you hadn't woken up."

I think back to the voice I heard and the kiss on my head, Alex. He was here in this room.

"He didn't stay long?" I ask as my heart begins to quicken.

"No, miss. He was ushered out of here pretty quickly. We only have room for family to wait. I believe he was hoping to see you awake. Where would you like these?"

If Alex left quickly, I doubt he wanted to see me awake. I'm sure he was hoping to leave these flowers with the nurse to deliver. The walls around my heart immediately erect themselves.

"You can place them with the others, ma'am."

"Really? As you wish. I've learned a bit about flowers since I've worked here. Do you know what the purple rose stands for?"

Interested I reply, "No, ma'am."

"Well, the saying goes that the purple rose stands for true love at first sight; that the sender of the flower finds the recipient irresistible, they are enchanted by that person."

Tears spill from my eyes as I wonder if he was aware of their meaning.

"Dear, are you ok?" she asks as I swipe at my eyes with my good hand.

I respond, "Yes, ma'am. I am, or I will be." Allowing the pain meds to take control of my body, I find myself drifting back off to sleep.

I receive visits from Madison and my family and then by Annie and Stephanie the next day. Annie and Stephanie sit with me for a few hours and we discuss trivial things and gossip about the office. They try to keep the topics lighthearted after what Stephanie and I have

endured. I let Stephanie know that Madison is still
looking for a tenant in my old home and she hops at the
chance to move from her parent's place. With a hug, I
thank Annie for acting quickly and saving my life. I owe
a great debt to her. Stephanie and I both do. To think no
one would have found us if I hadn't agreed to dinner that
night.

Later in the week, Nancy and Fred both drop in
with sandwiches from our favorite deli. They get the
chance to meet my parents and chat with them like old
friends. It's amazing how quickly they form a bond,
mostly to look out for me.

On Wednesday, Dr. Young comes into my room
and helps me locate a therapist in the area that can work
on my shoulder. By now most of the wrappings have
been removed from my body and I've been allowed to
shower and brush my hair. Bradley seems to notice the
change.

"Mallory, you should set up your first
appointment on Monday since we will be discharging
you on Saturday morning. Your coworker mentioned you
are taking some time off?"

"Yes, they are granting me two weeks of medical
leave."

"That sounds great. Your arm and hip are healing
fast since they were only small breaks so you should be
out of your cast in about five weeks. Your ribs may
continue to hurt from the bruising, though." Closing his
clipboard Bradley looks up at me and continues, "Well,
Ms. Winston, it has been a pleasure working with you.
The rest of the week I am off rotation so I will be leaving

you in Drs. Chang and Epperly's care. They will make sure you're ready to be discharged on Saturday. If you have any questions about your therapy don't hesitate to call me."

Dr. Young hands me his card with an additional number scrolled across the back.

Before leaving he adds, "Also, Mallory, I am sure you have heard from the nurses that I have paid special attention to your care. I think you are a very beautiful and lovely woman. I don't ever date my patients, but since you will no longer be my patient in the coming days, I would like to take you out once you feel up to it."

I smile at the handsome doctor and say, "Thank you, Bradley. I've recently gotten out of a relationship that broke my heart, but maybe we can see each other as friends first."

"That would be fine by me, Mallory."

"Thank you, Dr. Young, for everything."

"You're welcome, Mallory; I wish you a fast healing."

Moving from my bed, he comes to stand close to my head. Bradley leans in, placing his hand under my chin, and plants a small, subtle kiss onto my lips.

"You have my number, Mallory. Please, call me soon," he whispers and I don't respond to his words but a shy smile crosses my face.
I sigh back into my pillow as he exits my room.

My daytime nurse comes in later. She is the older woman named Francis that I have gotten to know over the past few days.

"Did he ask you out? Did he kiss you? Please tell me he kissed you!" she asks as she runs up to my bed.

I laugh at her need for an office soap opera and tell her, "He kissed me; just a soft peck after he asked me out."

"Oh my goodness, to be young again."

"Francis, I had my heart broken by the love of my life. Bradley and I will only ever be friends."

"Well at least give the man a shot. Let love decide who wins your heart."

I contemplate her words as she checks my stats and asks, "Mallory, have you called someone to pick you up on Saturday?"

"No, my parent's needed to go back home, but I think I know who I'll call."

"Ok, well, I'll leave you for now, but I will come back to gossip about Dr. Sexy later."

"Sure thing." I reply laughing at the nickname Madison and I gave Dr. Young.

Francis hands me my phone on her way out and I scroll through my contacts. I'm not 100% sure who to call, but I know I will need to make sure that they can get here in time. As I land on the number I have been contemplating, I gaze around the flowers in my room and stare at the purple roses in the far corner. I make my decision and press the call button.

"Hello?"

"Hi, it's Mallory. I'm being discharged from the hospital and I was hoping you could pick me up on Saturday."

"Really? Message me the time and I will be there."

"I will text you Saturday morning when I know. Thank you."

"You are most welcome, beautiful."

(To be continued in Make Me Yours.)

RENEE HARLESS

If you enjoyed Make me yours, please leave a review.

Keep reading for a look at the Book Two in The Stone Trilogy, **Make you mine**.

RENEE HARLESS

Acknowledgments

An enormous thank you goes out to Monika, Courtney, Brianna, Mimi, Chris, Tish and Vanessa. You all took the time to read and critique my work, not holding anything back. Your words of encouragement helped me to pursue my writing and come up with an amazing story for Mallory and Alex. Vanessa, I truly appreciate all your help in the beginning stages of my work and I know it helped to bring life to the scenes.

I wouldn't have been able to chase this dream without the support of my family. To my husband and children, thank you for allowing me many late nights and days locked away to put my ideas onto paper, or rather type out onto cyberspace.

As mentioned in the novel, Prader Willi is a syndrome that affects approximately 12,000-15,000 people. This rare genetic disorder affects appetite, growth, metabolism, cognitive function and behavior. This syndrome is close to my heart and I hope that as a reader you will take the time to learn more about this disorder. (Information taken from www.pwsausa.org) Thank you,
Renee Harless

RENEE HARLESS

RENEE HARLESS

I feared the shadows. My life became a sequence of seconds, minutes, and hours; nothing more, nothing less. I needed an escape and my job was going to offer it. But Europe contained the one thing I couldn't have – him.

Or have the tables turned?

My trust is shredded, only a sliver of faith remaining and he uses it to his advantage. Except Alex says it's different this time around.

But how can I believe a man that lives in a world shrouded in secrets?

Prologue

MY BODY IS TREMBLING as his rough fingertips glide up along my thighs, inching their way past my skirt and wandering to my warm center. His touch sets my skin on fire and I beg him to move faster. My pleading only causes him to chuckle as he slides his fingers around the opening of my panties and drags them down my legs.

Sitting back on his heels he says, "Take off your clothes, Mallory."

Fingers shaking, I unfasten each button of my blouse and free my arms from the material, tossing the fabric onto the floor. I slowly trail my fingers across my chest, caressing my breasts as I reach down to remove my skirt. The screech of the zipper is the only noise that can be heard over our heavy breathing.

Once I'm completely naked and lying on his satin sheets, he says, "So beautiful. Absolutely perfect," as his fingers skim over the heated skin of my stomach.

"Please, I need you," I whisper.

"I know, beautiful."

Leaning forward, resting his body on top of mine, he punishes my mouth in a devouring kiss. His nimble fingers cup my breasts and I moan into his mouth as I feel the heat building in my core. Nudging my sensitive spot with the tip of his penis, he rocks against me, increasing my desperate need for him as he continues to knead my breasts and assault my mouth. Knowing that my release is pending, he swaps the hand on my breast for his mouth and rubs his hand on my clit, instantly forcing my climax.

As I come down from my release, he thrusts his large manhood into my center, causing me to gasp at the fullness. As he stares down at me, not moving, I can't help but feel an indescribable peace. Only he does this to me, makes me feel as if I'm a part of him, and nothing else around us matters. But with the electricity crackling through my veins, I don't have long to wonder about this sense of peace - I need him to move.

Rocking my hips against him, he begins to thrust, slowly at first, gradually increasing to a breath-taking pace. Wrapping my legs around his waist, he takes that as a cue to thrust harder. The noise of the bed creaking against the wall can't be heard over our moans and my screams of ecstasy.

Suddenly he stills above me, and I feel his erection grow thicker before the warm release of his seed rushes into me. Resting on his elbows, he stares lovingly into my eyes while brushing the sweat-drenched hair away from my face.

"That was amazing," he whispers, "I don't know what you do to me, Mallory, but everything with you is just… better."

"I know what you mean."

Wrapping me in his arms, he pulls me across his satin sheets and drapes my body across his own, tucking me against his side. His fingers slide through my hair as I lie there, listening to his steady heartbeat.

I realize I must have dozed off for a few minutes as I feel a darkness wash over me. Reaching across the bed, I feel nothing; no warm body, no cold sheets, just air. Assuming I have moved to the edge of the bed, I turn over and open my eyes, only to come face to face with plastic railing.

Beep...... Beep.... Beep. Beep. Beep. Beep.

A glowing monitor looms over me, and I witness my heartbeat increase to an alarming rate.

Sitting up in the bed, I rub my eyes and look around the frigid room. I can't believe I dreamed of him again. And I dreamed that kind of dream. It was so real. I felt him, every part of him.

A few moments pass and a nurse walks in to checks my vitals, frowning as she notes my increased heart rate.

"Dearie, this is the fifth night you've had an accelerated heart rate. What's got you so worked up? Is it the accident? Are you having nightmares? The doctor can prescribe some sleeping medication if you'd like."

"No medicine, but yes it's the accident," I lie.

It's not an accident that keeps me up at night. It's the face, the voice, the feel, the essence of the man that completely transformed my world and stole my heart.

Alex.

Purchase: myBook.to/stonetrilogy2

RENEE HARLESS

About the Author

Renee Harless is a romance writer with an affinity for wine and a passion for telling a good story.

Renee Harless, her husband, and children live in Blue Ridge Mountains of Virginia. She studied Communication, specifically Public Relations, at Radford University.

Growing up, Renee always found a way to pursue her creativity. It began by watching endless runs of White Christmas- yes even in the summer – and learning every word and dance from the movie. She could still sing "Sister Sister" if requested. In high school, she joined the show choir and a community theatre group, The Troubadours. After marrying the man of her dreams and moving from her hometown she sought out a different artistic outlet – writing.

To say that Renee is a romance addict would be an understatement. When she isn't chasing her toddler or preschooler around the house, working her day job, or writing, she jumps head first into a romance novel.

Reader group: Renee Harless' Risque Readers
https://www.facebook.com/groups/reneeharlessrisquereaders/
Facebook: facebook.com/authorreneeharless
Amazon: www.amazon.com/Renee-Harless/e/B00VAHGAWE
Bookbub: www.bookbub.com/authors/renee-harless
Newsletter: www.reneeharless.com/newsletter
Instagram: @Renee_harless
Twitter: @Renee_harless
Snapchat: @renee_harless

RENEE HARLESS

Made in the USA
Columbia, SC
10 June 2021